WITHDRAWN

MR. NICHOLAS

Also by David Ely

WALKING DAVIS

POOR DEVILS

TIME OUT

THE TOUR

SECONDS

TROT

MR. NICHOLAS

by David Ely

G. P. Putnam's Sons, New York

To Nancy and Sylvain,
Allen and Daniel

MR. NICHOLAS

Part One

THERE was a lull in the late afternoon. The office was hushed; the intercommunications box was still.

He sat behind his desk, looking down at a report that lay open before him. He read a page. Then he read it again. He hadn't really paid attention to it. He'd been concentrating hour after hour during the noise and rush of the business day, and now, in this slack period of the afternoon, he had a disconnected feeling, as though everyone else had gone, leaving him in an empty building where the elevators were locked and the stairways closed off . . . which was nonsense, of course. He was merely alone in a quiet office. It ought to be a relief. But it wasn't.

He looked carefully around. The door to the adjoining conference room was closed. So was the main door, which led to the outer office, where his secretary, Miss Prince, had her desk. Usually he kept that door open, except when he had

3

meetings, but now it happened to be shut. He supposed that his last visitor had closed it. No matter.

He resumed reading the report. It wasn't a difficult subject, and the material was clearly presented. Why, then, couldn't he keep his mind on it? He glanced around the office again. The silence was distracting him. It was a peculiar sort of silence; it came piling slowly in, layer on layer, until it seemed to share with him the possession of the room. It was as if someone else were there.

He had had that sensation before. He had tried to ignore it then; he resolved to try harder this time. *I'm alone*, he told himself. *There's no one else here. Absolutely no one.*

Still, his gaze would sometimes swing up to the walls, to the ceiling, or over to the door of the conference room. Once he checked his wristwatch to see how much time was left before the end of the day. He glanced at it stealthily, almost as though someone were watching who might, with disapproval, interpret this as evidence of his desire to leave work early—which was ridiculous. No one was there; no one was watching. Anyway, if he wanted to leave early, he could do so. He was the president of the company, after all.

"Mr. Haddock—?"

The disembodied voice startled him for an instant. But it was only Miss Prince on the intercom, asking about a change in his appointments schedule for the next day.

"Yes, yes," he said into the box. "That'll be all right, Miss Prince. . . ."

His voice sounded choked and thick. It showed how nervous he was—but he had reason to be nervous. He'd held the presidency for less than a month. No one could be expected to handle a difficult and demanding job properly in such a short time without showing signs of strain.

4

He found himself glancing around the walls again.

That made him angry. *Stop it, Haddock,* he ordered. He was perspiring. He had to pull out his handkerchief and wipe his forehead and the palms of his hands. Oh, he knew he was tense, terribly tense. But that's all it was. It couldn't be anything else. He was alone. He was without the slightest possible doubt alone.

He leaned forward and stared at the opposite wall.

"All right," he said aloud in a challenging voice—and he laughed to show he realized how foolish it was, speaking to a blank wall in an empty office, but his voice was unsteady and his laughter forced.

He couldn't help speaking again, but softly this time, as though he were ashamed to be speaking at all.

"All right," he repeated. "All right." Then he whispered: "All right, Mr. Nicholas. Are you there?"

Of course he knew perfectly well that Mr. Nicholas wasn't there. No one was there. Mr. Nicholas was living in retirement on an estate in eastern Pennsylvania—or at least so Haddock had been told, and he had no reason to doubt it. As it happened, he had never met Mr. Nicholas, nor had he ever had occasion to speak to him by telephone or exchange so much as a letter with him. In fact, he'd heard virtually nothing about him at all—which in itself was a bit unusual, for Mr. Nicholas had founded the company.

At the time of its establishment the company consisted of no more than a few technicians working in warehouse space in Paterson, New Jersey, fabricating electrical parts for war contractors. Mr. Nicholas' chief contribution had been to select several aggressive young administrators under whose

5

management the company had prospered. After a generation of mergers and expansions it had become one of the larger electronic manufacturers in the country, turning out thousands of items of equipment, its principal product being communications systems for large industrial and municipal customers.

Mr. Nicholas himself had soon receded into the background. Although he had served both as president and as chairman of the board in the early period, and had continued for years as a director, he had become a forgotten figure even before his actual retirement. Since then, he had not once visited the company's headquarters in New York, nor had he attended the annual banquets or stockholders' meetings. His name remained on the mailing list for company publications, but he gave no indication that he bothered to read them or that he retained any interest whatever in the business.

The younger executives—and those who, like Haddock, had been hired away from other companies in recent years—had never even seen him. The older men, who had once worked with him, remembered him only dimly. Even on ceremonial occasions, Mr. Nicholas' deeds were not gratefully recalled in speeches, and his name was only rarely mentioned.

Indeed, it was purely by chance that Henry Haddock had become aware of him at all—and this, characteristically, had come about not through Mr. Nicholas' presence but because of his absence. Or what seemed to be his absence.

It had happened on the day of Haddock's election.

The president of the company, Charles Mersey, had died

of a heart attack on January 2 that year. The board of directors had not unduly protracted its deliberations on the question of his successor. Haddock was the obvious choice. Two or three other executives were tougher and more experienced, but none of them had what he so abundantly possessed—the style, the manner, the presence. He *looked* like a company president.

At the age of forty-six he was still youthful, with sandy hair handsomely graying, and alert features. When he smiled (and he smiled a lot), he had a boyish charm. He was almost six feet in height, but the quickness of his movements made him seem shorter. In disposition he was brisk and cheerful. He was a first-rate listener, and when he spoke, he spoke well.

In the six years since he'd come east from Chicago to join the company as director of national sales, he had been impressively successful. He wasn't only an engaging and attractive fellow; he had a good-natured enthusiasm that people couldn't resist because it was so sincere. He possessed that evangelical streak Midwesterners sometimes have—an enlarged capacity for belief that can be irritatingly righteous, but wasn't in his case because of his disarming modesty. Haddock's beliefs centered on the company. His career was his life; his life was the company. And the company wasn't just any company. It was special; it had a mission to perform, and as the company's chief salesman, he'd become its most energetic and persuasive spokesman.

"Information is our product," he'd say to prospective clients (or to his sales staff or perhaps, just for practice, to his neighbor in a plane). "All kinds of information, on a great variety of levels—an incredible quantity of information, but at the same time precise and exact and absolutely reliable, to

7

an extent that nobody could have dreamed thirty years ago."

And depending on where he might be at the time, he'd pace up and down the room or lean across the table or tap his neighbor on the knee.

"We've got giant systems standing guard over entire automated plants to keep the supervisors constantly informed about their production programs—and on the other end of the scale we've got elaborate microsystems for medical and biological research. We can monitor what goes on inside the human body, and we can enable you to participate, as a spectator, in the actual growth of plant cells—the cells of a living plant!

"And then, of course, we've got our practical, everyday systems, like the traffic monitors we install at trouble points on the highways to permit the rapid deployment of police units to maintain vehicle flow—and there are protective systems, too, like camera units in banks and in payroll trucks, and installations in the corridors of apartment buildings that allow one guard to observe a dozen floors from a single central control point—and there's no end to the examples I could cite, but what does it all add up to? That's the real question." And here Haddock might rise to his feet (if he wasn't already pacing) or rub his hands together lightly with a keen, expectant smile. "To me, communications is a method of rationalizing the entire spectrum of a society which has rapidly grown denser, more complex, more sophisticated, more potentially chaotic. Chaos—that's what we're fighting against! We've got to keep the factories running smoothly, we've got to avoid traffic jam-ups, we've got to protect society in general from breakdown from any source, and that includes the human breakdown of crime. In

8

short, we've got to make certain, through communications, that our civilization keeps on working properly!"

Haddock was, moreover, likable. His father, a druggist in Columbus, Ohio, had impressed him greatly once with the statement that people would like him if he liked them. Haddock had put this proposition to a test. He'd practiced liking his schoolmates, his teachers, and his family's friends, and he'd discovered right away that what his father had said was true. People did like him. They liked him a lot. He liked them even more for that. He liked them at Ohio State University (where he was president of the senior class) and at graduate business school, and he kept on liking them in the business he'd begun his career with. By the time he accepted the offer to join the company Mr. Nicholas had founded, he was a formidably likable man.

Liking people wasn't just Haddock's way of getting along smoothly in the world (although it worked very well for him that way). It was also a moral principle. "When you like someone," he was fond of saying, "you bring out the best in them—and they'll do the same for you. But it's got to be honest, it's got to be sincere, it's got to be genuine!"

He did genuinely like people—and not just some of them, but all of them. He liked his friends, his associates, and his superiors. He liked his subordinates just as much. He also liked the manager of the residential hotel where he lived in New York, he liked the elevator men and the cleaning women, and he liked the news vendor, the shoeshine boy, taxi drivers, characters in novels, television personalities, and the politicians he read about in the newspapers.

He'd liked his wife, too—and it had been chiefly for this reason that his marriage had collapsed. He'd been too busy to see much of her, and then when he did see her, he was invariably courteous, pleasant, and charming. That is, he behaved toward Joyce just as he behaved toward everyone else. When she realized this fully, she found it intolerable. "Loving and liking are two different things," she'd cried out at him. "I don't *want* you to like me—you like everybody! Don't you know what love is? . . . Oh, for God's sake, stop smiling! Don't you dare smile at me that way! That's how you smile at people in the street!" He'd tried to explain that a man's personality was inevitably influenced by the work he did, and he conceded that perhaps he'd spread himself too thin emotionally—but then the telephone would ring, or he would have to hurry off to catch a plane or attend a meeting, and although he was terribly dispirited when she finally went off to get the divorce, he also was relieved for her sake, for he knew he'd failed to make her happy, and he hoped she'd find happiness elsewhere.

That had been five years ago. Now he and Joyce exchanged amicable letters each Christmas, and Haddock, having met her new husband, liked him, and the husband liked him in return. As for Joyce, even in her darkest days with Haddock, she hadn't been able to help liking him. Everyone liked him, particularly those who worked with him, and so as Haddock walked through the corridors toward the conference room on the afternoon of January 10, there was a gratified hush in the offices he passed on his way, for virtually the entire staff knew in advance that he was to be the new president, and no more popular choice would have been possible.

When the board's decision had been officially announced to

Haddock, there'd been the usual ritual of congratulations as the directors welcomed the new president with remarks appropriate to the occasion. Once these formalities had been disposed of, they gathered up their papers and their briefcases and departed, leaving Haddock alone with the chairman, old Mr. Elphinstone, for a review of certain questions of company policy. After this, Mr. Elphinstone decided to conclude the meeting on an informal note, and so he settled back in his chair and began reminiscing about the early days of the enterprise.

Haddock listened politely to these stories without paying much attention to them. He kept glancing about the conference room. Everything there was solid and secure: the high-backed chairs, covered in dark green leather, and the huge oval conference table, and the formal portraits of eight company notables that hung along the walls—men depicted at the height of their dignity and authority, presidents and chairmen of the board who in their time had met in that very room to determine policies that had concerned the livelihood of thousands of employees and the disposition of millions of dollars of investment capital.

"I remember the time . . ." went on Mr. Elphinstone in his high, crackling voice, and Haddock thought of all the past meetings he had attended in the conference room and how different his awareness of it had suddenly become. Until today he had been merely another high-ranking executive; the conference room had meant nothing in particular to him. Now he found himself in charge of the entire company, a responsibility for which he would be answerable to the board of directors, assembled around that table—and so the room took on, in his imagination, something of the authority of the board itself. The empty chairs sat gravely, like judges;

the majestic oval table, polished by a thousand executive sleeves, seemed charged with a tremendous permanence, as though it had thrust its ponderous legs through the carpet and all the way down—fifty stories and more—into the sub-soil of the city, while the portraits on the walls appeared to cast severe and measuring glances at the newcomer, as though skeptical of his ability to guide the enterprise they had so laboriously created.

Mr. Elphinstone, reminiscing, happened to mention the name of Edgar Nicholas.

Haddock looked again at the portraits. All the great figures of the company were there, including Mr. Elphinstone himself. But the founder was not represented.

When Mr. Elphinstone next paused for breath, Haddock commented on this omission.

Mr. Elphinstone craned about, peering at the portraits. "No," he said. "Edgar never had his picture painted. He didn't care for public appearances at all—speeches, dinners, that kind of thing—and I suppose he didn't even want his portrait hanging where other people could look at it. He placed a high value on his privacy," said Mr. Elphinstone, "and he still does. I've only seen him once myself since his retirement, and that's been—well, eight or nine years now. He doesn't encourage visits, not even from old friends. He doesn't see anyone now. Even in his active years, he had a retiring sort of manner. He preferred to work behind the scenes. Why, I don't think Edgar ever made a speech in his whole life. A man of few words, Henry. Not that he didn't keep up," the old chairman added. "No, far from it. Edgar was devoted to the company, and he put in long hours, I can tell you. He had a passion for detail. Nothing escaped his eye. And he was always prompt for board meetings. First to arrive, last to leave. That sort of thing. Even if you came ahead of time, you'd find Edgar already there—here, that is, in this room. We even joked about it. You know, saying that he must sleep here and have his meals brought in. Actually, that's what made his final year on the board so difficult. He suffered from lumbago or something of the sort," said Mr. Elphinstone, screwing up his leathery features in the effort of recollection. "In any case, the doctors forbade him to travel, so he had to stay home. But it's indicative of the quiet determination of the man that he didn't miss a single meeting all that year, as far as I know."

Haddock looked at the chairman inquiringly. "How could he do that?"

"It was quite simple," said Mr. Elphinstone. "He arranged to monitor the meetings. I'd completely forgotten about that until you asked about him."

"He had a closed-circuit system installed, you mean?"

"That's what he did," said Mr. Elphinstone. "And of course this permitted him to 'attend' our meetings without stirring from his fireside. Whenever he had anything to say, he merely picked up his telephone and called us. It was a one-way system, of course."

"He had it installed here?"

"Right in this room," said Mr. Elphinstone. "And a very neat job it was. You couldn't tell it was here at all. I didn't know where it was myself." He stifled a yawn and blinked down at his watch. "As I told you, Edgar was a retiring sort of fellow. He didn't want to call attention to himself by having a lot of equipment hanging on the walls."

"I see," said Haddock, and he couldn't resist the impulse to glance about the walls. There was nothing to see, of course, apart from the portraits and the windows.

Mr. Elphinstone was gathering his papers together and putting them into his briefcase.

"How long was it here?" Haddock asked.

"The monitor?" Mr. Elphinstone pondered the matter for a few moments. "I really can't say, but it's interesting to note that this was an early version of what we're now producing in our special-projects division, Henry."

Haddock took a look at the ceiling. Only an ordinary light fixture was there.

"Of course, Edgar was a rather silent man—always let the other fellow do the talking—so he didn't participate much in those meetings," Mr. Elphinstone continued. "I don't suppose he phoned us more than three or four times altogether."

"He just watched?"

"As far as I know."

"You couldn't tell whether he was watching or not, then?"

"I suppose not." Mr. Elphinstone snapped the catches of the briefcase. "No, you're right, Henry. There wasn't any way of telling, as I recall."

"Did the other directors object?"

"Object?"

"To the monitor."

"Oh. Well, I doubt that they did. I really don't remember. This was years ago, Henry. Years ago."

Haddock looked around the room again. The portraits stared back at him with their cold and disapproving eyes. "And I suppose it was taken out when Mr. Nicholas retired," he remarked.

Mr. Elphinstone, rising creakily to his feet, didn't answer.

Haddock stood, too. "Would you remember when that was?" he asked.

"When what was?"

"When the monitor was removed."

"I'm afraid not, Henry." Mr. Elphinstone was tired. He had no further interest in the topic. He moved stiffly toward the door.

"The office records would show that, of course," Haddock added.

"Yes, yes," Mr. Elphinstone muttered. He paused, his hand on the doorknob. "A lot of the original group departed in that period, Henry," he said. "We all got old then. Some retired, like Edgar, and others . . . well, they passed away. Of that old board, I'm the only active survivor."

They went outside into the corridor. "Those days are gone now," said Mr. Elphinstone glumly. "But . . . new days, Henry. And new men." He gave Haddock a bony hand to shake. "Again, my best wishes for your success."

"Thank you, Mr. Elphinstone," said Haddock, shutting the conference room door behind them.

For the remainder of that first day he had been too busy to think about the little story Mr. Elphinstone had told him.

People were stopping by to congratulate him—not only his fellow executives but also the secretaries, all of whom had been in love with him at one time or another—so his office was crowded, and his own secretary, Miss Prince, who had worshiped him for years, became so flustered that she misaddressed three letters.

Before long, telephone calls began coming in from his friends and business acquaintances outside the company. Haddock's cheeks ached from grinning, and his hand tingled from all the shakes it had made. He found time to telephone his mother at her nursing home in Florida. "They should have made you president years ago," his mother told him, and then, as she always did, she asked when he was coming down for another visit and why he didn't remarry.

"I'm president now," he kept thinking. "I'm really president." Snow was sifting down over Manhattan. To him it looked like confetti, flung out of the windows in his honor. A band was playing at some municipal ceremony a block or two away, and this, too, seemed to have been arranged for his benefit. He went to the window to look out at the snow and to listen to the faint, triumphal music. Then the public-relations man hurried in with the draft of a press release on his election, which had to be reworked and approved and gotten to the papers right away, and after that there was a heavy hour with the corporation counsel to dispose of the formal aspects of the presidential takeover, and on top of this, Haddock had several important pending matters in his own department to take care of and the usual correspondence to check and sign.

At the end of the day he had a rather uncomfortable meeting with the executive vice president, George Imry, who had expected all along to get the presidency and was stunned to find that it had been thrown away on a popinjay salesman like Henry Haddock. "I'm willing to serve under you, Henry," Imry said several times, which indicated how sorely he felt the fact that until that very day, Haddock had been serving under him. He looked sick and angry, and he sweat a lot. Haddock tried to soothe him by saying that the executive vice president was really the key man in the company and that the president was merely a handshaker and speech-maker and front man, which modest assurances did little to

16

comfort Imry, even though there was a good deal of truth in them.

It wasn't until the following morning that he had decided to satisfy his curiosity by seeing what the files contained on the subject of Mr. Nicholas' monitor. He thought first of having Miss Prince do the checking for him. Then he changed his mind, judging that it would be better for him to do it himself, in view of Mr. Elphinstone's emphasis on the founder's desire for privacy. It would do no good, Haddock thought, to spread that little story around, trivial though it was. Besides, Miss Prince was terribly busy on more immediate work. So was he, of course, and when the file folders were brought up to him from the company library, he set them aside.

Only during odd moments in the next few days had he been able to examine the files. They were voluminous, for they contained the records, year by year, of everything that concerned the establishment and upkeep of the company headquarters: purchases of furniture, of rugs, lamps, and office machines; job orders for painting and redecoration; contracts for all kinds of maintenance and repair work, from the installation of air conditioning down to the replacement of a toilet handle in the secretaries' bathroom. No item seemed too insignificant to be included; no category appeared to have been overlooked. From these files one might reconstruct the physical history of the headquarters establishment, office by office.

And yet there was no reference to the removal of the monitor.

The files indicated that it had been installed ten years before, almost to the day. An official permit had been obtained, and there were various memos concerning the necessary replastering and repainting work—but the folders for subsequent years contained no further records on the monitor.

He found that annoying. Of course, it didn't matter, really. Perhaps no official permit had been required when it came time to take the thing out. In any event, it wasn't worth bothering about.

He began going through the files a second time.

He had moved into the president's office. It was handsome, spacious, and modern in design. From the large window, overlooking Fifth Avenue, he obtained a splendid panorama of the city, and through the main doorway (which he kept open to encourage the other executives to bring in their problems) came the busy sounds of the company's activity—the tapping of the typewriters, the hum of voices, the rise and fall of steps along the corridors.

When he wanted to concentrate on some difficult subject, he would go into the adjoining conference room, entering by the side door. There, sitting in one of the high-backed chairs at the huge oval table, he could study and reflect in a tranquil and untroubled atmosphere.

He decided to take the files into the conference room and re-examine them there.

He also took along a report on personnel policy that he needed to review—and he would review it, if anyone happened to enter the conference room, for he would just as soon not be found there going over such paltry material as the housekeeping files.

As was his custom, when he had seated himself at the table,

he took a long look all around the walls, glancing at the portraits of the past presidents and chairmen with a deferential expression. After all, it was their room, just as the company was their company, and he wanted to show them the proper respect—not the portraits, of course, but the men, and since the men were deceased (with the exception of Mr. Elphinstone), the portraits remained to represent them. There, above the bookcase where the black-bound annual reports were shelved, was old Maurice Carpenter, who'd been the real driving force back in the early days of the company; to his left hung Albert Cagle (whose bulk had been tastefully deemphasized by the artist); then there was J. J. James, who had preceded Mr. Elphinstone as chairman, and John Sims Day, the financial expert, and Carl Brandt, who more than any other man had gotten the company established in the defense and space industries, and Walter Wyse, and finally Mersey, whose portrait had been finished just before his death. All were gathered there along the walls as though assembled for a meeting. Haddock smiled at them with polite good humor, and in his mind composed an appropriate greeting: *Good afternoon, gentlemen. I hope I'm not late. Mr. Carpenter, would you be kind enough to take the chair today? And is everyone here so we can begin . . . ?*

Edgar Nicholas wasn't there.

Haddock frowned down at the files that lay on the table in front of him. The monitor had been removed years ago. He could safely assume that. And if the written evidence hadn't turned up . . . well, it might have been lost or misfiled or put in under some other heading somewhere. In any event, he'd wasted too much time on it already.

He shoved the files aside. As far as he was concerned, the subject was closed.

19

He'd kept on thinking about it, though. Every time he entered the conference room—and sometimes when he merely glanced at the conference room door from his desk in the office—it insinuated itself into his thoughts. In the middle of meetings he would catch himself wondering about it. Where, exactly, would it have been? On that wall over there . . . ? In the space between the portraits of Messrs. Day and Brandt? Or maybe in the ceiling. Not overhead, but off to one side, to obtain a good viewing angle.

One day he informed Miss Prince that he didn't want to be disturbed by calls or visitors. He closed his office door and went into the conference room, shutting that door behind him and making certain that the main entrance, too, was closed.

Then he made a careful inspection of the room, at one point climbing up on the oval table (first having removed his shoes) to get a closer look at the ceiling. Wherever the monitor had been, he thought, its removal might have left some tiny trace—an extra layer of plaster or the mark of a painter's retouching. But he saw no such signs anywhere. He even went around the room tilting the portraits so that he could peer at the spaces behind them. He found nothing.

Very well, he thought. It had been removed as expertly as it had been installed, then. And as for the missing records, they might have been retained by the company technical personnel who would have taken the equipment out. He could try to check on that by phoning the research and development center over in New Jersey.

He decided not to bother. He had plenty of serious preoccupations; he had no business fretting over petty distractions. The presidency weighed on him. It wasn't so much the work; it was more the sensation that something tangible yet invisible enfolded him, isolating him from the others. It was like the magic cloak in a child's fable he remembered—easy to put on, impossible to remove. Everything seemed calculated to remind him that he was president. The new company letterhead, engraved on stationery and memorandum sheets, bore his name and title, as did the new office directory and his incoming mail. His fellow executives, now his subordinates, appeared to hesitate just a fraction of a second before speaking to him, as though they were suddenly remembering that it wasn't just Henry Haddock they were confronting but the president as well—and Haddock, sensing this, became afflicted by the same hesitancy. He found that he was consciously selecting his words in advance, even for the most casual responses.

Outwardly little had changed. Those who had called him by his first name continued to do so, and the same executive group got together for lunch at the same places and talked about the same things, and no one deferred to him particularly or acted as though anything more important had happened to him than a switch in office locations.

The signs of friendliness remained. If anything, they increased. But there was a hollowness about them. When someone made a joke, Haddock had the impression that everyone automatically flashed a look at him before laughing, as though the joke were a program proposal on which his reaction would indicate the general policy line. When the usual luncheon group got up to leave the restaurant, the others didn't give him precedence, but it seemed to him that they deliberately didn't give him precedence. It was as though they were determined not to embarrass him by standing aside for him, and yet they had to allow for the possibility that he would decide to go out first, so even in this simple

21

daily act of leaving the restaurant was an awkward reminder that he wasn't what he'd been before and that everything had changed.

He felt lonely. His friends within the company were Haddock's friends, not the president's. And yet the president was always there, a shadow that sat with him at his desk, a ghost that trailed him when he walked the corridors, a presence whose existence he sensed only in the recognition it evoked in other people; and so the spirit of spontaneous companionship vanished, leaving only its forms behind. Even his friends outside the company regarded him a little differently now, he suspected, but he couldn't be sure of that, for he hardly saw them at all now, he was so busy.

He knew that he was magnifying the problem, if it really was a problem. He just wasn't accustomed to the presidency yet. In time, he knew, he'd manage to impose his own style on it. Charles Mersey had been a caustic president; that had suited him. And Brandt had been a cold, analytical president, for he'd been, in character, a remote and emotionless man. So Haddock, too, would re-create the presidency in his own image. He'd be a cheerful president, a likable president—yes, he'd be a decent, modest, enthusiastic president! He'd furnish the presidency with the personal qualities he'd so carefully acquired and nurtured through the years . . . and when he'd done that, then he'd feel at home in the job.

He didn't now, though. He was stiff and unsure of himself. His smile was wooden, his gestures tense. He'd lost that easy, genuine manner. "It'll come back, though," he assured himself. "I'm nervous now. It won't last long. I'll be all right again."

He was working hard. Mersey's death had delayed many

22

decisions that had to be disposed of, and since there were certain areas of the company that Haddock didn't know well—finance and research, for example—he spent long hours alone, studying memorandums and reports. At those times he was almost contented. He didn't consider himself to be a brilliant fellow, not by any means, but he'd always been diligent, and he prided himself on his common-sense judgment, so he felt that he could drive his way through his problems by energy and dogged effort.

It was tiring, though. Sometimes he'd slump wearily at his desk or at the big table in the conference room and push his papers aside for a while. He was working too hard . . . and for what purpose? To demonstrate his honest desire to do a good job? That was all very well, but the company cared only for results. Any nincompoop could put in long hours. Well, he was anxious. He had to admit that. Whatever anybody did anywhere in the company was, in a sense, his doing, and yet he couldn't possibly learn all he needed to know in order to shoulder such a burden, no matter how many hours he spent burrowing away in the papers on his desk. No, a president couldn't do the job just by reading reports and quizzing department heads. He needed a particular sensitivity that would let him know which detail was significant and when the surface of an event concealed its true meaning. A president had to develop a set of intuitive reactions to meet the challenge of his authority—and that's what the exercise of power was, wasn't it? The expansion of a man's personality under the force of events? Yes, and he, Haddock, would have to acquire that extra sense. There was something almost animal about it. A beast in the jungle knows instinctively when something's going on in its territory . . . even in silence and darkness, when nothing can be seen and nothing heard.

And could he, too, learn to see through the dark, to hear through the silence?

In the conference room one evening he worked right through the dinner hour without realizing how late it was. This pleased him in a way. It meant that he was really digging into the job.

He leaned back in his chair, savoring the sensations of fatigue and solitude. The building would be empty now, he supposed, except for a few cleaning women and the night guards. Perhaps one or two other conscientious executives would be working alone at their desks in remote offices far below. Through the side doorway he could see the corner of his desk in the president's office. A vase there held a single flower. Miss Prince brought in a fresh one every morning. As he watched, he saw a petal fall. Everything was so quiet that he listened, wondering if he could hear the tiny impact on the carpet. He couldn't. But it was quiet, remarkably quiet. He liked that. He'd come to feel harassed by the thousand noises of the busy daytime hours; each one might mean a new problem, a further drain on his energies. But now, in the stillness of the conference room, where there was no one to disturb him, he was at peace.

As he sat resting there, the quiet seemed slowly to assume a definite state, as though the lack of sound were itself a sound. The silence took the shape of the room. He might pass his hand through it and imagine its texture. And the fact that he was totally and completely alone began to produce a similar effect on him, for the prolonged absence of any other human being within the range of his senses made him aware of the solitude as possessing a sort of presence. Nothing was there. It was there, that nothing. He was enveloped by it. He couldn't touch it or taste it, he couldn't see it, couldn't hear it

... but it was in there with him. It was in the room. He knew it was there. He could sense it . . . something hidden, something secret—

He shuffled his papers together, rustling them deliberately, and glanced swiftly around. It was a dead room: empty chairs, inert table, lifeless painted faces ranged about the walls. And yet . . . the light struck the portraits oddly. It almost seemed that the eyes were fixed on him. He knew it was only a trick of his imagination, but still he felt it—a gaze of steadfast, mindless penetration, remotely hostile, as though he were an intruder.

He rose to his feet. *Don't be a fool, Haddock,* he told himself. Obviously he'd been working too hard. He was overwrought.

Still . . . he paused, frowning, and he listened. He heard the sound of silence, he sensed the presence of nonbeing.

Then he turned and walked to the doorway, snapped off the lights, and passed into his own office, closing the door behind him. He closed it tightly, so that the catch snapped.

And he decided that in the future he would do all his work in the office. He really had no need to go into the conference room.

His sense of isolation increased when at the end of January he moved into the midtown apartment that the company maintained as a presidential residence, as well as for informal conferences and business entertaining. (Mrs. Mersey, the widow of his predecessor, had moved down to Florida to live.)

At his hotel Haddock had been on friendly terms with everybody. He had stopped to chat with the desk clerk every day and joked with the waitress in the coffee shop where he ate breakfast, and he usually shared a taxi with two other residents of the hotel who also worked in midtown.

He had no companionship now. The apartment was splendid and spacious; he felt lost in it. An elderly butler and cook, Mr. and Mrs. Frey, occupied two rooms beyond the kitchen, but he didn't feel at ease with them. Frey was formal and aloof; his wife seldom appeared when Haddock was present, and when she did, her expression was dour.

Haddock was served breakfast in his room each morning. When he left for work, he took an automatic elevator to the ground floor and nodded to the doorman as he hurried outside to the street, where his chauffeured limousine was waiting to carry him to the office. The driver, a solemn, bulky man named Mackensen, didn't initiate any conversation, and Haddock was so intent on the problems he'd face when he arrived at work that he opened his attaché case the moment he'd settled himself in the car. At the end of the day the limousine brought him back to the apartment, and again he conscientiously used the time to study memorandums and reports. After he'd eaten his solitary supper in the dining room, he worked some more before going to bed. For days at a time, he realized, he didn't exchange a friendly word with another soul. He didn't have time. He was too tired, too preoccupied, too anxious . . . and yet he knew he needed some human contact, a touch of someone else's life each day to lighten his mood.

With whom? Frey, the butler, was too remote and frosty, and the doorman too obsequious. His chauffeur seemed a more promising prospect; professional drivers usually were eager to relieve the boredom of their jobs by talk.

"Well, Mackensen," Haddock said one morning, "I guess you get a lot of reading done."

"Reading, Mr. Haddock?"

"When you're not driving, I mean. You've got a lot of time on your hands during the day, after all."

"That's right, Mr. Haddock, but I'm not much for reading."

"No?"

"I'll tell you what I do, though, to pass the time, and it's I train my memory."

"Ah."

"I practice on license numbers. When I'm parked somewhere waiting, I memorize the numbers of all the parked cars, and then I turn around so I can't see them, and I write them down, see, and then I check to see if I got them right."

"Is that so?"

"But what I'm working on most now is lipreading, Mr. Haddock."

"Lipreading."

"Right, and that's pretty tough, I can tell you, and I have to practice a lot. At home I practice with no sound on the TV, and I go to movies with plugs in my ears."

"How about that."

"The trick is you got to watch people, not just their lips but their hands and their faces, and you got to learn to do it without their realizing. I mean, you can't go around staring them in the face like some nut, Mr. Haddock."

"They mustn't know."

"That's it, Mr. Haddock."

"But suppose they *do* know, Mackensen? I mean, suppose they know you're over there reading their lips? How would *you* know that they know?"

"Well, I never thought of that, Mr. Haddock, but it's not likely they'd know about the lipreading. I mean, they might notice me watching them, and I might read them saying something like 'who is that guy over there staring at us like

27

that?' but lipreading, it's uncommon, and I doubt they'd guess."

"I see. Well, put yourself in the other fellow's shoes, Mackensen. Suppose you suspected that somebody was reading your lips, but you couldn't be sure. How would you feel about that?"

"I honestly couldn't say, Mr. Haddock, but in my case, I don't think I'd worry. I mean, whatever I've got to say, I don't care who hears me. I don't talk dirty or anything like that, Mr. Haddock—and here we are, sir," said Mackensen, pulling up at the Fifth Avenue entrance to the building, into which Haddock strode with a display of vigor he didn't quite feel, for his long hours of work had begun to leave their mark.

Before his election Haddock had always stepped smartly out of the elevator into the company lobby with a grin for the receptionist and a wink for the secretaries he passed on his way to his office. He'd be whistling, too, or humming some popular tune, and on overcast days, when he carried his umbrella, he might spin it a few times like a drum major's baton or even twirl his hat around on its tip.

His election had sobered his style. He was genial, but dignified. No more grins and winks; no more juggling with hats and umbrellas. He smiled at the secretaries gently, even sadly; the sight of them reminded him of more carefree times.

As he neared his office, his smile became fixed, his step heavier, and his gaze anxiously expectant, as though he were about to enter a meeting for which he was ill prepared. Miss

Prince, in the anteroom, gave him her usual blush and breathless "Good morning, Mr. Haddock," but he returned no more than a distracted nod as he crossed his office threshold. She rose and followed him with the morning mail, which she had opened and sorted as usual. He didn't notice her. He had paused in front of his desk and was glancing all around the room. Slipping past him to put the mail on his desk, Miss Prince startled him. He exclaimed in surprise and pulled back, then quickly caught himself. "Sorry, Miss Prince! I, ah—" He laughed, and to cover his awkwardness, he went over to the closet to dispose of his hat and overcoat. Then he turned, poised and smiling; Miss Prince flashed him a shy and tender glance and left.

He plunged into his customary routine: conferences, telephone calls, letters, reports to be analyzed, memorandums to be scanned—that endless flow of words written and spoken that seemed to act both as a stimulant and a depressant as the day wore on, for he could feel keenly excited one moment and sluggish and dull the next. He dictated part of a speech he had to deliver the following month, he roughed out plans for a contract-lobbying trip to Washington, and in the middle of all this he had to rush off downtown for lunch with the board of directors' finance committee, three elderly bankers whose sourness drew heavily on his reserves of charm.

In midafternoon he caught himself dozing at his desk. His head snapped up, and he glanced guiltily around the room, as though someone were there watching him disapprovingly—and then he shook his head, rubbed his eyes, and resumed reading the report that had put him to sleep. He couldn't concentrate on it. Something was troubling him. That little nap of his—why couldn't he take a nap if he wanted to? Lots of busy executives took midday naps in the office. It was a sound, healthy practice. Even a few minutes' rest was enough to refresh a man.

He wasn't refreshed. He felt oppressed. *All right, Haddock,* he told himself. *Nobody home. Just you. Now, back to work.*

He looked down at the report again, but he wasn't reading it. He was listening. And then his gaze walked the walls once more. He saw nothing, heard nothing. Nothing was there. It was there again, that nothing.

The door to the conference room was closed. He checked it first thing every morning, just to be sure. As a matter of fact, he checked it several times a day. It was closed. He could see that. No point in getting up and going over to test the knob.

He got up and went over and tested the knob. It was definitely closed, all right.

He still had that strange feeling. It angered him. He was willing to admit that his imagination might play tricks on him at night when he was tired and alone on a deserted floor of offices—but not during the day when the whole building was alive with activity, when he could hear the tick-tick of a dozen typewriters, the hum of voices, even the faint rattle of traffic drifting up from the avenue, where pedestrians by the hundreds were hurrying along on that bright, frosty winter afternoon. It wasn't reasonable, it wasn't fair, especially since he'd been working so hard for the company. He determined to put it out of his mind.

He buzzed for Miss Prince.

"Yes, Mr. Haddock?"

"Miss Prince, will you get me whatever files we happen to have on Mr. Edgar Nicholas, please?"

He had lowered his voice so much she had to ask him to repeat what he'd said.

She came back later with a dozen fat folders, all of them old. He sat frowning down at them, fingering their edges. He started to open the top one, but he stopped. He glanced at the door to the conference room.

He pressed the buzzer again.

"Miss Prince, I'd like to check these folders out and take them home. Would you wrap them up and have a boy run them over to the apartment for me, please?"

She picked up the folders and took them away again.

He sat for several minutes pondering certain physical sensations: his pulse was fast, his hands were cold, his forehead slightly damp. He wondered if he were coming down with a fever. But he didn't feel shaky.

Then, in a rush of annoyance, he told himself he'd better come to grips with what was bothering him, openly and honestly.

All right—suppose it was still there? So what? It would be dead. It would be useless. After ten years . . . ? Why, even the most modern system couldn't be guaranteed to function that long.

Of course, he had to admit that his technical information came entirely from the civilian side of the company's operations. The defense research was conducted on a restricted basis. He'd never had occasion to get involved with that. He really ought to check that situation out before long, not because of Mr. Nicholas but because it formed a part of the general picture the president had to be acquainted with.

As for Mr. Nicholas' monitor—well, it would be in the conference room. That's where it had been installed, and if it

31

hadn't been removed, then that's where it would still be.

He strolled around the office, examining the walls, the ceiling, the baseboard at the edges of the carpeting. Nothing out of the ordinary, nothing at all. Yet the same thing could be said about the conference room, couldn't it? And the two rooms were adjacent, after all.

He returned abruptly to his desk, sat down, and buzzed for Miss Prince.

"Yes, Mr. Haddock?"

He'd forgotten what he wanted. "Never mind," he mumbled. "It's nothing—sorry."

There was only one installation. Mr. Elphinstone had mentioned just the one. Of course, Mr. Elphinstone might not know about a second one—and even if there was only one, it might serve both rooms at the same time, mightn't it?

"Stop it, Haddock," he whispered. "Stop worrying about it."

He couldn't stop.

He thought about it every day, each time he was alone. He kept reminding himself that the whole thing was next to impossible. And yet he couldn't help wondering: if something could be set up in one room, couldn't it be set up in another?

So it was, late one afternoon, that he leaned forward in his chair, stared at the opposite wall, and spoke.

"All right, Mr. Nicholas. Are you there?"

Part Two

FROM that time on, he never really felt alone in his office. And he kept thinking about it.

It was just nerves. He was convinced of that. "There isn't any monitor," he'd tell himself. "There was once, but not now. They took it out. That's almost certain." Anyway, he knew it had been in the conference room, not the office. And even if it had covered both rooms—a remote contingency at best—it hadn't been in operation for years. It would be rusting away in some forgotten crevice. Mr. Nicholas himself probably couldn't remember its exact location. So the monitor was no problem.

He was the problem. He knew that he had suffered what amounted to a mild psychological shock because of his election. This had obviously activated certain latent weaknesses within him and forced them up to the surface, in this particular guise.

What was it, really? Nothing but a phantom created by his

own imagination, and since he had called it into being, he had the power to dismiss it, too. And he would. He'd do that in due time. Right now, he reasoned, it undoubtedly served a useful function by focusing the neurotic tendencies that the presidency had shaken loose in him. Yes, it was a convenience to have these little vagaries collected in one spot, so he could keep a sharp eye on them. And if he chose to give this psychological servant the name of Mr. Nicholas—well, that was an amusing touch of primitivism, and when the whole episode was over, he could make quite a neat little after-dinner story out of it.

The more he thought about it, the more he came to find a symbolic propriety in the form that this temporary fixation had taken. It was, one might say, a shadowy representation of the power and responsibility of his office. That is, he was being watched by the presidency itself. Or, to put it less fancifully, it was his own presidential awareness that he felt. And that was undoubtedly a useful reaction. In fact, it might be the beginning of that animal instinct of watchfulness that he knew he'd have to develop somehow. Of course, it had taken a rather peculiar form, he had to admit.

These thoughts comforted him. What he sometimes so foolishly imagined to be a hidden monitor was actually his own anxiety. He wanted to be a good president, and he was worried about it. When he'd gotten a grip on the job, then the anxiety would recede, leaving him free to behave as he always had, in the most normal, natural, and easy manner possible.

Then, one evening at the apartment, he came across the only item in the body of files on Edgar Nicholas that was in the least unusual—and even this wasn't really unusual. In fact, it made no particular impression on him when he first read it. It seemed to be just another dull, commonplace memorandum, tucked away in a dusty folder, curling at the edges with age.

Edgar Nicholas had been the one who proposed that the company acquire an apartment for the use of its presidents.

That next morning he woke suddenly and sat bolt upright in bed, staring around the room.

He knew he'd had a nightmare, although he could remember nothing about it. His mouth was dry. The skin on the back of his neck tingled, as if the hair there had risen. Nightmares weren't unusual for him. He had them now and then. This one had been stronger, though. It had left him shaken and confused and with the sensation that there was something not quite right about the room itself.

Which was nonsense. Everything was in its accustomed place. Quite a nice room, really. It was much larger than his old room at the residential hotel and was equipped with all sorts of conveniences. A button by the bed permitted him to open the draperies and let the sunlight enter. He pushed the button, and the draperies obediently parted. But it was an overcast day; the light that came in was dull.

He couldn't quite define the feeling he had about the room. He didn't wânt to define it, actually. He occupied his thoughts by reminding himself how fortunate he was to be living in such a spacious apartment. There were two other bedrooms, for guests, and several other rooms besides: the living room, with a commanding view of the city; the dining room (its table, when fully extended, could seat twenty persons); a sizable terrace with potted plants and smog-proof chairs; a study, and finally, the kitchen and pantry and the

37

quarters occupied by Mr. and Mrs. Frey, who had nothing to do but tend to his needs. So he was a lucky man, wasn't he?

He raised himself up on his elbows and looked carefully around the walls. "A lucky man," he said softly, smiling. He eyed the ceiling. Not even a flyspeck up there. Smooth as glass it was. Nothing to worry about, then. Nothing at all. And he wasn't worried. He wasn't exactly at his ease, but he certainly wasn't worried. A poor night of sleep was bound to make anybody a little jumpy—well, not jumpy, but feeling... out of sorts. It had nothing to do with the room. He'd slept well enough there for more than a month now. So there was no reason suddenly to feel compelled to goggle at the walls.

Then he remembered what he'd read in the files on Edgar Nicholas the night before. That's what had done it. That suggestive little item had lodged in his mind somehow—no doubt it had been responsible for his nightmare—and now, having gnawed right through his subconscious, here it was, out in the open!

Of course the idea was so patently ridiculous that it was laughable. He started to laugh out loud, in fact, but didn't quite manage it. He grinned instead and, grinning, looked all about the room. Yes, it was a really incredible idea. He resolved to ignore it.

He could always telephone Mr. Elphinstone and ask him about it.

No, he couldn't. In the first place, if Mr. Elphinstone knew about it, he would certainly have told him. So Mr. Elphinstone didn't know. And in the second place, Mr. Elphinstone might think it odd for Haddock to mention such an extraordinary thing. The next time he saw Mr. Elphinstone he might allude to it in a roundabout way—except how could one allude casually to such a monstrous possibility? He'd better not say anything to Mr. Elphinstone.

He got briskly out of bed, went to the bathroom, and showered and shaved. It was his custom to go back to the bedroom nude, put on his underwear and dressing gown, and await the butler, Frey, who brought in his breakfast at 7:30. But today, without thinking about it, really, he reentered the bedroom wrapped in his towel, picked up his underwear and dressing gown, carried them back into the bathroom, and put them on there, with the door closed. Then he returned to the bedroom.

He was glad when the punctual butler arrived with the breakfast tray.

"Good morning, Mr. Haddock."

"Good morning, Frey—and my compliments to Mrs. Frey on this fine morning!"

"Thank you, sir."

Frey was a model butler—reserved, dignified, and close-mouthed, an almost invisible man. He placed the tray on the table by the bed. Then he went to the closet for Haddock's clothes.

"Will it be the gray tweed today, sir?"

"Oh, the brown, I think, but give me a bit of color with the tie. Something with red in it. Something heartfelt, if you know what I mean."

"Very good, sir."

"Tell me something, Frey. You and your wife have been here a long time, haven't you?"

"From the beginning, Mr. Haddock."

"From the beginning? Oh, you mean from the time the company established the apartment."

"Yes, sir. That's ten years now, sir."

"And before that?"

"Before that we served Mr. Brandt, sir, when he was president, and we moved here with him, you see."

"Well, and I suppose you also were in service at one time with Mr. Nicholas; am I right?"

Frey hesitated, his smooth old face impassive. "We never had that honor, sir."

"I was just guessing, Frey. When I think of the company, naturally I think of Mr. Nicholas, and I just thought of him in this connection, too. In connection with the apartment, I mean."

Frey made no comment.

"He did take an initial interest in the apartment," Haddock went on, buttering a French roll. "I happen to know that, Frey. And I'd be willing to bet he took a hand in supervising the layout and decoration of the place."

"I honestly couldn't say, Mr. Haddock."

"Oh, I'm sure he must have," said Haddock, smiling affably, watching Frey's face. "It has that special touch. I don't mean to say that I know Mr. Nicholas personally, for I haven't had that pleasure, but it just strikes me that—well, a place like this, it's really a company facility, and after all, Mr. Nicholas founded the company, so the two things naturally go together; wouldn't you say so, Frey?"

"I'd never thought of it in quite that way, sir."

"I mean, one might say that the apartment and the company both bear the stamp of a single personality," said Haddock, struggling to keep his smile in a casual, genial mold. It was too tight, though. He could feel it. "The mark of the creator, Frey. That is, when a man creates something— whether it's an entire new corporate enterprise or the design

40

of an apartment—he leaves his mark on it, and it always' retains some little, indefinable something of his spirit, so it's almost as if he were still present, in a way."

He caught himself. Had he gone too far? Frey made no response except to incline his pale, gray dome in polite acknowledgment.

"Just a manner of speaking, Frey," Haddock added. "Just a manner of speaking."

Frey betrayed nothing. Not so much as a sidelong glance at—at what? Nothing, probably.

"Will there be anything else, sir?"

"Ah, no. Nothing, Frey, thank you."

"Very good, sir," said Frey, backing off a pace. He turned and noiselessly departed.

"My compliments to Mrs. Frey on this fine morning!" Haddock called cheerfully after him before realizing that he'd said the same thing earlier. "Erase that," he muttered automatically, as though he were dictating onto a tape, but then he pursed his lips disapprovingly, for he didn't want to fall into the habit of talking out loud when he was alone.

If he was alone.

In the limousine that morning he sat silently for a while. Then his eyes met those of his chauffeur in the rearview mirror, and he felt obliged to make some sort of conversation.

"Well, Mackensen," he said, "read any good lips lately?"

"I'm still working at it, Mr. Haddock."

"Fine, fine."

"It takes a lot of practice, though. You've got to keep doing it every day."

"I can believe that."

"You just don't pick up a skill like that in a couple of weeks, Mr. Haddock."

"I guess not. Listen, there's one thing that puzzles me about your lipreading."

"What's that, Mr. Haddock?"

"How can you verify your results? For example, you read somebody's lips and you think you've understood what they've said, but you can't check it out with them, so how can you be sure?"

"Well, I've gotten my wife to work with me on that. She stands off at different distances and in different conditions of light, you know, and she says things silently, and then I tell her what she's said, and she corrects me when I'm wrong."

"So you're accustomed to reading her lips, but what about other people, Mackensen? You need to practice on more than one person, don't you?"

"That's very true, Mr. Haddock, and it's a weak point in my training. When you get into lipreading, you realize that no two pairs of lips are the same. A person with fat lips speaks one way, and a person with thin lips speaks another way, and then you've got people with a thin upper and a fat lower or the other way around. My wife, now, she's a thin-lipped woman, so I can read thin-lipped people pretty well. What I need is someone with fat lips to work with. It's not easy, Mr. Haddock. You don't find many people with the kind of lips I'm looking for, and sometimes they can't speak natural when they know I'm reading them, so they're not much good to me. And then a lot of people just don't want to get involved."

"Why not? They don't care for the idea of someone reading their fat lips?"

"I guess they don't."

"Maybe they think it's an invasion of privacy."

"Well, it sure isn't that, Mr. Haddock. I do all my reading in public. I don't sneak into a man's house to read his lips."

"What about my lips, Mackensen?"

"Sir?"

"Would you read my lips?"

"I can't read lips while I'm driving, Mr. Haddock."

"No, I mean would you read my lips if you had the chance, when you weren't driving?"

"Well, I sure wouldn't read your lips if you didn't want me to, Mr. Haddock."

"But ordinarily you read every set of lips you can, right?"

"It's my hobby, Mr. Haddock. Nothing personal about it, believe me."

"I believe you, Mackensen," said Haddock, and he let the subject drop, for they were nearing the office, and he wanted to rest for a minute or two before pulling himself together for another working day. He was tired already.

He had a heavy schedule. He welcomed it, though, for it sent memorandums flowing across his desk, it kept his telephone ringing, it brought in visitor after visitor, and finally, he hoped, the day would be devoured and he could leave.

But inevitably there came that midafternoon pause, the American siesta, when the other executives were overtaken by lethargy. They didn't make the calls they might have made, they couldn't muster the energy to walk down the hall to Haddock's office, and they tinkered drowsily with memorandums that needed no improvements. Haddock was left in a vacuum. There was work to be done, but the pressure to do it was gone. He was too tired to generate it himself.

For a time he sat slackly at his desk. Then he crossed the office and went into the bathroom. He washed his hands, cleaned his fingernails, and checked his suit for lint. When he'd done that, he washed his hands again. Then he adjusted the knot of his necktie. He was dawdling there; he really didn't want to go back into the office. Perhaps the phone would ring. Someone might buzz him on the intercom. He cocked his head, listening through the door, left ajar. He heard nothing. Nothing was in his office; nothing was awaiting him there.

He strode back in aggressively, his head slightly lowered, wading through that nothing. It was stronger now. It seemed to thrive on that dead midafternoon time. "Steady," he whispered, but then it occurred to him that whatever was watching him—if anything was—would be listening as well. The company produced equipment so sensitive that the slightest murmur could be picked up and amplified a thousandfold if need be.

So it would be better not to muse aloud. But his very footsteps on the carpet could be captured, couldn't they? Even the rhythm of his breathing and the beating of his heart might be electronically possessed by someone far away, unknown to him. And then, visually, the merest hint of an expression on his face could be caught, enlarged, and registered in precise definition, so that the fleeting emotions that would be effectively hidden from someone sitting right across the desk from him might be transparent to that distant observer.

He began pacing the room. It was better to keep moving. That way his image would be more difficult to home in on.

But he couldn't walk all day. He stopped. *Reason it out,*

Haddock, he thought. *One point at a time.* Granted, Mr. Nicholas had made the original installation years ago in the conference room, and—for the sake of argument—one could assume that the old man had decided to cover the adjoining presidential office, too, while he was at it.

Very well. But that didn't mean that he stayed glued to the set all day long, did it? Mr. Nicholas had better things to do than watch a man in an office. Even commercial television wasn't that dull. Besides, he would have to take time out for meals, wouldn't he? He couldn't watch every damned minute.

But when *didn't* he watch? You couldn't tell.

Surely Mr. Nicholas would tune in only for important meetings, when basic issues were up for decision. A man of his stature wouldn't be interested in anything trivial.

Haddock resumed his seat behind the desk, somewhat relieved. Right—Mr. Nicholas watched, but two or three times a year, a half-dozen at the maximum. He might make a few spot checks now and then, though. He might flip the thing on once in a while just for the hell of it, to see what was going on at the office back in New York.

And if now happened to be one of those times, he'd see his new president sitting vacantly behind his desk, wasting time.

Haddock picked up a memorandum, pursed his lips, and began reading. He couldn't concentrate on it. He kept thinking about the monitor problem.

If Mr. Nicholas really wanted to keep himself informed on significant events at the company—which he probably had the right, as founder, to do—then tuning in just on board meetings wouldn't be satisfactory. The most important business only rarely took place there. No, the key decisions were hammered out as events themselves demanded—haphazardly, for the most part, in response to a combination of factors that simply wouldn't submit to scheduling—and as Mr. Nicholas would undoubtedly realize from his own experience, he'd miss most of the real action unless he kept a very strict watch on things day by day. And that was impractical.

Unless . . . well, suppose he had his equipment rigged to start grinding away in response to a subtle alteration in the acid content of the air? Men under the emotional pressure of making tough decisions started pumping all sorts of fluids through their bodies, didn't they? Adrenaline or something. And no matter how cool they appeared on the surface, they exuded the stuff into the air, which could be detected by special equipment that in turn could trigger Mr. Nicholas' screen. Ring a bell, maybe. Signals would start popping all over the place when executive juices flowed.

It might be happening now. He was actually perspiring a little. The hand that was holding the memo wasn't steady. And his breath was quick. So right at this moment the damned thing could be pounding away like mad, and the old man would be hustling into the viewing room to see on the gigantic screen the company president magnified thrice life-size, a man alone in his office—a sweating, gasping, shuddering Haddock.

"Jesus," he muttered. He stood, turned toward the window, snatched out his handkerchief, and mopped his damp face.

Had to get hold of himself.

Smile.

He smiled—but then he realized that this made him look asinine. A man smiling at no one, at nothing?

He had to get some other human creature in there with him fast. He buzzed his secretary.

He felt a surge of relief as she entered.

"Miss Prince, I thought I'd better take another crack at that speech for the business news editors convention, if you wouldn't mind getting the last draft."

"I'll get it, Mr. Haddock."

She returned with a sheaf of typed manuscript, laid it on his desk before him, and then took her chair, her pencil and dictation pad ready, waiting for him to begin.

He realized that he had made another error. Miss Prince's love for him glowed from her every look, her every gesture. He, for his part, had accepted her silent adoration in a gentlemanly way, without once departing from an attitude of kindly correctness. Everyone knew that she loved him, but such harmless little passions were customary around the place, so no one thought a thing about it, particularly as she was careful to maintain in public a proper reserve. Only when they were alone did she permit her eyes timidly to caress him, her cheeks to bloom, and tiny sighs to warm her dutiful responses.

As she was doing now.

She thought they were alone, but they weren't. Probably they weren't. He couldn't say a thing to her about what he suspected. That was out of the question.

"Well, are we ready, Miss Prince?"

"Ready, Mr. Haddock."

She uttered the words with a soft little quaver in her voice. She didn't realize how obvious she was being. And her eyes—Haddock stole a quick look at them—her eyes were moist with tenderness.

Oh, God, he thought. She was making a fool of herself, poor creature. And what was Mr. Nicholas doing now? Staring with growing suspicion and disapproval at the two of them emblazoned on the screen before him—or cackling with amusement at the spectacle?

If he was watching. Surely he wasn't watching.

Haddock rose, frowning, and began to pace, holding the draft manuscript in one hand. "Well, here we go, Miss Prince." He remained as far away from her as he could, at the far end of the room. That way only one of them could be viewed in close-up. "I want to expand that paragraph at the top of page seven, so this will be a substitute for that material, OK?"

"Yes, Mr. Haddock."

She might as well have plainly said: "I love you, Mr. Haddock."

Haddock was so accustomed to dictating speeches that he didn't have to struggle to get his thoughts in order. He had that knack. Right now he wasn't giving much thought to what was coming out of his mouth. The words sounded all right, but he wasn't really listening. He was dictating to the walls. He didn't dare look at her. He had only to glance at her to make her blush, and he had to admit that in the past he occasionally had let his eyes linger on her a bit, which hardly made him a cad, but still he couldn't honestly say that he was totally guiltless, even though another man in his place might have taken advantage of such a sweet, young, innocent girl. . . .

Good God. He realized that for two or three fateful moments he had been doing precisely what he'd just been thinking about—gazing directly into her eyes.

She seemed ready to faint.

And what sort of nonsense had he been dictating? He was sure he'd strayed off the point somewhere.

"Better strike that last stuff," he said.

She struck it. She would have struck herself had he asked her to.

"What was it that came before that, Miss Prince?"

" 'in the forefront of the battle for public information,' " she quoted tenderly.

"Right," said Haddock, pacing again. "You as editors and we as producers of communications systems are in the forefront of the battle for public information. If a corporation is to be truly responsive to the public of which it is a part, then its actions must be reported widely and accurately, with nothing essential withheld or kept hidden. Everything must be subjected to full scrutiny, down to the most minute details, at every moment of the day—"

He broke off, confused. That wasn't what he had intended to say. He grimaced and ran his fingers through his hair. Miss Prince watched his fingers. She couldn't hold back a little tremor.

"That'll be all for now, Miss Prince." He couldn't go on. He had to get her out of there. She made him too nervous. Still, he needed a secretary. If he couldn't bring Miss Prince into his office without going through all this agony, what was he supposed to do?

Well, he'd manage somehow. It was a question of getting accustomed to the new order of things. Being watched wasn't so bad. It was the uncertainty that made a man jumpy. Goddamn it, was the old fellow watching or not?

He wanted to shout at the walls: "Hey, Edgar. Look at this." And then unzip his fly or something.

To be watched, watched, watched . . . and not to know, not

to be sure? Every instant of the day. Maybe the night as well—?

When the working day was over, he didn't feel much easier. He escaped the office—only to go to the apartment. And then next morning he'd get out of the apartment to return to the office, and this would be the pattern of his days, being shuttled from one to the other, and the only relief he could count on would be those brief periods in transit by limousine.

At a stop light he caught Mackensen's gaze in the rearview mirror.

"Listen, Mackensen, have my lips been moving?"

"Your lips? Not to my knowledge, Mr. Haddock."

"All right, but if you happen to notice my lips moving anytime, just tell me, will you? You know, a man sometimes gets to muttering to himself without realizing it, and I'd like to know about it if I start doing it."

"You want me to read what you mutter, sir?"

"No, no. I mean, just tell me if I start doing it."

"Sure will, Mr. Haddock. I'll keep an eye on you, sir."

Haddock watched the filthy streets slip by. Black snow was heaped like coal in the gutters. His gloved hands ached. He glanced down at them, wondering why. Oh, yes. He had them tightly clenched.

I can't go on this way, he thought. No, it was stupid. He couldn't do useful work under such conditions. He'd have to take immediate action. Right. First thing tomorrow he'd telephone Mr. Elphinstone and inform him that he was going to have a crew of technicians from the research center in New Jersey come over, locate the transmitter in the conference room, and remove it. And the reason? Well, he'd simply say that it was contrary to prudent security to have the company's private discussions subject to a monitoring system controlled by someone who—founder or not—wasn't a member of the present board. And then, did Mr. Elphinstone know for certain that the system was still in Mr. Nicholas' hands? Evidently he didn't. He didn't know a thing about it. Obviously the only thing to do was to get rid of it at once, and Mr. Elphinstone could, as a matter of courtesy, inform Mr. Nicholas of Haddock's decision.

So that would take care of the conference room—but what about the president's office? What about the apartment?

Well, that might be another matter. He could imagine Mr. Elphinstone's withered old face freezing with suspicion when he was told about the other installations. Haddock's story wouldn't be credible, not without proof. Mr. Elphinstone would wonder what sort of paranoid personality had gotten into the president's chair.

All right, he could have the technicians do the job without telling Mr. Elphinstone. Just have them come in and get it done. But they might have to rip into all the walls and the ceilings as well. He could hardly risk having the office, conference room, and apartment virtually dismantled without at least advising the chairman in advance, and a solidly based explanation would have to be provided.

He could have the technicians come in just to locate the installations. Fine—then he'd have the proof, and the work of removal could proceed. But suppose they couldn't tell where the damned things were without some exploratory chipping away? And in any event, the word would spread through the company, so if his suspicions weren't verified, he'd look pretty silly. He might ask a private detective agency to do the job on the sly . . . but no, he couldn't do that.

Suppose the story got out somehow? That the president of one of the nation's top electronic manufacturers had called in outside detectives on such a matter!

Well, damn it, why couldn't he just telephone directly to Mr. Nicholas? *Excuse me, Mr. Nicholas, but are you watching your little old set a lot these days, sir? And do you happen to have the apartment tuned in, too? . . . No, no, I don't mind it, Mr. Nicholas. Not in the least. I just called to see if there wasn't something I could do on my end, sir, to help you. Like moving a chair or something to give you a better angle . . .*

Yes, but it wasn't funny. It really wasn't funny. If he wasn't careful, if he didn't reason the whole thing out step by step and act only when he was sure of his ground, then he might find himself in real trouble.

But he *was* in real trouble. Wasn't he? It felt that way.

"Your lips moved, Mr. Haddock."

"What?"

"I said your lips moved, sir."

"Oh. Well, I just smiled, Mackensen. That's all. I smiled."

"There's something that's been troubling me, Doctor."

"Yes?"

"It may sound sort of odd, but I've had the feeling that I'm . . . being watched."

"Being watched, Mr. Haddock?"

"You know, kept under observation."

"I see," said Dr. Despard with an understanding smile. Haddock had just completed his annual physical checkup and was having a final conference with the internist, who encouraged his patients to disclose their private worries to him so that his analysis could be complete.

52

"Obviously it's some sort of neurotic reaction," Haddock went on, "but I thought I'd mention it."

"Yes, yes," said Dr. Despard. "I'm glad you did. That's what we're here for, Mr. Haddock. That's our job." He was a medical version of Haddock, a smooth and dapper fellow who radiated a warm sincerity. "Tell me," he asked, "how long have you had this feeling?"

"Well, about two months. It started shortly after I was made president of my company, so I've wondered if there might be some connection there."

"There may indeed, Mr. Haddock. There may indeed." Dr. Despard smiled knowledgeably and made a little note in Haddock's file. "And this sensation of being under observation . . . you feel it at the office, I suppose?"

"Yes, that's right." Haddock hesitated. He wondered whether he ought to mention the apartment, too, but he was wary of going that far. That might make him seem really unbalanced. Besides, the apartment was just an extension of the same basic problem, so he wasn't concealing anything of importance.

"At the office," Dr. Despard repeated. "I see. And you feel this is all subjective on your part? Purely imaginary, would you say?"

"Absolutely imaginary," Haddock replied. "I mean, nobody's really watching me. It's completely subjective, as you say." He glanced about the consulting room. Its restrained but expensive professional elegance reassured him. Mr. Nicholas seemed remote now, hardly more than a bad dream. "Just a nervous reaction," he added more confidently. "I knew that's what it was right from the beginning, and I'm all the more convinced of it now."

"Ah," said Dr. Despard with a wise and sympathetic smile.

53

"Well, I think I can make some tentative comment on what's bothering you, Mr. Haddock, unless you have something further to add at this point."

"Nothing to add, really," said Haddock, and he settled back, awaiting Dr. Despard's judgment that he was being plagued by a common neurosis that would in time fade completely away.

"I'd like to say," the internist began, "that your physical condition is excellent. You're a little tired, but fundamentally you're a healthy male animal, Mr. Haddock, and your career achievement record demonstrates you to be sane, responsible, socially well integrated, and all the rest of it. Now," Dr. Despard added in a tone of genial paternalism, "when such a man comes to me and tells me that he has a problem of the kind you've just indicated, do you know what my assumption is?"

Haddock smiled at him expectantly.

"My assumption," said Dr. Despard, "is that there is some real basis for it."

Haddock stirred uneasily in his chair. "What do you mean by that, Doctor?"

Dr. Despard, pleased by Haddock's reaction, sat smiling at him complacently. "I mean precisely what I said, my friend. You have the sensation that you're being watched. Well, Mr. Haddock, you *are* being watched!"

"Good God, Doctor!"

Dr. Despard chuckled soothingly. "Don't be alarmed, Mr. Haddock. It's really quite simple, quite normal, quite ordinary."

Haddock looked at him doubtfully.

"As president of your company," the doctor continued, "you've suddenly taken on a vastly increased importance in

54

the eyes of your co-workers, and so they're sensitive to every-thing about you—what you say, what you leave unsaid, your daily moods, your preferences and your dislikes, and so forth. All these things are of real concern to them now—and so they're keeping an eye on you. I don't mean they're peeking through your keyhole or anything like that, but they're definitely watching you, for good reason, too, and your awareness of this situation—which you may not fully acknowledge on a conscious level—has helped produce this little anxiety of yours."

"Yes, yes," said Haddock, much relieved. "That's right, Doctor. I knew that, of course, but—"

"But you just didn't give it proper weight, is that it?"

"That's it."

"And believe me, Mr. Haddock, your complaint is a com-mon one. We ought to call it the New President Syndrome or something!" Dr. Despard laughed cheerily; Haddock laughed, too. "Just be patient, Mr. Haddock," the doctor added. "I won't say that you'll be freed from this problem, because you never will be, not entirely, for it's a real problem, not an imaginary one, and it's a part of your situational apparatus as president, you understand."

"I certainly understand that," said Haddock in eager agreement. "I just wish I'd been able to think of it that way sooner."

"And another thing," said Dr. Despard with a satisfied expression. "You ought to remember that this watching business works both ways. They're watching you—and you're watching *them*. Am I right?"

"Well, I guess I am."

"You've got to. It's part of your job. Again, I don't mean you spy on them. I mean you have supervisory authority over them, so you have to keep yourself adequately informed on their job performances, isn't that so?"

"Yes, yes. Of course."

"Now, there's a further wrinkle in this thing, Mr. Haddock. Do you know who's keeping the closest watch on you of all?"

Haddock glanced at him with an inquiring smile.

"Do you know who's watching you every minute of the day while you're seated at your desk in the office?"

Haddock's smile faded.

"Every minute of the day," the doctor repeated with a glint of humor in his eye, "and every minute of the night as well—in the office, Mr. Haddock, and in your very own home, too?"

Haddock was staring at him in wonder and alarm.

"Do you know who, Mr. Haddock?" asked Dr. Despard, smiling in triumphant anticipation.

"Well, I think so," Haddock mumbled in confusion, "I mean—"

But Dr. Despard hadn't heard him. "I'll tell you who that is, Mr. Haddock. It's you yourself!"

"*Me.*"

"Exactly!" Dr. Despard settled back in his chair, gratified by the effect of his little performance. "Your understandable anxiety about your abilities as president has caused you to keep a strict and unremitting guard upon your every thought and action, or I miss my guess!"

Haddock began chuckling. His palms were damp. He wiped them on his trouser legs. "You meant me all along, is that right, Doctor?"

"Of course, Mr. Haddock!"

Haddock couldn't stop chuckling. He was laughing outright, in fact. "You had me mystified there for a minute, Doctor," he gasped between bursts of laughter. "I mean, I thought you were going to . . . well, I didn't know *what* you were driving at. And it turns out to be me!"

"But you're not really surprised at my conclusion, are you?"

"No, no," said Haddock, striving to compose himself. It wasn't easy. "Not at all."

"So you're the real culprit, Mr. Haddock," said Dr. Despard cheerfully. "The people in your office are contributing to the situation, of course, but it's an internal matter, too, and that part of it you'll be able to deal with soon enough, if I'm any judge of your determination and character."

"I'm sure you're right," said Haddock, wiping his eyes. A stray chuckle escaped. "Honestly," he added with sincere gratitude, "you've helped me a lot, Doctor. You've put your finger on the problem, all right. I feel a hundred percent better right now; I really do." And he did. He was light and relaxed, as though a physical burden had been lifted from him, and this buoyant sense of freedom remained in full force after he'd said good-bye to Dr. Despard and taken a taxi back to the apartment.

When he arrived, he celebrated by asking Frey to make him a martini. He took it into the living room with a copy of the afternoon paper and sat down on the sofa to browse through the news columns.

And then he glanced around the walls, and he couldn't help wondering: if it was installed in the master bedroom —and it wasn't, of course, it wasn't—but just suppose, for the sake of argument, that it had been. Then . . .

Would it be there in the living room, too?

* * *

He knew he had to put Mr. Nicholas out of his mind. It was no longer a distraction. It had become an obsession. He could hardly think of anything else. Whenever he set himself to work on some problem, his attention would be sapped by the suspicion that Mr. Nicholas was there, and struggle against it as he might, it refused to give way. It grew stronger. It became a certainty. Mr. Nicholas was reading over his shoulder! Mr. Nicholas was peering into his face! Mr. Nicholas was devouring him with his terrible electronic gaze! And so, angrily shoving his papers aside, Haddock would rise to his feet and pace about the office and then return to his desk and try again . . . and again the awareness of Mr. Nicholas would edge into his thoughts; again Mr. Nicholas would swell like a genie, filling the room with his presence.

"Go away!" he shouted once. "In the name of God, go away and leave me in peace!"

Miss Prince hurried in, alarmed.

He told her he'd been bothered by a fly. "It's gone now," he said as she glanced about, puzzled—a fly in March? "When it comes back, I'll swat it."

But he couldn't swat Mr. Nicholas.

His work was suffering, not only because his capacity to concentrate was impaired but also because the sensation of being watched deflated his self-confidence. If only Mr. Nicholas would appear in person to argue with him over this decision or that, if only he'd come storming into the office, red-faced and outraged over some error! It was the silence that shook Haddock's nerves. What was the old man thinking? Why didn't he make some comment or other? If he didn't like the way Haddock was managing things, let him say so!

Well, no one was watching. He knew that. He did have a

creepy sensation to the contrary, but that was only nerves. He had to conquer it. He set his jaw so hard that his teeth ached, and for the thousandth time he told himself: "I don't believe any of it. I don't believe. I don't believe in Mr. Nicholas."

And yet he couldn't help returning to the idea that there might be some useful purpose in this fantasy of his. For the first time since his childhood he was really lonely, and he knew that lonely people try to fill the emptiness around them with their imaginings. Hadn't he done just that when he'd been a boy? He'd invented imaginary playmates. He hadn't been able to see them, either, had he? And then to calm himself at night, when he'd been terrified by ghosts and witches and by the horrible things that hid in the corners of his bedroom waiting until he closed his eyes, he had invented his own guardian monster. It was a hideous creature—it had to be hideous, to keep the others at bay—but even while he'd been frightened by it, he'd known that it wasn't really going to harm him.

Was Mr. Nicholas the friendly monster of his presidency? Was Mr. Nicholas really a protection against something worse?

Sometimes he thought that he'd better settle for Mr. Nicholas. "After all," he reflected, "I know Mr. Nicholas. Well, I don't really *know* him, but . . ."

In any event, he seemed powerless in the matter. But he told himself that it wouldn't be so hard. He'd get used to it after a while. He ought to think of Mr. Nicholas in a more positive way—as the founding father of the company, as his benefactor perched up in the walls somewhere (or maybe in the ceiling), keeping a kindly eye on him. Yes, Mr. Nicholas: his friend.

He would like Mr. Nicholas. He was starting to like him a

little bit already. *Mr. Nicholas* ... why, the very name sounded like Christmas! A time of happiness and friendship and love! Yes, he'd take that attitude! He'd like Mr. Nicholas—and Mr. Nicholas would like him, too!

He cast his warmest smile around the empty office. *Let him know that you know, Haddock. Let him know that you don't mind a bit. Let him know that you really enjoy it!*

One evening in March he had a dozen guests in for dinner, as a belated sort of housewarming, for he'd been too busy to do any entertaining earlier.

These were Haddock's personal friends, men and women from business and the professions who were dynamic, successful and unattached. Some of them had been married, several still had husbands or wives in the background somewhere, but their careers were of chief importance to them, and so for companionship they sought out those who felt the same way they did. Within the set there were casual affairs, in which the partners changed from time to time without causing any particular fuss or stir. Haddock himself had spent occasional weekends with each of the women; but if Ginny, for example, were to decline such an invitation in order to go skiing with Walter instead, Haddock wouldn't have felt the slightest pang—nor would Walter if the situation were reversed. Jealousy and rivalry were out of style in the set, and anybody who started betraying such passions simply didn't get included anymore.

As they began arriving at the apartment, Haddock realized what a mistake he'd made in not having them over sooner. Their high spirits brightened the rooms and filled the emptiness he'd found there. They admired everything they saw. They found the view magnificent and the furnishings in excellent taste. Everyone had some compliment to make, to which Haddock responded with a natural grace he hadn't possessed in weeks. He was surprised by this and grateful for it. Surrounded by these agreeable people, he felt cheerful and relaxed, and he permitted himself to accept a second cocktail from the tray that Frey brought around instead of limiting himself to only one. He'd completely forgotten about Mr. Nicholas. Well, he hadn't forgotten, exactly, but the question seemed less important at the moment. He was actually enjoying himself!

By the time dinner was served, he was in an ebullient mood. The dining room was lighted by candles whose flames, multiplied in the mirrors and windows, gleamed like the lights of the city itself. Its walls glowed from the brilliance of the silver and crystal on the bright cloth. Looking at the lively faces of the men and women assembled at the table, Haddock felt a surge of optimism. With such friends as these, what could possibly trouble him?

Being a good host was more or less like being a good president, he reflected. One selected the right combination of guests and arranged their seating order with care, and then made certain that no one was neglected and that the conversation remained within the bounds of civility and friendliness. And as a matter of fact, he perceived that a disagreement was developing to his left, where a stockbroker named Paul Jaspard was beginning to dispute warmly with a lawyer, Larry Bolling, who was condemning the space program as a waste of public funds and a misdirection of technical energies. Their voices were rising above the level Haddock thought proper for the dinner table, and so he decided to enter the discussion on Jaspard's side, to turn Bolling's attention his way, after which he'd be able to deflect the conversation into some less controversial channel.

His satisfaction at the success of his little party caused him to take Jaspard's part too jauntily, evidently. Bolling was ruffled and gave him a sharp glance. Then he asked in his sarcastic courtroom voice whether Haddock's company held space-agency contracts.

"Sure we do, Larry," Haddock replied with an engaging grin. "Any company worth its salt has some interest in that program, but are you suggesting that my views are influenced by that fact?"

"It wouldn't be unnatural," Bolling retorted.

Haddock's grin broadened. "What—do you think I'm some sort of propagandist? That I'm an agent in the pay of a domestic power?"

There was laughter at this remark. It annoyed Bolling all the more. He thought Haddock was poking fun at him. "You do a lot of military work, don't you, Had?" he said aggressively.

"Space isn't military, Larry."

"What about the spy satellites? You help make those, I'm willing to bet. Those things that can read the trademark on a golf ball from forty thousand feet up?"

Haddock laughed and replied that the only golf-ball trademarks he'd helped anybody in Washington to read were those on the fairways of the country clubs down there, but when Bolling persisted in pressing him, he smilingly reminded him that he could say little on defense subjects, owing to security restrictions. "I can tell you anything you want to know about our civilian systems, Larry," he said.

Bolling was still irritated. "All right, Had. Tell me about the wiretapping equipment you make, then."

Haddock hesitated. "Well, Larry, we make a lot of electronic equipment, and if you're talking about the authorized and legal use of—"

"I'm talking about wiretapping equipment."

Haddock put fresh energy into his smile. "Larry," he said in his most candid manner, "if you want me to take an oath that the equipment we manufacture is never put to uses which are improper, obviously I can't do that, anymore than an automobile manufacturer can guarantee you that one of his cars won't be used in a bank robbery. Speaking of cars," he added, trying to leave the wiretapping question behind, "one of our most successful communications systems is in the area of traffic control. . . ." And he went on briefly to describe the traffic monitor system until Bolling, not yet mollified, interrupted him.

"Why do you keep referring to that equipment as being communications equipment?"

"That's what it is, Larry."

"Well, communications equipment to me means a telephone. Some device that enables people to communicate with each other. But your monitoring systems are surveillance systems. They don't fit into a definition of communications at all."

"Well, I believe they do, Larry," said Haddock. The other conversations along the table were ceasing, as the attention of the guests had been caught by the hostility in Bolling's voice. "We don't happen to manufacture telephones, but we're still working on the assumption that communications is our business," he added, more sharply than he'd intended to. Twelve faces were turned his way. (And was there a thirteenth?) "The telephone is quite frankly a pretty old-fashioned instrument, Larry. I'm not saying it still isn't important and useful as a basic tool—obviously it is—but we couldn't possibly cope with the demands of the modern world if we hadn't gone far beyond that. If Edison were alive today, I can assure you that he'd be working on sensors and monitors right in the vanguard of communications research."

"Surveillance research," said Bolling.

Haddock grinned. "Honestly, Larry, it seems to me that you're too concerned about definitions, and maybe we need to coin a new word here, but the word 'surveillance' doesn't bother me, I can assure you." It did bother him, though. It was a word that hardly ever appeared in company memorandums. He glanced smilingly along the table; then his gaze lifted to the opposite wall and lingered there briefly. He knew that, as host, he should turn this subject aside with a joking remark; but he had other obligations as well, didn't he? The very essence of his company's function was being questioned right there in the presence of . . . well, it didn't matter in whose presence. He simply couldn't let Bolling's remarks go unanswered. "All right, let's call it 'surveillance,' " he went on. "But let's take a good, hard look at what it amounts to in reality. I've mentioned traffic control. The object of that is to save lives and prevent property damage. The same thing is true in the case of the systems we install in apartment buildings. They act as a deterrent to crime, because the criminal realizes that he can't act unobserved. We're putting them in banks and subways, too, and also in public toilets, to discourage perversion and vandalism, and as for those so-called spy satellites, they also act as a deterrent, for a potential enemy realizes that he can't make offensive preparations undetected. So you can call it surveillance if you want to, Larry, but to me it's something that

64

promotes security, prosperity, and peace, and no label you can try to stick on it is going to make me anything but proud and honored to be associated with it."

Bolling cleared his throat, but Haddock, leaning forward with an ingratiating smile, forestalled him. "Now, I realize that as a lawyer, Larry," he continued, "you may feel that there could be a certain potential abuse, by which I mean the invasion of the privacy of law-abiding people, but I can assure you that this concern is absolutely and completely groundless. We're not invading privacy, we're protecting it. We're protecting the right of people to enjoy their privacy without fear. You might even say that we're waging war against fear." He smiled at his guests, confident that he had scored a telling point . . . but was his tone a bit strident? His voice too loud? "Fear—that's the real enemy, Larry," he said, but he wasn't speaking to the lawyer anymore. His voice was raised; his eyes were, too. He was smiling at that dim opposite wall, where the candlelight cast shadows. "It's fear that invades a man's privacy," he said. A plate clanged. Someone's fork had slipped. It startled him, and he swung halfway around to glance at the wall behind him. "Fear," he repeated. Then he turned back. "The world is full of unknown threats and dangers, Larry. What we're trying to do is to reduce the worry that people have by increasing their knowledge of these dangers. We're shining the light of communications into dark places! We're translating the unknown into the known! And it's the unknown that creates fear."

He broke off. Was there something wrong? He searched the faces of his likable friends. He found no clues there. Perhaps he had spoken a bit dramatically. His hands might be shaking just a trifle. He wiped them on his napkin.

"That's all very interesting, Had," Bolling said, "but how

do you know that some of your customers aren't using your systems to get information they shouldn't be getting?"

"Larry, I can promise you we take every precaution," Haddock said quickly, but he didn't at all care for the way this discussion had been going, and he was grateful when Carla Cox broke in with a story about the elaborate measures her fashion house took to prevent its dress designs from being copied in advance of the seasonal showings.

After dinner he recovered his good spirits. Several guests had to leave early—luckily Bolling was one of them—but the others remained. Haddock put some records on for dancing. Lily Estival, by request, did a few of her impersonations, and Paul did several magic tricks with his disappearing cards. Later there was general amusement when Jenny Schwartz said she was convinced that her ex-husband was following her movements electronically. "What do you mean?" someone asked. And she answered, "He's got me bugged," at which everybody laughed. Haddock laughed the loudest. "He's just communicating with you," someone else remarked. "Right, Had?" And Haddock laughed some more. Jenny turned toward him. "Seriously," she said, "could he really do that? Could he plant something on me I wouldn't know about?" Which question Haddock smilingly ducked. "There's only one way to find out," he said. "We'll just have to debug you, bit by bit. Volunteers?" he called out to the men, and if the circumstances and mood of the party had been different, his joking suggestion might have led to something, but as it was, everyone simply laughed, and the subject was dropped. Around midnight they all thanked Haddock for a wonderful evening and took their leave.

He went down to the street with the last of them. "Good night, good night," he called out, shivering in the chill wind, the filthy snow smearing his shoes. He was sorry to see them go. Reluctantly he turned back to the building, where the night guard stood waiting for him in the entrance. In the lobby he glanced about to see if there was a central monitor. No, there wasn't. Odd that he hadn't noticed this before. Well, there was a sales possibility right there in his own building, wasn't there?

It was worse that night. He couldn't sleep.

First he tried making the bedroom dark. He adjusted the draperies so that no light could enter from the outside. He stuffed a twist of tissue paper into the keyhole of the door. But as he lay in bed staring into the darkness, he wasn't satisfied. He suspected that the absence of light wouldn't guarantee him his privacy. The system—if there were a system—might be one of those types that generated its own light. It might even use the heat of his body as its source of power. In that case, the only solution would be to turn himself off. A dead man was cold. Then he realized that a cadaver didn't cool all at once. The image of his corpse would fade slowly. It would be visible for hours. This somehow seemed grossly unfair.

He switched on every lamp in the room. He picked up a mystery novel, but he couldn't concentrate his attention on it. Was someone reading over his shoulder? Well, if so, he wouldn't object. He didn't want to hog the book. The problem was, he couldn't tell at what rate he ought to turn the pages. He'd better assume that Mr. Nicholas read quickly, and if the old man happened to get caught up by the story, he'd get impatient waiting for Haddock to turn the next page.

He cast the book angrily aside. How childishly he was behaving! There *was* no Mr. Nicholas. Well, there was a Mr. Nicholas, but he was living in retirement down in Pennsylvania. The Mr. Nicholas who dwelt in his walls was a pure and absolute invention. Haddock's little neurosis. And the best way to handle a neurosis was openly and honestly. Coax it out. Get acquainted with it. Make friends with it, so to speak.

Yes, recognize the damned thing. Talk to it. He opened his mouth. No words came out. He was silenced by his prejudice against talking to himself. It wasn't a healthy habit.

He resolved on a stratagem. He always kept a pocket tape recorder handy so that he could dictate memorandums whenever the need arose. It was there on his bed table. Now he could address himself directly to his problem by speaking aloud in a natural and acceptable manner.

He picked up the tiny machine. It had an official feel in his hand that counseled him not to make his remarks too personal. Suppose somebody got hold of the tape and heard him babbling a lot of nonsense to some nonexistent person?

"Following are some observations for possible future use in speech material," he began self-consciously. "On communications," he added, glancing sheepishly about. He paused to take a breath. His heart was banging away. My God, he was having a little stage fright. "My own career," he went on uncertainly, "has been devoted to communications, and now I have the deep personal honor to head one of the biggest companies in this highly complex and demanding field." That sounded safe enough. No one could object to that.

He began pacing about the room, the tape recorder in one hand. It was nearly two o'clock in the morning, and he was bleary with fatigue. He really wanted to go back to bed and try to get some sleep, but now that he'd begun dictating so portentously, he didn't feel that he could just abandon it. That might look strange.

"Communications," he repeated, frowning, trying to focus his thoughts. "Communications is more important than ever in our overcrowded world. . . ." He hesitated. He wasn't exactly having that man-to-man chat with Mr. Nicholas he'd envisaged, but no matter; he'd work around to it. "When men are living jammed together in large numbers, their safety and convenience require constant watchfulness. We've got to know what the other fellow is doing so we don't step on his toes or bump into him when we go around the corner—and he's got to know what we're doing, too, for the same reason, and so the more everybody knows about what everybody else is doing . . . well, the safer things are, aren't they? Damned right they are! And as for personal privacy in the old-fashioned meaning of the word—well, you can't expect to have your cake and eat it, too. No, if you want to enjoy the benefits of an expanding industrial society on a safe and secure basis, you've got to be prepared to pay the admission price. And as the president of a company that is helping in an important way to make all this possible, I've got to set a good example! I realize that fully! And I don't object—not in the slightest!"

He shivered. The heat had been turned down for the night. He set the recorder on the bed table while he went to the closet for his bathrobe. He put it on and knotted the belt firmly.

"It's an honor, actually," he resumed. "I really and truly believe that. It isn't every man who could stand this sort of thing, but I'm fully aware of the responsibility involved, and

69

I accept it without any reservations whatever." He smoothed his hair with his free hand and glanced about the room, smiling. "My life has been an open book. I don't mean I'm perfect, but I've never done anything to be ashamed of. I believe in the brotherhood of man, and by that I mean that I'm convinced that no man does evil, provided he has a genuine understanding of his fellow man . . . and he can't obtain that understanding if he's alone and cut off from them. No, he's got to be in touch somehow. That's where communications comes in. To help us understand, to help us behave like decent human beings." He glanced about the room again. "Yes, that's what it really is," he said fervently, smiling all the more. "The man who uses communications to observe his fellow men, he's doing it in order to adjust his behavior to their needs, in a positive way! That is, he observes in order to gain understanding—and for what purpose? To avoid harmful actions! To perform beneficial ones! Exactly! Therefore such a man is bound to be motivated by the desire to do good! And the act of observation—why, that's the very essence of goodness!"

He pressed the button that operated the draperies. They parted, revealing the dark cut of the East River below and the lights of Queens beyond. He wandered up to the window. Reflected there, as on a dim, gigantic screen, was his own image, a weary man in a bathrobe, clutching a tiny machine.

"All brothers out there," he said into the recorder, speaking low, almost whispering. "Living their separate little lives. And yet if they could join hands, in a symbolic sense, if they could only touch one another somehow. To touch, that's the thing." He swung around, smiling at the walls. "That's what it's all about, isn't it? Some kind of contact? Not touching, maybe. You can't literally touch everybody. But a contact of the senses, that's the principle involved!" He felt a rush of hope, as though he were on the verge of an important discovery. "Right! And the only sense that can do the job is the visual one. In brief, the human eye!"

He smiled with genuine enthusiasm. He felt that he had expressed himself clumsily, but that didn't matter. Mr. Nicholas would understand. In fact, Mr. Nicholas would have known already. The old man no doubt had been silently urging him along this very line of thought in order to arrive at that conclusion!

"Brotherhood!" Haddock said excitedly into the tape recorder. "Human decency and understanding! Communication via the eye of man, electronically assisted!"

But as he gazed eagerly about the room, vainly seeking some sign of acknowledgment and approval, he realized that there was nothing human there apart from himself and that he was exhausted and beaded with a chill perspiration.

He clicked off the tape recorder, went back to bed, and switched off the lights. The last thing he did was to run the tape back to the beginning. Then he erased everything he'd said.

In the morning he told Mackensen to drive him to the company's research and development center in New Jersey.

It was a raw day. A bitter wind blew in the streets. Haddock was warm and secure in the car, however. He felt a little groggy from the lack of sleep, but he was more confident of his position. He was president, after all. He was fully outfitted in the trappings of command—armored in a good thousand dollars' worth of clothing, including gloves, hat, and overcoat, and mounted, so to speak, on a great, sleek

71

limousine fit for royalty—and he was moving aggressively on to the attack.

He was going to determine once and for all precisely what technical possibilities were available to Mr. Nicholas. That was the first step and perhaps the most important of all. Suppose it turned out that every type of system required a certain amount of light? Well, he couldn't conduct his business in a darkened office, but at least his nights would be secure. He could switch off the lights, hop in bed, and sleep in the blissful certainty that he was quite alone, in every sense of the word. Let Mr. Nicholas watch him all he pleased the rest of the time, as long as those eight blessed hours of slumber were guaranteed.

True, he'd have to be circumspect in his questioning. It wouldn't do to let the technical people know what his real interest was. Word might filter back somehow. As it was, he was taking a bit of a chance by going directly to the laboratories. Normally a president would summon the research director to the head office, wouldn't he? "The hell with that," he told himself. "I just need to remember that I'm president, and I can do whatever I want to. I don't owe explanations to anybody. They're the ones who have to do the explaining. I've got to radiate confidence, that's all."

He practiced radiating confidence. He put a keen glint in his eyes and cocked his head at an arrogant angle. Too bad there wasn't a mirror in the car. Well, there was, but it was the rearview mirror up front.

He leaned forward. "Mackensen, suppose somebody didn't want you reading his lips, so he grew a mustache. How would you handle that?"

"A mustache, Mr. Haddock? Well, that would depend. If it didn't droop down over the upper lip, it wouldn't bother me.

72

Actually, a full-bearded man is easier to read than a clean-shaven one, because his beard will give you a good, dark background for the lips, so they stand out nice and clear."

"Yes, but with a mustache, Mackensen. Suppose it did droop down over the upper lip?"

"Oh, well. In that case, I wouldn't have enough to work on. You can't read just one lip, Mr. Haddock."

"I see. Thank you for that information, Mackensen."

"Anytime, Mr. Haddock."

Twenty minutes after they left the Turnpike, they arrived at the research center, a group of long, low buildings set in a smoggy industrial valley. Smokestack discharges had turned the snow that clung in nearby thickets to a brilliant hue of orange.

Haddock had been there on several past occasions, although never as president, and he was acquainted with the top staff members. He walked briskly through the halls straight to the office of the research director, Andrew Cooley, a tall, thin fellow who worked in his shirt sleeves with his cuffs rolled up above the elbow. Cooley was surprised at the unexpected appearance of the company's new president and seemed to be ill at ease even after Haddock told him he'd come to New Jersey on other business and, finding himself so close to the labs, had decided to drop by to say hello. Haddock then went on to say that he knew too little about certain areas of company operations, such as research, so he wanted to take every available opportunity to educate himself. He noticed with some satisfaction that his genial manner was having a soothing effect on his research director—and then he realized that he was doing the opposite of what he'd intended to do; that is, he wasn't being confident and commanding, he was simply being ingratiating, as though his chief purpose was to win Cooley's friendship. "I'm not tough enough," he admonished himself. "I've got to quit being nice."

"Wonder if I could check over your monitor research, Andy," he said with a glance at his watch, as though to show he was in a hurry. "I don't mean the civilian side of it. As you know, I'm pretty well acquainted with that."

"Right, Henry." Cooley remained motionless in his chair, however. Haddock expected that he would pick up the phone to advise the appropriate technicians that a visit was in store for them, but he didn't.

"You call it 'special projects,' I believe," Haddock added.

"That's it, Henry. That's right." Still Cooley did nothing. He seemed embarrassed.

"This won't create any problem for you, will it, Andy?" Haddock put a little tartness into his tone.

"No, no," said Cooley hastily. He hesitated. "Well, Henry, you know that area is restricted."

"Of course."

"It's not our security, it's a Defense Department requirement."

"I realize that, Andy."

"So access is denied to anybody who isn't specifically cleared—and, well, you just aren't on the cleared list, Henry. I mean, you aren't on it yet."

"Oh. I see."

"If I'd known in advance, we could have tried to get special clearance. It's just one of those red-tape things, you know."

Haddock nodded. He was immeasurably disappointed. He'd counted on finding out what he wanted to know that very day.

"I know it doesn't make sense for the president of a company not to be able to see everything his own company's doing, Henry," the research director went on unhappily, "but when you're tied in with Defense, you do it their way on security. They're pretty picky about that."

Haddock had two choices. He could bluster and roar and announce he'd take full responsibility and be damned to the Defense Department, or he could withdraw gracefully.

"Oh, it doesn't make any difference, Andy," he said with an understanding smile. "I'll get the clearance business going once I get back to the office, and I'm glad you reminded me about it. In the meantime, I'll just take a look at some other aspect of your operations."

"Henry, I'm glad you understand our little problem," said Cooley gratefully, and Haddock knew that he'd certainly cemented his friendship with this important member of the company team, even if he'd failed completely in the purpose of his visit. He spent a dull forty minutes inspecting visual-aid education devices, responding politely to the explanations of the engineers, and when Cooley accompanied him out to his car, he inquired casually how long the clearance process usually took. "Oh, for you they'll ram it right through," Cooley replied encouragingly. "I'd say you could get it inside of two months for sure."

Two months.

"Thanks a lot, Andy," Haddock said with a friendly smile.

It was twenty minutes past eleven when he arrived at the office. George Imry, the executive vice president, and three other executives were waiting for him there. He'd forgotten that he'd scheduled a meeting with them for eleven sharp. "Terribly sorry, gentlemen," he said, hanging up his coat

75

and hat. "That traffic is really something today. I was just—"
He broke off. He didn't need to explain. He was president.

"Henry, why don't we go into the conference room?" Imry
suggested. "We can spread out more in there."

"No, no," Haddock said quickly. He hurried to his desk
and sat behind it, to forestall a move. Not that it mattered.
"It's sunnier in here," he added, smiling. It wasn't sunnier,
really. "I don't want to waste another second of your time,"
he said, spreading his smile from one face to another. They
didn't respond to it very well, though. What was wrong? Did
he look rattled? He felt rattled. His defeat at the laboratories
had shaken him. *Two more months. Sixty days, sixty nights.*

He frowned down at the folders on his desk and tried to
compose his thoughts for the meeting.

"Well, gentlemen—" he began, but Imry interrupted him.

"By the way, Henry," he said, "I understand that you
dropped by the R and D labs this morning."

Haddock glanced up. He could feel himself paling. He
took a swift look around the walls and at the ceiling.

"Andy gave me a call a little while ago," Imry went on. "He
said you wanted to get a special security clearance."

Haddock wanted to rise and leave the room, he wanted to
throw a handful of memorandums in Imry's thick potato
face—anything to stop him—but he could only sit there
wordlessly staring, his mouth dry, a sensation of chill descending into his stomach. He tried to shrug, to show his
indifference. All he did was twitch. Worse—now he was
grinning, but he shouldn't be grinning. He'd been caught
like a schoolboy. Somebody had snitched to the teacher, and
now the teacher was reprimanding him in the principal's
office. And the principal was probably watching.

"Sorry you didn't check with me beforehand, Henry,"

Imry said, his little eyes alert. He seemed surprised by Haddock's discomfiture but pleased by it, too. He'd never forgiven Haddock for having gotten the presidency. "I could have saved you the trip."

"It doesn't matter," Haddock said hoarsely.

"You wanted to see the special-projects division, I believe."

"No, no. That is, I just happened to mention it to Andy in passing, that's all." Haddock was aware that they were all wondering why he was so visibly upset. "There's no point wasting time on this now, George," he added, but his tone of voice wasn't firm, it was pleading.

"I just wanted to clear up one little point that Andy evidently neglected to tell you, Henry," Imry said. "As you may know, clearance is requested on a need-to-know basis. We've got to provide a reasonable justification."

Haddock nodded. He made no reply. Now, he felt, there was no possibility of escape. He glanced quickly at the walls—a glance of timid defiance. *Yes, I tried. I failed. So here I am. Back again.*

"Well, Henry," said Imry, studying Haddock's features attentively, "was there any particular reason why you wanted to see special projects?"

"Actually no, George. I merely—"

"Andy said you asked to see the monitor work there, is that right?"

"Well, I don't specifically recall mentioning that, George, but—"

"Unless we can cite a real reason, I don't see how we can go ahead on a request."

"Just a minute, George," said Haddock. He glanced down at his hands, clasped together on the top of the desk. The knuckles were white. He could feel the perspiration forming

77

at his hairline. "I was under the evidently mistaken impression that as president of this company, I would be able to visit any department or division within the company, purely and simply for the purpose of finding out what they're doing there, as a matter of my own information and background as president, but apparently it isn't quite that simple." He gave an amused, ironic little laugh. It came out broken, a half sob.

"Position alone doesn't qualify as a need-to-know reason under the regulations, Henry." Imry was watching him with relish. "Mr. Elphinstone isn't cleared, and neither am I. Chuck Mersey did have clearance, but he was the one who set the thing up, and as a matter of fact, I believe his clearance lapsed last year."

Haddock's breath came short. He felt winded. "Well, frankly," he said unevenly, "what bothers me a little is the principle involved. The labs are part of the company, after all."

"Only in a superficial sense. In reality, Defense has hired a piece of our research outfit—brains, tools, space—and as long as the contract lasts, it's theirs." Imry never once looked away from Haddock's face. "I'm sure you can understand that this is a special situation, Henry."

"Of course I understand that, and I certainly have no desire to butt my head against existing arrangements, but—"

"And at this particular time, when we're trying to increase our participation in Defense programs being set up for the next fiscal year, I for one would be reluctant to see us pushing on even a minor security matter without really solid justification."

"I can appreciate that, George." Haddock felt transfixed by Imry's curious, penetrating gaze. The other men, he saw, were looking away from him now, as if unwilling to witness his . . . his what? His humiliation? Was it that bad? "My point was only this, George," he said, swallowing. "I simply wanted to drop by the labs to get acquainted with the men working there, and I find it a little difficult to understand why I should be prevented from doing that when, after all, I have to bear the ultimate responsibility for that program." He had to raise his hand quickly to wipe away a drop of perspiration that was rolling down his forehead. "How can I undertake program review if I don't know the guts of the program itself?"

Imry gave him a sly look. "It's only the technical stuff that's restricted, Henry. All the cost and production factors are available anytime you want. We can go over the whole thing this afternoon if you like."

"Yes, of course," said Haddock. He didn't know what else to say. Sweat was gathering under his arms. "We can talk about that later, George." He opened the folders in front of him. "Now, maybe we'd better—"

"I just want to wind this up, Henry," said Imry. "We'll certainly go ahead with your clearance request if you want."

"Well, I don't think that'll be necessary—"

"Maybe I can make an unofficial inquiry down there beforehand."

Haddock gazed hopelessly down at his folders.

"Just let me make a note of this, Henry." Imry scratched something down on his memorandum pad. "Now, you wanted to see the monitor operation, is that right?"

"Well, no, not exactly."

"Wasn't that the reason you went to the labs?"

"Actually no, not that."

"You had another reason, then?"

"No," said Haddock in a low voice, almost whispering. "There wasn't any reason."

"What was that, Henry?"

"I said there wasn't any reason!" Haddock snapped out. "No reason whatever, is that clear?" He was trembling. He wiped his forehead with the palm of his hand. "Sorry, George," he muttered, lowering his eyes. He didn't want to see the malicious triumph on Imry's face. "Let's get on to the subject of our meeting, shall we?" he went on, trying to keep his voice steady. He looked at the folders. He'd actually forgotten what the meeting was about. Oh, yes. A proposed plant-expansion program. More monitors.

The March meeting of the board of directors was held that afternoon. It was the second Haddock had attended as president; it was also the first time he had been in the conference room in weeks.

He entered with a vigorous step, greeted Mr. Elphinstone and the other directors, and took his chair with self-assurance. Then, smiling, he took a long look around the room. Yes, the eight portraits were all in place, and the huge oval table was right under his fingertips. He rubbed the surface; its solidity pleased him. He felt surprisingly secure in the conference room. Well, he knew what was there, he knew it beyond any reasonable doubt, whereas in his office and in the apartment he wasn't absolutely sure. It was better to know. Things were more honest that way, more out in the open—well, not precisely out in the open, but—

Imry, sitting next to him, gave him a nudge. Haddock realized that the vice chairman, Mr. Nammers, was addressing a question to him, apparently for the second time.

"Sorry," he said hastily, grinning in apology. "I didn't quite get that, sir."

Mr. Nammers repeated the question once more.

"Right," said Haddock briskly. The question concerned the financial balance sheet. He knew the answer, so he provided it with ready certainty. Imry nudged him again, whispering something in his ear. "Sorry, gentlemen," said Haddock with a rueful smile. It seemed he'd given them the figures from last year. He corrected himself.

That little episode worried him. *Stay alert,* he told himself. *Pay attention. Keep smiling.* He did keep smiling, but evidently his efforts to pay attention weren't so successful, for before long he realized that his was the only smile in the room. Everyone else was looking stern. Why was that? Ah—they were discussing the renegotiation of a labor contract. It was a prickly situation. The union might call a strike. Shouldn't he join the discussion? Yes, he'd better do that. A president oughtn't to sit there like a mummy while an important issue was being reviewed. He leaned forward with a show of eagerness, waiting for an opportunity to speak, and as he waited, he flashed a look here and there at the walls. Now, if he had installed the monitor, he'd have put it right behind that big portrait of old Maurice Carpenter, so the lens would look out of one of Carpenter's eyes or maybe one of the buttons on his coat. The portrait was centrally located. You could cover the whole room pretty well from there. . . .

"You have something to add, Henry?" That was old Mr. Elphinstone, inviting him to speak.

"Right," said Haddock crisply. He realized that he'd been leaning forward with his eager expression for some little time, perhaps a minute, who knew? Now he'd have the chance to recoup that little blunder he'd made earlier. "Well, in my judgment, gentlemen," he said with a keen, tight-lipped smile, and he went on to deliver a succinct opinion on the labor negotiation, an opinion that became even more succinct when he perceived that they weren't looking at him but were exchanging puzzled glances and clearing their throats. Something was wrong. He broke off.

Mr. Elphinstone informed him dryly that although his views on the labor matter were welcome, the board had in fact left that subject entirely. They were discussing something else.

"Right," said Haddock. "I just wanted to get myself on the record." *Carry it off with a smile, Haddock.* He smiled. But Mr. Elphinstone wasn't smiling back. Neither was Mr. Nammers. They were staring at him, staring without disapproval or scorn, staring as though they were impervious to any emotion whatever and proof against any appeal. He was alarmed. What was happening to him? Why couldn't he keep up? He kept glancing from one director to another, smiling anxiously, searching for some clue that might help him, but each face looked more or less like the next one—great, round, expressionless pudding faces that from time to time turned toward him, and he felt hopelessly confused, with his dignity draining out of him smile by smile.

The meeting apparently was continuing. He observed mouths that opened and he heard words that came out of them, but he couldn't seem to understand what was going on. What *was* going on? He was being stared at. That's what was going on. How could he manage to follow the superficial chatter of those voices when the real purpose of the meeting was to stare at him? He was weary, confused, distracted. Eyes glinted at him behind glasses. He had just enough energy left to ward them off with his only weapon, his smile. *Keep smiling, Haddock.* They'd bought his smile, hadn't they? They'd elected that smile as their president. Well, then—let them have it. He smiled his repertory of conference smiles: judicious smiles, skeptical smiles, smiles that crinkled the skin around the eyes while leaving the mouth alone, analytical smiles (lots of delicate eyebrow work in those), and a subtle masterpiece of ambiguity, in which he smiled with the left side and frowned with the right. He lay down a barrage of smiles, each one different, no two alike. Not enough. The stares kept coming.

"... perhaps you could enlighten us on that point, Henry."

"Right," said Haddock. What point? He grinned, bewildered. "Actually, Mr. Elphinstone, I think I'll have to defer a response on that one until I've had a chance to give it a good, thorough analysis, sir." He waited for Imry's nudge, for Imry's whisper. But Imry wasn't nudging. Imry was inching away. "I'd hate to commit myself on that subject without being absolutely certain of my facts, Mr. Elphinstone." That sounded safe enough, but it wasn't. Mr. Elphinstone was hunched there glaring at him like a spider monkey. Haddock glanced around the table, taking a quick poll. Yes, they were all staring, and doing a good job of it, too. Suppose he simply spread his hands apologetically and told them: "Well, gentlemen, I'm just having a bad day." Wouldn't they be disarmed by such frankness and leave him alone?

They were leaving him alone. Imry was doing a lot of talking now. Their questions were being directed to him. Haddock remained neatly erect in his chair, wearing the faint smile of the attentive listener. But he wasn't listening. He couldn't manage it. He was exhausted. It was all he could do to keep from tilting forward inch by inch until his head came to rest on the surface of the conference table. Why couldn't he do that? He wasn't participating anymore. For him the meeting had been adjourned. They were talking about personnel policy; he knew a lot about that, for he'd studied the basic documents just the day before, but if he delivered an opinion on the matter, it might turn out to be a different subject altogether, as it had before. So it was better just to sit silently, smiling. But he ought to choose one smile and stick to it. He had the impression that he was running rapidly through the whole repertory again, one smile rushed in after another, which, if true, might be making him look a bit foolish.

They were still staring at him, one or two at a time, sometimes all together. The portraits were staring, too, now. Or were they? He couldn't tell. The faces all looked the same. The paint didn't make much difference, actually. The eyes were staring. That's what counted. As he sat there smiling, he imagined that all those stares were merging into one pair of eyes—into a single eye, in fact. One enormous eye, unwaveringly fixed on him. One huge, lidless eye . . .

He rose to his feet. *Gentlemen, there's just one point I'd like to make. While you're staring at me, don't you realize that something else is staring at you? Something that sees without being seen, that listens secretly in silence? Don't you realize that you're under constant observation, gentlemen?*

But no, he didn't actually say that. He simply muttered something about wanting to be excused.

As he left the conference room, he was smiling a controlled smile of well-bred regret, and this same smile was on his face when he crossed his office and entered the bathroom.

He looked in the mirror, still smiling. Then he shut the door, put the lid down on the toilet, sat down there, and

—very carefully laying a towel across his lap—bowed his head into his hands and began silently weeping.

"Mr. Elphinstone, I'd like to apologize for what happened at the meeting this afternoon. I haven't been feeling too well lately, I'm afraid."

"You look tired, Henry."

"Well, I haven't slept well, and I've got a cold, but anyway, I wanted to express my regrets."

"Think nothing of it, Henry." Mr. Elphinstone was not a kindly man. There was a touch of impatience in his manner, as though he would have preferred to say: "Got something wrong with you? Well, take care of it, then!"

"One other little matter," Haddock said. He glanced about nervously. He had caught Mr. Elphinstone leaving after the meeting. "Could I have a word with you in private, sir?" Mr. Elphinstone seemed puzzled. All the other men had left, and they were alone in the conference room. "I don't want to delay you, I mean," Haddock said, hastily correcting himself, and smilingly he guided Mr. Elphinstone out into the corridor that led to the elevators. "It's just a little idea I had," he said as they walked along. "I haven't ever had the opportunity of meeting Mr. Nicholas, and I thought—"

"Speak up, Henry. I can't hear you."

"Well, I thought it might be a courteous thing to do if I paid my respects in person."

"Who's that you're talking about?"

"Um, Mr. Nicholas, sir. After all, he's the founder of the company, and I thought that a little courtesy visit might not be out of order, but of course I wanted to check it with you first."

85

"You say you want to go to see him?"

"Well, that's more or less the idea, yes."

"I'm afraid not, Henry."

"Sir?"

"I don't think you'd be able to see him."

"I hope he isn't ill, Mr. Elphinstone."

"No, no. He's in good health. I spoke to his nephew just last week. His nephew stays with him now."

"I see. Well, I'm glad to hear—"

"Edgar simply doesn't care to meet people."

"Ah."

"He never did, even when he had to. Now he doesn't have to, so he won't."

"Well, I suppose he's busy with one thing or another."

"He has his little hobbies, I imagine——"

"Hobbies? What hobbies?"

"I don't know what his hobbies are, Henry. I'm simply saying that he lives a quiet life and insists on his privacy."

"Privacy, yes. I see."

"So I'm afraid you wouldn't be able to see him, Henry. It was a thoughtful idea, though."

"Well, I might just telephone the nephew anyway, on the off-chance—"

"You'd be wasting your time, Henry."

"I see. Well, in that case—"

"Henry, I have a suggestion to make. You could use a little vacation. You've been working too hard."

"Well—"

"Take a week off. Don't delay. Get into the sun and bake that cold out of your system."

"Yes, but the company—"

"Don't worry about the company. I should say that George

Imry could keep things going for a week in your absence," Mr. Elphinstone said pointedly. "Don't you agree?"

"Yes, Mr. Elphinstone."

Three days later Haddock caught a morning flight to Miami. He rented an automobile at the airport and drove north some fifty miles to the rest home where his mother had been living since his father's death four years earlier.

As usual, his mother's pleasure at seeing him took the form of a detailed description of her own interests and preoccupations, such as her pinochle games, the food, the weather, and the eccentricities of her neighbors. She also related the latest gossip, which concerned the shocking behavior of one of the nurses with the resident physician, Dr. Feldman. "And he's a married man," she said disapprovingly. She regarded her son for a moment. "Well, Henry. What about you? Aren't you ever going to get married?"

"Dr. Feldman doesn't seem much of a recommendation."

"He reminded me, that's all. You know what I mean." Mrs. Haddock was a pretty little woman with cottony hair and shrewd blue eyes that noticed hardly anything. She'd even complimented Haddock on how rested he looked. "Every man needs a wife," she said. "It's not right to live alone the way you do."

"I'm never alone."

"You're what?" She was hard of hearing but refused to wear a hearing aid.

"I said I've got a butler and a cook."

"Oh. Well, that's very convenient, I'm sure, but it's hardly the same thing as a loving wife, Henry. Your poor father, now . . ." She plunged vigorously into reminiscence. Haddock, feigning sympathetic attention, let his thoughts wander. His mother was lucky. She could play pinochle and gossip as much as she liked, and when she wanted to enjoy her privacy, she could shut her door, sit by the window, and gaze out at the ocean, and if she didn't care for the ocean, she could draw the blinds and curl up by herself like a periwinkle in its shell. He glanced enviously about the room. Then he saw something above the door.

"*What's that, Mother?*"

"Great heavens, Henry!"

"*How did that get in here?*"

"What are you shouting for, Henry? I can hear you perfectly well—"

"*Mother, do you know what that is?*"

"Oh, you gave me such a turn, leaping up."

"*Mother—*"

"What's the matter with you, Henry? You're all pink and spotty."

"Sorry, Mother, but I'm asking you something."

"And what in the world are you doing pointing like that?"

"Mother, I want to know if you know what that is."

"What *what* is? Oh, that. Why, of course I know. It's one of those things, I forget what they're called. They put them in last month, I think it was. Henry, you sit down and stop this fidgeting around."

"Listen, Mother. Did they explain to you what this was for?"

"Of course they did, and a very sensible idea it is, too. Why, just a few days ago Mrs. Stern fell out of bed, and they ran in to help her in no time at all. Just between the two of us, I'd say that Mrs. Stern may have nipped a bit too freely that evening—"

"What do you mean, 'just between the two of us'? Don't you realize what that thing does?"

"Henry, you're getting very loud again, and I can't for the life of me understand why, but if you're referring to that whatever-it-is, they only look, they don't listen."

"How do you know that?"

"You're acting very silly, Henry. What difference does it make? It's only Nurse Rennie out there, anyway, and I can assure you she's got better things to do than listen to a lot of old ladies chatter. *Hi there, Nurse Rennie!*"

"Mother, please don't do that. Don't wave at that monitor."

"I'm waving to Nurse Rennie, and I'm sure she sees me. Unless it's Nurse Phillips. Sometimes they switch afternoons. Anyway, it's a great comfort to have it, Henry. Why, it's your own company that makes them, I do believe. Would that be one of yours, Henry, or a competing brand?"

"It doesn't matter, Mother."

"That's hardly the way for a man in your position to talk, but I suppose you know best. Do you know what Dr. Feldman calls them? Our faithful companions, that's what he calls them—and that's precisely what they are. It's always there, you know. And at night when you wake up, you can see its friendly little red eye glowing up there . . . why don't you quit pacing around and sit down, Henry? Where are you going?"

"I've got an appointment, Mother. I'll come back to see you tomorrow."

"Honestly, Henry. You're as nervous as a cat. What you need is a wife, do you hear? You need a good woman to look after you!"

His real purpose in flying to Florida was to visit Mrs. Mersey, who had moved into a comfortable retirement community north of Palm Beach. He had taken the precaution of telephoning her from New York to ask if he might drop by; she had been flattered and pleased.

It was late afternoon when he arrived from the rest home. Mrs. Mersey served tea on the terrace. The ocean, ironed flat by an overcast sky, stretched out blankly in the distance. On the horizon three tiny tankers inched along.

". . . and how do you like the apartment?" Mrs. Mersey was saying.

"Oh, it's—" He couldn't think of the right word to use. He smiled. "You lived there seven years, didn't you?"

"Almost eight years," said Mrs. Mersey. She was a gentle, placid woman, with an expression of dreamy dignity. "I never felt it was really our home, though."

"No?" Haddock glanced at her. "Do you mean there was something about it that wasn't . . . homey?"

"Our children were grown then, you see."

"Oh."

"Charles and I were by ourselves there."

"I see. I suppose that might have made it lonely."

"Oh, no. I never felt lonely, not even when Charles was away on business. I always had a certain feeling about the apartment."

"Yes?"

"Well, you know each place has its own character, its own special . . ." She hesitated.

"Its own spirit," he prompted eagerly.

"Yes, you might say that."

"A resident spirit."

"Yes, I suppose that's what I mean," said Mrs. Mersey, smiling vaguely at the ocean.

"And?"

"Oh, well. I never mentioned this to Charles. He had little patience with such notions." She peered doubtfully at Haddock. "He would have called it 'hogwash.' That was his favorite word of disapproval. He came from Indiana."

"I certainly wouldn't call it hogwash, Mrs. Mersey. Tell me, this spirit—what was it? I mean, what kind did you feel it to be?"

"What kind?"

"Well, was it, um, favorably inclined? A pleasant sort of influence? You know, benign? Or—"

"Oh, it was certainly benign, Mr. Haddock."

"Oh," said Haddock, disappointed. "Benign." He produced an understanding smile. "And how did you sense its presence? I mean, did you have the sensation that it was observing you?"

Mrs. Mersey gazed at him, puzzled.

"Observing you from inside the walls, let's say? In a benign way, of course."

Mrs. Mersey regarded him reproachfully. "I think you're making fun of what I said, Mr. Haddock."

"Oh, I'm not at all, Mrs. Mersey," Haddock exclaimed earnestly. "Believe me, I'm not—"

"But really, spirits looking out of walls—"

"No, no. I'm dead serious about that, Mrs. Mersey. I've had the same feeling—"

"I didn't mean real spirits, Mr. Haddock. I'm not a spiritualist, you know."

"Neither am I, but—"

"I was simply referring to the atmosphere of the place where I lived, a poetic reference, you understand."

"Oh, I do understand, I understand perfectly, I assure

91

you. It's just that when you said you never felt alone there even when you were alone, that really struck a chord with me, because I've had that very same feeling."

"Yes, but surely not to the extent of—" she tittered like a schoolgirl "—of seeing ghosts in the walls!"

"No, no, no," Haddock responded with a merry laugh. "I didn't literally mean that, of course!" He laughed some more, despondently. He felt as though Mrs. Mersey had cleverly drawn him out with her ambiguous hints and then betrayed him. But he was determined to maintain his dignity. "When you're living alone, though, your imagination will sometimes carry you a little farther than other people's, Mrs. Mersey, and that's a fact. I mean to say that when a happily married wife and mother could sense the existence of a resident spirit—a poetic reference, I know—well, a lonely bachelor like myself, without a wife to talk to, he can very easily push that little idea another step or two along the way, and before long, he can have ghosts in the walls just by snapping his fingers!"

And Haddock, laughing, snapped his fingers—snapped them so sharply, indeed, that Mrs. Mersey blinked and pulled her head back, and from the glance she gave him, he suspected that she was thinking that Henry Haddock, despite his pleasant appearance and courteous manners, was a rather odd fellow.

"Um, did you happen to know Mr. Nicholas, Mrs. Mersey?"

"Mr. Nicholas? Oh, no. I never met him, but I feel as though I've known him very well."

"Really?" But Haddock was suspicious this time.

"Charles spoke of him often, you see."

"Yes. Well, what was his opinion? I ought to say that I've

never met Mr. Nicholas either, and he has nothing to do actively with the company, so that my interest is, at best, very remote, but of course he's quite a figure in a historical sense for us, so I'd be interested—mildly interested, as I say—in your husband's views on Mr. Nicholas."

Mrs. Mersey regarded Haddock curiously after this disclaimer. "Well, he thought highly of him," she said. "You see, Mr. Nicholas helped Charles get established in the company in the early days. He took a special interest in his work."

"Kept an eye on him, would you say?"

"Yes, he was very kind," said Mrs. Mersey. "And of course Charles was grateful."

"Naturally."

"He had the highest respect for him. He always said that Mr. Nicholas was a man of great vision."

Haddock raised his eyes, looking at the sky. The overcast had parted. Something gleamed, and gleamed again. The wingtip of a jet? But there was no vapor trail. It could be a satellite, tumbling there. He glanced down into his cup. It was empty.

"Well," he said, smiling. Mrs. Mersey had retreated into her placidity. She was regarding him vacantly. He found that he had no desire to ask further questions. The open sky was widening rapidly now. He looked at his wristwatch. "I guess I'd better be running along, Mrs. Mersey." He got to his feet. "I've got to get back to my mother." He chuckled. "You know how mothers are. She keeps after me all the time. 'Get married'—that's what she says the minute she lays eyes on me!"

"That might not be such a bad idea, Mr. Haddock," Mrs. Mersey observed, rising to accompany him out to the driveway.

* * *

93

"A good woman, Henry," his mother said. "A loving sort of woman. That's what you need."

He glanced up at the top of the door. "A faithful companion, Mother?"

"Someone to share your life, Henry. It's true that things didn't work out with you and Joyce, but that was so long ago." She was laying out a game of solitaire. Queen on king. "It's time to try again, before it's too late."

He cracked his knuckles.

"See how jumpy you are?" she remarked, sliding her glance his way. "You never used to be jumpy. You were the calmest, sunniest little fellow in the world." She destroyed her game, shuffled the cards, and began laying them out again. "You need someone to watch over you."

He laughed and cracked his knuckles again. She was frowning at her game. It hadn't come out properly. If she cheated, would Nurse Rennie see?

"Dratted cards," she grumbled. She leaned back. "Let's take a little walk along the beach, Henry."

"Not now," he said. He didn't like the room, but it was better than being outside, beneath that enormous sky. "I've got a little headache," he added, rising. "I think I'll go back to the motel and lie down for a while."

"Take an aspirin," his mother said, but he could tell she was thinking of something else. "There's a good movie on television this afternoon, Henry. Why don't you watch it with me?"

"Television hurts my eyes." He stooped to give her a kiss.

"Well, come by this evening, then," she said indifferently. Even before he'd left the room, her attention had returned to her game.

In his motel room he lay on the bed. His window was open.

The warm, ocean-scented air washed in, and he could hear the breakers slapping listlessly at the shore. For a long time he lay listening; then he went to the window. A gull was circling out there. It dived, thrashed in the water, rose up to circle once more, and dived again. From afar it looked tiny, no larger than a moth. And yet to a fish it was terrible—not because of its claws, its beak, or its wings. What made it formidable was its power of sight. From the heights the gull stared down, attentively scanning the wide screen of the sea. What it saw, it devoured. No fish near the surface was safe. To be observed was to die. And the fish had no warning—oh, perhaps a premonition, perhaps the glimpse of something flashing down, but too late, too late.

He turned back to his bed. The only protection was to inhabit the depths. There was danger below, but there were places to hide: reefs and rocks; the skeletons of wrecked ships; dark, subaqueous forests that waved as currents combed them. Even the wrinkles in the floor of the sea could camouflage a hunted creature. . . .

"You ought to marry a younger woman," his mother said that evening. "Face facts. You're not going to be young all your life. You'll need someone to take care of you later."

"I'll marry Nurse Rennie, then."

"Don't be flippant. A wife has to be something of a nurse, though, I can tell you, and a psychiatrist, too, and believe me, your father wouldn't have lived as long as he did if I hadn't been there to coddle him when he needed it. He used to come home as stiff as a board from all the tensions of his work—"

"What was he afraid of?"

"Afraid? He wasn't afraid. I didn't say he was afraid. He was tense, I said, and I comforted him. I always had a funny

95

story to tell him to make him laugh and a good strong cup of tea for his stomach."

"The women I know don't serve tea."

"They serve cocktails, I suppose. Well, I'm not narrow-minded. It's love that counts."

"All right, Mother."

"All right what?"

"I'll get married."

"Oh, you're just saying that."

"No, I'm not. I mean it."

"Well, you don't want to be too hasty. Don't rush into something before—"

"I am going to rush, Mother. That's exactly what I'm going to do—rush!"

He didn't want to get married. He only wanted a woman to live with him. But he knew that the company wouldn't care to have its president maintaining a concubine in the official residence. So marriage it would have to be, and the sooner, the better.

On his flight back to New York he made a list of the women he knew. Some already had husbands, even if they weren't living with them. Others were opposed to marriage on principle. Still others, while having no such objections (they'd had plenty of husbands), kept several affairs going all the time, which wouldn't suit his present purposes too well. He kept going over the names on his list, crossing some out, putting question marks beside others, and scribbling marginal notes concerning the nature and habits of his candidates, whom he knew fairly intimately, as he had passed an occasional night with each one.

By the time his plane landed, the name least marked by penciled doubts was that of Jenny Schwartz. So be it, he thought. She didn't have Belle's chic or Ginny's wit, but she was energetic and good-tempered. His mother would call her "wholesome" (provided she didn't know how many men Jenny had slept with). So he certainly could do worse. His impulse was to propose to her right away. He could telephone her while he waited at the terminal for his luggage. She could take a cab to the apartment and meet him there.

Well, he knew that wouldn't work. She might not want to marry him. In any event, she would obviously expect certain preliminaries—not courtship in the old-fashioned sense, for Jenny had a modern contempt for that sort of thing, but he'd have to provide a good explanation. She'd insist on that. And he'd have to be honest about it, too. Anything less would be not only dishonorable but also impractical, for he wanted her to share his burden, and she obviously would have to know what it was right from the outset. Exactly. The only question was how to tell her. He reviewed possible approaches as his taxi took him into the city.

"Jenny, there's a fine old gentleman by the name of Edgar Nicholas who's going to be . . . well, he'll be sort of sharing the apartment with us."

"He'll be living here?"

"Um, yes. That is, he won't actually be living with us, but he'll be . . . present in a certain sense."

"Had, I don't understand—"

"I'll try to explain it more clearly, Jenny, but let me assure you that he's a very quiet person, and you won't even know he's around. . . ."

Or he might try something a bit more brisk and direct:

"Jenny, I'd like you to meet an old friend of mine, Mr. Edgar Nicholas, the founder of my company."

"*All right, I'll meet him if you like.*"

"*And Mr. Nicholas, let me present the future Mrs. Haddock.*"

"*Who are you talking to, Had?*"

"*I'm speaking to Mr. Nicholas, dear.*"

"*Are you kidding? There's nobody else here.*"

"*In a literal, physical sense, you're right, of course. But from an electronic point of view, Mr. Nicholas is quite probably present at this very moment.*"

No, that wouldn't do. He'd have to take her aside—in her place, not in the apartment—and tell her the whole story, step by step, from the beginning. He began to rehearse it. "*As you know, my company produces electronic equipment, including television monitors. Well, it seems that . . .*"

But he had no proof. He couldn't unfold such an improbable tale to her any more than he could to Mr. Elphinstone. She would be more sympathetic, but in the end her reaction would be the same—poor Haddock, slipped over the edge. His experience with Mrs. Mersey ought to be sufficient warning of what people would think of him if he attempted to broach such a topic.

So the direct approach was out. He couldn't expect Jenny to marry a madman. What could he do? Nothing, probably. His taxi arrived. Gloomily he entered the building and took the elevator up to the apartment. Mr. and Mrs. Frey greeted him in the foyer.

"Welcome home, Mr. Haddock."

"Thank you, Frey."

"I hope you had a restful vacation, Mr. Haddock."

"And thank you, Mrs. Frey. Yes, I certainly did. Very restful."

In the living room he paused. (*"Welcome home, Henry." "Thank you, Mr. Nicholas. Thank you very much, sir."*) He smiled, but his teeth were grinding. He could feel the presence, more forcefully than ever. The very air seemed heavy with it.

And then he thought: *Let her feel it, too.*

Yes, that was the answer. He'd invite her up for a drink, and then they'd sit chatting companionably in the living room for a while, and after a bit she'd give a little shiver and glance uncertainly around.

"What's the matter, Jenny? Are you chilly?"

"No, no. It's just . . . "

"What?"

"Oh, nothing."

"No, tell me."

"Well . . . I had a funny feeling, that's all."

"What do you mean, a funny feeling?"

"Oh, it's silly, but . . . well, I felt as though someone else were here with us."

"Someone else?"

"I told you it was silly. I mean, there isn't anyone here, and yet . . ."

"Yes?"

"Well, I do have this odd feeling, Had."

"Of . . . being watched?"

"Yes, something like that."

"Well, I'm interested to hear you say that, Jenny, because to tell you the truth, every once in a while I have the very same feeling myself."

"You do? Oh, I'm glad. I don't mean I'm glad, but I was beginning to think—"

"I know what you mean. Yes, it's better when two people feel the same thing. Well, on that little subject, there's a story I'd like to tell you. . . ."

Yes, that's how it would happen, more or less. Mr. Nicholas, in effect, would introduce himself.

* * *

He telephoned Jenny at once and found that she was free the following evening. He suggested that they have a drink at his apartment before going out to a restaurant. His own sense of Mr. Nicholas' presence was so strong that he was sure she'd feel it pretty quickly.

So as they sat in the living room chatting together, he kept watching her, confidently awaiting the initial indications.

"What's the matter, Jenny? Are you chilly?"

"No, not at all. I'm fine."

"Oh, I thought . . . no matter."

"Why? Are you chilly, Had?"

"Oh, no. It's just that there are drafts sometimes."

He decided that his presence might be delaying things. If he could manage to leave her alone there for a bit, she would become aware of Mr. Nicholas all the sooner.

"Listen, Jenny. I'm sorry, but I've got to phone a man I couldn't reach earlier. I promise you it won't take ten minutes, all right?"

"Of course, Had. Go ahead."

He went back to his bedroom and lifted the telephone receiver off its base. It wouldn't do to have the phone ring while he was supposed to be using it. Then he tiptoed back along the hallway to a point from which he could glimpse her through the doorway. Nothing would happen at first. He knew that. He'd have to be patient.

She remained seated on the divan, gazing out at the view of the city, from time to time sipping her drink. She picked up a magazine, flipped through a few pages, and put it back down. After that she lighted a cigarette and practiced a few smoke rings, and then she yawned several times, scratched herself under one arm at the bra strap, removed her left shoe, massaged her foot, wriggled her toes, put the shoe back on, took another sip of her drink, stubbed out the cigarette, fished a mirror from her purse and checked her eye makeup, and all the time Haddock was watching from the shadowy hall, intent on catching the first little signs.

There was nothing unusual in what she had been doing. She was behaving normally . . . or was she being just a shade too deliberate in her movements? He couldn't be sure. But he suspected that there was something wooden about her casualness, as though she were beginning to be slightly troubled by the first faint glimmerings of a suspicion that someone might be watching her. Well, *he* was watching her. Maybe he shouldn't. It might be confusing her growing awareness of Mr. Nicholas. He backed off a few paces so that he couldn't see her. Then he moved forward again. He didn't want to miss the opportunity of finding out just how Jenny reacted to this situation. If she were totally insensitive to it, then perhaps he'd have to try someone else. So it was important for him to watch. His future—and hers—might depend on it. To be sure, he didn't much care to be lurking in the hallway, spying on her. He'd never done anything like that in his life or at least not since he and some other boys had tried to sneak a look into the girls' locker room at the junior high school gym back in Columbus.

Ah . . . now there was a change. She was betraying a certain restlessness. She was frowning slightly. He sucked in his breath, waiting, and he held himself rigidly still. Yes, now . . . she was casting a glance around the room!

He took a quick look at his watch. Good Lord. He'd told her he'd be gone no more than ten minutes, and almost half an hour had passed. He hurried back to the bedroom, replaced the telephone receiver, and returned to the living room, apologizing to her for his absence. He was annoyed with himself. He'd managed things badly. She'd looked around the living room, all right, but now he didn't know why. She might simply have been impatient waiting for him to return.

He tried to be jolly at the restaurant, but it was one of those lugubrious little places where the clatter of a spoon on a plate sends a shudder around the room. He peered across the table at Jenny, shrouding his anxiety with a genial smile. He couldn't speak to her frankly about the situation, for even if she had sensed something back in the living room, she wouldn't be ready for a full disclosure. He might allude to it in a roundabout way, though.

"Well, what do you think of the apartment?" he inquired casually.

"Um, it's sort of big, Had." She ate zestfully, with ample forkfuls. "It's not a cozy nook, you know."

"It gets lonely sometimes," he said, watching her. She was short and bosomy; not fat, but fleshy. She'd been a juvenile swimming star. Perhaps he'd be better off with a more delicate mate. "But it has its own atmosphere, don't you think?"

"Oh, I'm sure it does."

"Didn't you feel it when you were waiting for me to finish my call?"

"Um." She buttered another roll.

"How would you describe it, Jenny?"

"Oh." She popped half the roll into her mouth.

"Sort of . . ." He smiled, trying to prompt her. "Wouldn't you say it was . . . ?"

"Well, empty."

"Yes, exactly. Empty. But there's a special sort of emptiness about it." He was watching her closely. It wasn't easy. Their table had been allotted only one candle.

She smiled at him blankly. She didn't know what he was talking about.

"Well," he went on, "it's almost as though the emptiness weren't quite as empty as it seems. It's empty, of course, but empty in a certain way. That is, the emptiness seems to be occupied by something, but at the same time it remains empty, if you see what I mean."

Had he gone too far? No. He could tell by her expression that he hadn't gone anywhere.

She glanced at his plate. "Aren't you hungry, Had? You've hardly touched a thing."

"Right," he said cheerfully, and he took a bite. "Tell you what," he said with decision. "Let's go back there for a nightcap, all right? I'd really like you to have the chance to soak in your impressions of the apartment and tell me what you think."

As they left the restaurant, his spirits lightened. He was still nervous, but it was excitement he felt, not apprehension. The closer the taxi brought them to the apartment, the more animated he became, chattering away to Jenny, laughing at the jokes he made, and laughing even when he didn't make jokes. He was eager to reach the apartment. Mr. Nicholas would be waiting for them there. Mr. Nicholas might be a little excited, too. Perhaps he had dusted off his screen for the occasion. And Jenny was becoming more lively, as though she realized that this was a special evening and wanted to do her best to make things go off smoothly. Haddock glanced at her with an approving grin as they entered the elevator. How bright and fresh she looked! Mr. Nicholas wouldn't be able to resist her. Why, the old man might go so far as to telephone them. At the very least, he'd send them a generous wedding gift.

The Freys had retired to their own quarters for the night, leaving a light in the foyer.

"Well, here we are!" said Haddock gaily, tossing his hat onto a chair. He helped Jenny remove her coat and then ushered her ceremoniously into the living room, snapping on the lights. "Here we are!" he called out again, gazing hopefully around. Would the meeting succeed? Would they recognize each other? He realized that he was behaving as though the marriage were to be arranged between Jenny and Mr. Nicholas—which wasn't too far from the truth, actually, for the three of them would be very close in the future.

He rubbed his hands together and glanced encouragingly at the ceiling. He smiled at Jenny. "Well, what do you think of it?"

She was regarding him soberly.

"No, no," he cautioned her with mock reproof. "Don't look at me. I'm not the one you need to be thinking about. Just pretend I'm not here." He chuckled and swept the walls with a meaningful glance, to show her how it was done. "Pretend you're here in the room by yourself . . . and yet not really by yourself—"

"Listen, Had."

"You know what I mean already, don't you?" he said eagerly. "You feel it just a little bit?"

"Had." She walked up to him and laid one hand on his arm. "You've been working too hard lately."

He laughed, dismayed. "Not at all," he said. "I just got back from a week in Florida. But seriously, don't worry about me now. It's the room I want you to concentrate on."

"Had, I don't care about the room. I care about you. We all do."

104

He patted her hand. "If you'd only concentrate for fifteen minutes—"

"We're concerned, Had. I've talked to Belle and the others. You haven't been seeing anybody for weeks now. And here you are, all tensed up like this." She gave his wrist a little squeeze. "You've got to snap out of it, Had. You've got to relax."

"You're right, Jenny, but that's not the main point," he began to protest. He was confused, though. She was studying him intently, a friendly and affectionate expression on her face; she was paying no attention whatever to the room. But that might be the way, after all. Who knew? He was so charged with the consciousness of Mr. Nicholas' presence that she would be bound to discover it through him. He was, in a limited sense, a manifestation of Mr. Nicholas' personality, just as, quite probably, Mr. Nicholas had been influenced by him in turn, for in any human relationship—even in one as unorthodox as this—a certain psychological interchange takes place.

". . . what you need," she was saying. He hadn't been listening, and so when she turned, picked up her purse, and walked out of the room, he hurried after her, afraid that she might be leaving. But she was simply heading for the bathroom.

He returned to the living room. "Sorry," he said with an ingratiating smile. "Don't worry. Honestly. She'll catch on soon enough. Give her time." Then he began experimenting with the lamps in an effort to arrive at the most appropriate arrangement of light, making certain that no bulb cast its glare against the walls, which might interfere with the reception.

He heard her calling him, her voice faint because of the distance. "Had . . . ? Had . . . ?" She might have had some trouble with the plumbing. "Coming," he announced as he reached the hallway. Could be a jammed faucet. "I'm on my way," he called out. Where was she, exactly? Which room?

"Had . . . ?"

He realized that she'd chosen the master bathroom. She wasn't there now, though. She was in the bedroom.

"Oh, Had. I thought you'd be, you know, ready."

She was ready. She was stretched out on his big double bed, covered by the sheet. Her clothing lay folded on a chair.

He stood transfixed in the doorway.

"Come on, Had." She smiled invitingly and extended her plump, bare arms. Her plentiful bosom arched beneath the sheet.

Instinctively he pressed the wall switch. But the overhead lights hadn't been on—she'd lighted only the two little bed-side lamps—so that now, instead of throwing the room into darkness, he illuminated it vividly. She sat up, smiling, and the sheet fell away. In the instant before he pressed the switch again, the flesh tones of her body glowed brilliantly, every detail blazingly clear.

"Come on," she repeated.

He rushed to the bed. He had to cover her. He had to turn those little lamps off. Cover her in darkness. Quick, the lamps. The spread.

She mistook his frantic fumblings for passion and laughed merrily. He'd sprawled across her, wrenching at the spread with one hand, grasping at one lamp with the other.

"Hey, you've still got your *suit* on," she cried out, and she began hauling his jacket from his shoulders. As he managed to pull part of the spread over her, she got one of his arms out

106

of the jacket. "You *have* been away a long time, haven't you?" she exclaimed, giggling. He sat up, tearing the rest of the jacket off, and as she pushed the spread aside, he flung the jacket on her and made a plunge for the other light. Got that one. But she'd left the bathroom light on. He swung off the bed and rushed for it. The room was dark now . . . but he knew that might not matter. He had to get her covered.

He stumbled back to the bed and began trying to wrap her up again. "Wow," she said. "The new Haddock." His fervor was exciting her. Her fingers were busy with his clothing. "Remember Vermont?" she cooed. They'd spent a ski weekend there. He'd skied down her hot slopes. But that was then. They'd been alone. His hasty hands got her covered to the waist, but she was sitting up, working at his buttons, her full breasts free. In Vermont they'd bundled together before the fire. Now he was trying to bundle her up alone.

He couldn't cover her with anything but himself. He forced her down and lay on her, twisting to whisper in her ear. "Don't move. Don't say anything, please. Just stay there." She gave a wriggle. "Hey," she said. He kept her pressed flat. "Listen," he mumbled. "Just give me a minute. I've got to think. Don't move." She grunted from his weight. "Say, Had, what's the—" He buried his face in her neck, a despairing nuzzle. She giggled; it tickled. "Please don't move," he whispered. He had to keep her quiet. "Just stay as you are, don't move, don't say anything, not a word, I'm sorry. . . ." What a fool he'd been. A marriage like this? Night after night, hiding in bed, exchanging furtive caresses? ". . . I've got to think a minute, just a little minute . . ." He couldn't tell her. She wouldn't believe him. Even if she did, how could he ask her to live like this? She struggled. "Please don't," he whispered. "Not yet. Wait. A minute." Well, he could move out of the damned apartment. But there'd still be the office. And how could he explain? There'd be suspicions. Mr. Nicholas had been neutral up to now, hadn't he? But suppose he were offended?

She twisted free, easing herself aside, pushing him off. "What's wrong, Had?"

"Nothing." He lay face down. "Cover yourself," he whispered. "Please cover yourself."

"Tell me—"

"No, please don't speak. Not yet." He lay rigid. "Don't turn on the light. Cover yourself."

"Had—"

"Cover yourself." He was whispering. She had to bend near him to hear. "Cover yourself, stay covered. . . ." No, he couldn't leave the apartment. The company was his life. A man couldn't simply move out of his own life.

"What's the matter, Had?"

"We're being watched," he said, but so low that she couldn't hear him. "I'm always watched. I've been watched for . . . for years." He lay there in the darkness, his lips moving. He felt her hand stroke his hair. *Watched for years. Yes, for years.* "They keep an eye on you and they bring you along step by step, higher and higher. . . ." *For years.* The difference was that now he knew. He could feel it. He was higher, closer.

"What *is* it, Had? You've got to tell me."

"Cover yourself," he whispered. "Please."

"Had—"

"Cover yourself!" he cried out.

She snapped on one lamp. He screwed his eyelids tight, still lying face down.

108

"Had, maybe you ought to see a doctor. Maybe you need a doctor."

"I need an electrician." He burst out laughing, his laughter muffled by the spread.

"If you want me to leave—"

"Oh, God, yes. Leave. I'm sorry. You've got to leave."

She was dressing now, in the light. He wouldn't turn his head to look. Nor would he listen to what she was saying. He jammed his head under a pillow. Then he saw himself as he was being seen—a grown man huddled hiding in bed—and he turned over suddenly, swung his legs over the edge of the bed, and stood.

"Jenny, I've got to explain."

She was zipping her dress up, gazing at him with a troubled face.

"I've had this terrible pain," he said, wincing. "Here." He pressed his stomach. "Sometimes it just knocks me out. It's awful." He managed a tired, tight smile of illness. "What a time to have it happen again."

"Poor Had." She wasn't completely convinced.

"You're right about a doctor." He surreptitiously rebuttoned his shirt. "I'll go tomorrow."

"Sounds like an ulcer, Had."

"That's what I'm afraid of." He winced again, guiding her out into the hallway. At the door he telephoned to the guard below, asking him to get a taxi. "I'll see you home, of course."

"Certainly not. Not in your condition."

"You don't know what pain does to a man," he said. She hesitated. "It's passing now," he assured her. "By morning it'll be gone. But I won't forget about the doctor."

She was still hesitant. He almost had to push her out and

into the waiting elevator. "Can you ever forgive me, Jenny?"

"There's nothing to forgive," she said. Then the doors closed. She was gone.

He returned to the bedroom and snapped on the overhead light. His jacket was crumpled on the floor; his tie trailed off the foot of the bed. He'd knocked over the clock. Slowly he began to put things in order. His hands shook. Searching for his slippers, he knelt by the bed, feeling around beneath it until he found them.

He remained there on his knees. He was tired. He closed his eyes.

Then he glanced up. "What is it you want of me?" he whispered. He looked all around, smiling. "What is it you want?"

Half an hour later he had left the apartment. It was only after he'd gotten into the taxicab that he remembered he hadn't left a note for Frey to explain his absence. But his absence would explain itself, wouldn't it? If he wasn't there in the morning, Frey would be capable of deducing that he was absent. Besides, if he'd written a note, Mr. Nicholas would have read it first.

"Where to?" the cab driver asked.

"Oh." He didn't know. "Well . . . oh, yes. Penn Station."

Fine. He'd decided on that much, anyway. He wasn't doing so badly, was he, in his first few minutes of being on his own? He'd catch a train. It didn't matter which one. He'd just take the first one, and then he'd stop in some city for a while. A few days. He didn't have enough clothes for more than that. He had simply stuffed a few shirts and changes of underwear into an overnight bag. But he'd forgotten extra socks, and he'd left his shaving kit behind—and worse, he realized that he wasn't wearing his topcoat. He had snatched up his hat, but he had rushed out without a coat. Oh, well. It was a mild night for March, and the trains would be heated.

He took a midnight train for Philadelphia. He rode in a rattling old coach, dusty and drafty and blazing with light. The train seemed to stop every few minutes; out of the shadows alongside the stations new passengers would appear, climb aboard, and fix him with unpleasant stares as they picked their way along the aisle. Haddock sat red-eyed with fatigue and sneezing from the dust, but smiling. He smiled at his muddy reflection in the window, at the smog-red moon outside; he smiled into his hat and down at his shoes and into the sour faces of the passengers, as though to say: "Go ahead and look at me all you want—I'm used to it!"

At Philadelphia he alighted and wandered about wondering what he ought to do next. "It doesn't matter," he thought. "I've gotten away from it at last, and that's all that counts." Then it occurred to him that instead of running away from Mr. Nicholas, he had run straight toward him. The old man's estate was a mere twenty miles from the city. "I'll go out there, that's what I'll do," he resolved. "I'll go out there and . . ." And what? Complain? Make a protest?

Mr. Nicholas, I don't mind your watching me—far from it. I'm flattered. But I've got to have one night off a week. Saturday night, let's say. . . . And do you mind if we put that in writing, sir? Saturday nights you swear you won't watch even for a minute, OK?

He sat sipping coffee at the counter of the all-night station café. "I ought to go out there with a lawyer," he told himself. "A contract—that's what I've got to have. I'd better get the whole thing spelled out in black and white." He gazed craftily about the walls of the café. "I could go to court on this, you

111

know," he whispered. "I could actually sue, understand?" Of course he knew Mr. Nicholas wasn't there. Mr. Nicholas no doubt was at that very moment furiously working the controls in his viewing room, electronically ransacking the presidential apartment, room by room, and checking the office as well. *Where was Haddock? Gone! How dare he!* Haddock chuckled. "Never mind where I am, Mr. Nicholas," he muttered. "You'll be seeing me soon enough—on your doorstep, accompanied by my attorney!"

But his lawyer was in New York, and clearly the problem was too complicated to be explained by telephone, so Haddock caught a 3 A.M. train back. He slept all the way and had to be shaken awake by the conductor after the train arrived at Penn Station. His nap made him more clearheaded, and he reexamined the question of a legal approach. In the first place, his lawyer was a cautious and elderly man who might be temperamentally unsuited to handle such an unusual matter. A more dashing and imaginative type was called for, someone with experience in the field of civil liberties. And then, too, Haddock wasn't at all sure he wanted to make a fight of it. A case like his would present tricky problems for which no precedents existed. It would cost thousands of dollars—and his position at the company would be jeopardized by the publicity. The directors might suspend him—or fire him outright.

He therefore determined that he'd make one last appeal to the founder, face to face, and so he bought another ticket for Philadelphia and took a 7:30 train back. Once more in the station there, he checked through the suburban directories and, rather to his surprise, found Mr. Nicholas' telephone number and address listed. He wrote them down but de-

112

cided against phoning in advance. "He'd probably tell me not to come," he thought. "I'll just take a cab out and present myself at the door and insist on an interview."

He went to a barbershop for a shave. That helped, but he still wasn't satisfied with his appearance. His suit was creased. There was a stain on one elbow. He went to a nearby hotel and took a room there, sending his suit down to be cleaned and pressed while he showered and lay down for a nap.

There was a television set in the room. It bothered him. First he unplugged it, then he covered its blank face with a bath towel, and finally he turned it around so that it faced the wall. That wasn't enough. He couldn't get to sleep. He disconnected the aerial wire and lugged the set out into the corridor.

He slept until the bellboy woke him bringing back his suit. Now he was presentable, but as he checked out at the desk, he realized the shakiness of his position. Mr. Nicholas would decline to see him. He'd know why he'd come, and he'd refuse him admittance. No, the only way to see Mr. Nicholas would be by some subterfuge or by means of an intermediary.

Mr. Elphinstone. Of course. The whole stupid business had begun with Mr. Elphinstone—it was Mr. Elphinstone's fault, in a way—and, moreover, Mr. Elphinstone was perhaps the only outsider who could, on the basis of his long friendship, gain admittance to see Mr. Nicholas. Once there, the old chairman could represent Haddock's position firmly with the best interests of the company in mind.... *Look here, Edgar, your arrangements must be modified. Henry Haddock is a sensitive fellow, and his work is beginning to suffer.* . . .

Exactly! Naturally he'd have to do a skillful job of persuasion in order to convince Mr. Elphinstone of the seriousness of the situation. He had shrunk from trying that before. Now he absolutely had to do it. It might be his only chance.

Haddock boarded a 6:30 P.M. train back to New York. By nine o'clock that evening, having completed his fourth passage of the day between the two cities, he was seated in a taxi, bound for Mr. Elphinstone's residence in the East Seventies.

The butler admitted him into the entryway, where several other persons were standing silently. As he passed by, one of them stepped up and addressed him. It was George Imry. "Listen, Henry," he said in a low voice. "We've been trying to reach you all day—"

'Personal business, George," Haddock replied. "Sorry." He went on to the stairs, where he recognized Mr. Elphinstone's daughter, Mrs. Lyle, slowly descending.

"I'm Henry Haddock, Mrs. Lyle," he said with a friendly smile.

She smiled back faintly, sadly. "Yes, Mr. Haddock. Thank you for coming." She glanced back up the stairs. "You wanted to see him?"

"If I may."

She turned and accompanied him up. More visitors were in the hallway there. Haddock wondered if it were some sort of party. A pretty lame party, he thought. Nobody was holding a drink.

"Here," said Mrs. Lyle softly.

Haddock entered a bedroom. The lights were turned low. Mr. Nammers, the vice chairman, was there, along with several others, all looking distressed.

Mr. Elphinstone was in bed. Haddock walked closer, oppressed by the lugubrious attitude of the guests. Well, no wonder. Mr. Elphinstone wasn't being a very lively host, lying in bed that way covered by a sheet.

The butler appeared in the doorway. "Mrs. Lyle?" he whispered. "The gentlemen from the undertaker's are here, ma'am."

"Thank you, Charles. . . . Um, Mr. Haddock, would you, um, mind . . . ?"

For Haddock had seized one of Mr. Elphinstone's icy hands and was squeezing it frantically, with tears rolling down his cheeks.

He thought that Mr. Nicholas would be sure to attend the funeral. But how would he recognize him? He leafed through the company's files of photographs. Mr. Nicholas was represented in group pictures as a round-faced man of medium height, stout and balding. He looked like anybody. Besides, he always had his eyes closed or cast down, as if he had deliberately set out to baffle the camera, knowing that a man without eyes couldn't be identified. Nor were the few individual portraits of any help, for they were outdated. The puffy youngish face of Mr. Nicholas gazed sleekly out of them with a hint of triumph. Yes, age would have disguised him. He'd counted on that. *(You won't find me so easily as all that, Henry!)*

At the entrance of the church Haddock spoke to the elderly comptroller, Mr. Probstein.

"Joe, can you do me a favor? You know Edgar Nicholas, don't you? I mean, would you recognize him?"

"Well, I knew him, Henry. It's been a long time, but I could pick him out."

"Would you mind checking to see if he's already gone in, and then if he hasn't, sort of watching the people as they come by? I'd really like to shake his hand, Joe, if you know what I mean."

"Certainly, Henry. I'll keep my eye out for him."

But Mr. Nicholas wasn't in the church. Nor did he arrive later.

That evening, at the apartment, Haddock dialed Mr. Nicholas' number in Pennsylvania.

A male voice, gruff and scratchy, answered: "Hello?"

"Mr. Nicholas?"

"Yes?"

"This is Henry Haddock, Mr. Nicholas, and I'm terribly sorry to bother you this way, sir, but frankly I'm at the end of my rope—"

"Excuse me, but—"

"—and I honestly don't think I can go on with this any longer."

"There must be some mistake. This is John Nicholas speaking."

"Oh."

"You may be trying to get some other Nicholas."

"Well, I checked this number—"

"I see. Well, it's listed under my name and also separately under my uncle, Edgar Nicholas, but surely you weren't calling him."

"As a matter of fact I was. I thought—"

"I'm sorry, but my uncle doesn't respond to telephone calls. He has an attorney in Philadelphia who handles his affairs. I could give you the name and address."

"No—no thank you. It doesn't matter."

"Well, then—"

116

"I'm sorry to have disturbed you, Mr. Nicholas."

"Not at all."

There was a click at the other end of the line. Haddock hung up his receiver, too. He went into the living room and sat down on the divan. He was alone there.

"Well, I wanted to tell you," he said, "that I'm at the end . . . at the end of my rope. And I can't go on. I'm sorry if I . . . if I breached security, sir, but . . . well, I don't really know the rules, if there are any rules, and—"

He stopped. Then he went back to his bedroom, undressed, and got into bed. He lay silently in the darkness, staring at the ceiling, where no shadows stirred.

Part Three

$\mathbf{B}$Y mid-April, Haddock had become president in name only. For the most part, he merely sat behind his desk, approving whatever George Imry sent in to him. When meetings were held, he presided with a show of decision, but he found himself agreeing with everything that anybody said, even when conflicting arguments were presented, and he made no attempt to reach any conclusions himself. None of it seemed to matter in the slightest.

"I'm finished," he thought. "It's all over. The only thing left to do is resign." Mr. Nammers, the vice chairman, had been officially installed as Mr. Elphinstone's successor, and Haddock supposed he ought to go to the new chairman with his offer to quit. He lacked the initiative to do so, however. It was almost as though he were waiting for Imry to prepare a resignation statement for his signature and then lead him in by the hand to present it. He didn't even worry about Mr. Nicholas anymore. Did Mr. Nicholas watch . . . or not? It seemed pointless. He simply didn't have the energy to mull it over any longer. Believing in Mr. Nicholas was easier than not believing, and so—languidly, passively—he believed.

He didn't like to be alone in the office. He kept calling people in on whatever pretexts he could think of, to explain issues that had been explained before or to review documents that had already been put in final form. Sometimes he went to their offices. He felt little relief at being away from his desk, however. He was made uneasy by the knowledge that he was preventing the others from going ahead with their work; then, too, he sensed that it was his duty—perhaps his only duty—to remain in his office. He had essentially nothing to do . . . and that nothing he was supposed to be doing in the president's office. And so he made his visits short and hurried back guiltily to sit behind his desk again.

He began relying more on his secretary. Miss Prince was assigned to serve his needs, after all, and as his chief need now was companionship, he summoned her often. The volume of his dictation grew substantially. Letters that normally would require a paragraph or two expanded to several pages. Speeches likewise became longer and underwent many drafts. In addition, he dictated speeches for future use, intended to meet hypothetical engagements. But these make-work efforts were self-defeating, for the more he dictated to Miss Prince, the longer she had to stay away afterward to get the necessary typing done.

"Wait a minute, Miss Prince," he said one day as she rose to leave with a full dictation pad. "You don't need to transcribe that." She hesitated, looking at him questioningly. "I mean," he amended, "you don't need to do it right this minute."

"Was there something else, Mr. Haddock?"

"No, no," he said briskly, glancing about his desk. It was

122

empty. He had nothing left to do. "It was just that I. . . ." His voice trailed off, and, from habit, he smiled. It was a bewildered smile. "Nothing else for the moment, Miss Prince," he said unhappily.

She started to leave.

"Please don't go," he said in a low voice. It startled her, and she turned, to see him smiling his bewildered smile this way and that as he glanced about the room. "If you wouldn't mind, Miss Prince," he said in an ordinary tone, indicating her customary chair. "Just for . . . a little while. I mean, there's something on my mind that I. . . ." He cleared his throat and sighed. There was nothing on his mind, really. "Of course, if you'd rather go—"

"No, no," she assured him.

"It'll come to me in a second or two," he said, but he only wanted her to stay with him, and he was so dispirited that he couldn't invent a reason. "Well," he said, and he rummaged in a desk drawer, pulled out some old memos, and sat fingering them. He cleared his throat again and frowned at the memos, as though summoning his thoughts. But it was hopeless. He laid the memos down and simply sat looking at her. She glanced at him timidly. She knew what he was going through, he thought. It made her unhappy, too. She was sorry for him. No one else was. See how nervous and distressed she was? Why, her eyes were getting a little teary. She had to give them a furtive wipe with her knuckles. He was touched by her emotion and gazed at her gratefully. Poor girl, he'd paid little attention to her before, as a matter of sound policy. But now the policy didn't seem so sound. None of his other policies seemed sound, either.

She wasn't bad-looking, really. Her nose was too long, and her hair was undistinguished, but she was slender and graceful, and her eyes were fine. What was her first name? Oh, yes. Lydia. That was it. An old-fashioned sort of name, but suitable, for Miss Prince was an old-fashioned sort of girl.

"It's a lonely job, Miss Prince," he said. She glanced up at him, surprised. He had always been kind to her, but he had never spoken to her except on company matters. And now he was sitting there regarding her with hurt and tender eyes, poor man, his handsome face all drawn and weary.

"And it helps, Miss Prince, to realize that there's someone who has a sympathetic understanding. I just wanted you to know that."

"Oh, I do. I mean, I hope—"

"And no matter what happens . . ." He hesitated, smiling ruefully. She was such a sweet and sensitive girl and so wholeheartedly devoted to him. Why hadn't he noticed her before?

In the following days Haddock found himself thinking of Miss Prince more and more. When she was with him, he kept looking at her. When she was away, he missed her. He began calling her in more often, and he kept her there as long as he could. Often they said nothing. He sat admiring her, while she remained before him, bewildered and agitated, trying unsuccessfully not to return his gaze. Sometimes when she was at her own desk in the anteroom, he would stroll over near the door to a point where he could glimpse her. She'd know he was there, and she'd glance shyly his way. Not wanting to embarrass her, he might pretend to be coming out of his office, but then, having nowhere to go, he'd find himself standing right by her desk, gazing down at her helplessly.

"Miss Prince," he'd say, but he'd be unable to think of

124

anything else, and so, after a pause, he'd say it again. "Miss Prince . . ."

"Y-yes, Mr. Haddock?"

Sometimes she'd dare to look straight up at him, trembling, until tears would stand in her eyes.

"Miss Prince," he'd repeat in a choked voice. "Miss . . . Prince . . ." Thus they would remain for an eternity of moments, until he would summon up a faint, sad shadow of one of his old salesman's smiles and turn away to go back to his office.

She was twenty years younger, he knew. But hadn't his own mother advised him to choose a younger woman —someone to invigorate his middle years and comfort him when he was old? Besides, Miss Prince loved him. She had loved him for years. He'd known that, of course. It just hadn't meant anything to him before. But now—

He caught himself abruptly. No, he had no business allowing himself to entertain romantic notions about his secretary. It wouldn't be fair to her, for one thing. And under present conditions, it was simply unthinkable. But those conditions could change. Yes, he could change them any time he chose, by doing what he'd been unable to bring himself to do for weeks . . . by resigning and leaving the company.

His gratitude to Miss Prince redoubled. Her loyalty, her sympathy, and her love had given him what he had lacked before—the impulse to take action. He didn't have to stay with the company, he kept telling himself with growing optimism. He could leave. He had that choice. He was free.

He left a message one morning for Mr. Nammers at his club and shortly thereafter received an answering call.

125

"You wanted to see me, Henry?"

"At your convenience, Mr. Nammers."

"Anything special?"

"Well, it's sort of personal, actually."

"All right. I'll be in about eleven, how about that?"

"That'll be fine, Mr. Nammers."

Following a company tradition, Mr. Nammers was a semiactive chairman of the board. He appeared at the company two or three times a week, using the conference room for his office as he discussed current problems with Haddock and other executives. Finance was his special province (he had risen to a partnership in an investment banking house and had been an assistant secretary of the Treasury in the first Eisenhower Administration), and he demanded figures on all occasions. In appearance, he shared with his predecessor an aspect many elderly men have of reversing evolution, but whereas Mr. Elphinstone had had a wizened, simian look about him, Mr. Nammers had gone farther back toward the source of life, the sea. With his squat, hunched figure, his warty skin, and luminous, protuberant eyes, he somewhat resembled an old frog. Haddock was frightened of him.

"Good morning, Henry," Mr. Nammers said with his customary air of menacing geniality. "Take a chair." He smiled a moist and wide-mouthed smile, as though Haddock were an unwary insect that had come within range.

Haddock glanced nervously around at the portraits. Their scorn was almost palpable. He had the impression that they would turn their backs on him if they could.

He took a deep breath and began. "What I wanted to talk to you about, Mr. Nammers," he said, "was to—well, to attempt to clarify certain factors relating to my present, um, position. . . ." As he spoke, he found that his knack for clear

126

phrasing had failed him. He was creeping about the subject instead of confronting it. Too late he realized that he should have memorized a short and pointed declaration. "The circumstances of the presidency are—um, they're not negligible ones, and on certain occasions I've felt that, with respect to the expectations of the board, in some ways perhaps my response to the particular requirements . . ." He felt trapped by his circumlocutions, but oddly enough, Mr. Nammers wasn't becoming restive. He was listening intently. His bulging eyes never left Haddock's face. ". . . and now with you, um, having acceded to the chairmanship," Haddock blundered on, unnerved by Mr. Nammers' unwinking gaze, "I thought there might be an occasion for a parallel—that is, a reexamination of . . ."

Mr. Nammers finally put an end to his floundering. "Henry, I think I know what's troubling you," he broke in forcefully. "It's been a difficult time for you, and you're worried about your job performance, am I right?"

"Well, yes. That's what I wanted—"

"Believe me, Henry, I realize what you've been going through. I well recall the early months of my own first experience in top responsibility. The pressure was intense. I felt that I was the focal point of crushing demands," said Mr. Nammers, his words rumbling up from the depths of his thick throat. "I was haunted by them, day and night. I couldn't sleep. I lost weight. I found it difficult to concentrate on the simplest item of business."

"You did?"

"Certainly. You can't tell me anything new on this subject, Henry. I was in a state of despair, frankly. I was persuaded that I'd failed—before I'd actually begun! And since not only my business career but my private life, too, had been sub-

127

merged by the terrible awareness of my responsibilities, I began to suspect that there was something personal involved. It was almost as if some malign force were persecuting me, determined to force me to my knees in surrender!"

"Well, I wouldn't say it was malign," Haddock interposed hastily with a placating smile at the ceiling.

"But then things began to change, Henry. Little by little, I discovered that I could handle the job. I felt more confident, more hopeful . . . and finally I was working at top efficiency! But do you know how long it was before that happened, Henry? Five months. Five whole months." Mr. Nammers leaned forward, his huge eyes hypnotically fixed on Haddock. "And how long have you been president, Henry? Why, it's been barely three months. It takes a little time to get the hang of things, you see, but once you do, it's plain sailing!"

"Well, maybe I was jumping to conclusions," Haddock mumbled uneasily, "but I was afraid that—"

"There's something special about being president," Mr. Nammers went on, beginning to wheeze, for he was troubled by asthma. "It makes fearful demands on a man. But it also provides rewards—and I don't mean only material rewards. The man who's had to deal with the realities of power is forced to understand himself and his world far, far better than the ordinary fellow. Look at those portraits on these walls, Henry." Haddock obediently looked. "They knew about power," the chairman continued. "It wasn't easy for them at first, either. But they persevered—and they earned their reward. They gained comprehension, Henry. They gained insight. They learned how to penetrate the surface of things and discover the truth that lies hidden within!"

Haddock glanced nervously about the walls of the room.

"Now, I'm far from being a sentimental man," said Mr.

128

Nammers. "What I rely on are facts. Give me the facts every time. But there's got to be more than that in the life of a business enterprise—and there is. Something you can't put your finger on. Something you can't literally see. But something that's there all the same."

"That's exactly it, Mr. Nammers."

"Ah," said Mr. Nammers. "So you've gotten an inkling of it, have you?"

"More than an inkling, Mr. Nammers."

"Fine. Well, it's urging you on, Henry. That's what it's doing—urging you on."

"Well, that wasn't exactly my interpre—"

"It makes you want to drive ahead, Henry. Those little promptings and whisperings you sense, those are the urgings of power. Power that wants to be used. Power that *demands* that you use it. Don't shrink back from those promptings, Henry. Follow them. Seize them. Seize them . . . and press on!"

Haddock gazed dubiously at the chairman, whose exhortations had empurpled his broad features and caused him to swell.

"That's your advice, then, Mr. Nammers?"

"Of course."

"And you really feel that I can do a decent job as president, then?"

"I'm convinced of it," said Mr. Nammers, slightly panting, for he was short of breath. "Let me put it to you plainly. You have outstanding leadership qualities in terms of personality, character, and presence. The only thing that's missing —temporarily missing, I mean—is the impulse of command. But that will come, Henry, and very soon, or I miss my guess. All the signs are there. I know those signs. I know them well.

129

And I don't say that blindly. We've been watching your work closely, Henry. Very closely."

Haddock edged back in his chair. "You've . . . been watching?"

"Of course we have," croaked the old chairman. "That's our job."

"Um, this watching . . . would you mind telling me about that? I mean, what exactly—"

"Henry, there are many ways of judging a man's performance, as you well know."

"Yes, of course, but I was thinking about one way in particular—"

Mr. Nammers dismissed his question with an impatient blink. "The point is, Henry, that while we're not satisfied *yet* with your handling of the job, we are certain that we *will* be satisfied." He hunched forward, his stubby fingers spread wide on the surface of the table. "Do you understand, Henry?" he said, his great eyes gleaming at Haddock. "We have great faith in you."

"I see," muttered Haddock. "I see." He sat in some bewilderment, unable to shift his gaze from Mr. Nammers' goggling stare. He felt numbed by it, his will congealed. Only in a distant corner of his mind did he remember that he had wanted to resign. But he hadn't resigned. Why, he hadn't even managed to utter the word. All he could do was sit there stupefied. "I see," he said again, but he didn't see at all.

Mr. Nammers had been wearied by his expenditure of energy. He appeared visibly to deflate; his eyes seemed to retract and then dulled as if veiled by a sleepy inner lid. "It's getting late," he observed, taking a look at his watch. "Unfortunately I've got an appointment downtown. Can't get out of it. Otherwise we might have lunch." He pushed against the

130

table, grunting as he rose to his feet. "Well, I hope my remarks have been of some encouragement to you, Henry."

"Oh, they have, they have," Haddock said hastily as he got up, too.

"Fine," said Mr. Nammers at the door. "Just remember what I've said. Give it a little more time, and everything will work out. Just follow your instincts, my boy."

Haddock, alone in the conference room, found the chairman's words echoing in his mind. Follow his instincts? Which instincts? He had quite a few of them, and they seemed to contradict one another. Perhaps that was why he had made such a botch of what was to have been his little speech of resignation. He probably hadn't been wholeheartedly intent on resigning, after all.

He took a cautious look at the portraits. Those faces weren't exactly kindly, were they? They were hard, in fact. Hard and cold and knowing. But Mr. Nammers had said they'd had their low moments. Perhaps they'd wanted to quit, too. Well, they hadn't. No, they'd driven stubbornly ahead—and was it completely out of the question to imagine that he might do the same?

He moved about the room, running his fingers over the surface of the walls. Mr. Nammers had faith in him. And the board of directors did, too. Mr. Nammers had made that clear. But it wasn't out of kindness. No, the directors weren't motivated by sentiment! If they had faith in him, they had sound reasons for it. The company was important to them —just as it had been important to the past presidents and chairmen whose portraits hung on the walls. They'd devoted their lives to the company, after all.

And so, Haddock reflected, had Mr. Nicholas. Why, the company was Mr. Nicholas' child, and a father doesn't aban-

131

don a child, does he? No, he watches over it with tenderness and love, trying not to intrude, but wanting always to be within reach. So that if Mr. Nicholas watched—if he really watched—then he did it because he cared. Mr. Nicholas cared a lot. He cared the most. He cared terribly! What else could explain the old man's self-effacing but unshakable attachment to the company and particularly to its president?

Yes, Haddock thought, Mr. Nicholas might be urging him on, too. Mr. Nicholas might have faith in him still. Mr. Nicholas wouldn't have tested him so severely if there hadn't been that faith—and wasn't it therefore his duty to respond with some faith of his own?

The next morning he awoke refreshed. "I slept better . . . why?" he kept asking himself, padding around the bedroom and casting tentative glances at the walls. "I feel better, too. I haven't felt like this for weeks!"

He ventured a smile. Did he dare speak out openly? He was afraid to. It might break the mood, a mood not of happiness exactly but of a premonition of happiness. Happiness? Was that possible? Well, in any event, he'd gotten a decent night's sleep. Perhaps he'd reached a turning point. Maybe the worst of it was over.

He had Frey send Mackensen back to the garage. "It's a fine spring morning, Frey," he said, "so I'm going to walk to work today." It had rained during the night, and the streets glistened as though they'd been scrubbed. An ocean breeze had cleared away the smog. He walked across a corner of the park. The trees were budding in the sunlight; squirrels raced about, and even the tramps looked cheerful. He paused to watch a fledgling balance itself high above his head. It wobbled on its perch, flexed its tiny wings, pitched forward—and flew. Haddock tipped his hat in a salute.

He arrived at the company glowing from his walk, strode past the secretaries with an authoritative step, and gave Miss Prince such a penetrating smile that she felt weak for an hour.

He sat down behind his desk, cleared his throat, arranged his features into an expression of resolution, and bent over the first memorandum that awaited him, determined to focus his attention on it by excluding from his mind all reflections about himself, Mr. Nicholas, Mr. Nammers, and even Miss Prince. It wasn't easy. He wanted to call Miss Prince in. She was wearing a new blouse. It suited her. He would like to mention that to her. How prettily she would color at his words! Well, he might do that later when he had a real reason to summon her. Right now it was that memorandum that counted. He had read it once without grasping its significance; he had to start in at the beginning again.

The second time he read the memo he understood almost all of it. That was encouraging. He hadn't really understood anything for weeks. If he read it a third time, he might grasp the whole thing. He did read it a third time, and now it was clear to him. He even had an idea on the subject involved and hastened to jot it down. Wonderful. But of course he couldn't read everything three times. He would have to improve on that.

By the end of a day of fierce concentration, in which he had his lunch sent in so he wouldn't lose a minute, he discovered that he could do the job in most cases with but a single reading. He was exhausted, but it was a contented exhaustion, and when Miss Prince made her final entry, bringing him some correspondence to sign, she found him leaning back in his chair with a weary smile on his lips.

"I saw an interesting thing in the park this morning, Miss Prince," he remarked as he signed the letters. "It was a baby bird, ready to take its first flight. It had wings, Miss Prince, but it didn't know how to use them. As far as that bird was concerned, those wings were useless impediments. They weighed that little fellow down. Well, there it was, teetering on its twig, looking lost and despondent, and then it turned its tiny head up toward the sun, and it saw the other birds flying about in the sky—and then suddenly, Miss Prince, it knew what it had to do. Yes, it *knew*. And so it plunged out bravely into the empty air. It leaped into the void, you might say. And those wings, which had seemed so useless . . . well, that little bird gave them a few flaps—clumsily at first, of course, but he didn't give up or get discouraged. No, he kept straining and flapping and fluttering, and in a matter of seconds he ws flying about as smartly as you please!"

"Oh, I'm glad of that, Mr. Haddock."

Haddock completed his last signature. "Here we are, Miss Prince."

"Thank you, Mr. Haddock."

She gathered up the letters and took them out. It was only after she had left the office that he remembered he'd neglected to compliment her on her blouse. Oh, well, he thought. He'd make a note to do that the next time she wore it.

As the weeks went by, his new determination to concentrate on his work began to produce results. He was less troubled by the uncertainties that had slowed him before. He became keener and more confident. Sometimes he had only to scan a report in order to perceive its significance and to discover its omissions, its errors, and its relation to other elements that bore on the subject. Before, he'd felt suffocated by the sheer mass of work; now he was disposing in minutes of matters that earlier might have taken hours.

Each day he addressed himself more vigorously to his work, marking his opinions on the various items with bolder strokes of the pen—"yes" to this, "no" to that, and frequently scribbling sharp phrases of criticism or admonition: "We'll have to do better than this!" or "OK, but get moving on it fast!"

There was also a change in his relations with his subordinate officers, which first appeared in the routine morning briefings they gave him on current problems. The other executives liked Haddock personally, but they knew that Imry was the real boss. When they entered the president's office, they slouched indolently into the chairs, knowing that if Imry were absent, nothing would be decided, and that whatever questions Haddock might venture would be asked not so much for enlightenment as to show that he had a sympathetic appreciation of their efforts.

Now, however, Haddock was starting to ask lots of questions, and his questions were real questions. He asked them mildly but insistently. One by one, his subordinates found themselves subjected to a grilling for which they weren't prepared. They were surprised and a little amused. What had gotten into Haddock? Had he decided that he wanted to play president?

"Wait a minute, John," he'd say, studying a report. "What you've just told me doesn't quite jibe with the material your

135

people assembled here last month. It says here quite clearly that . . ."

"Well, I can explain that, Henry. You see . . ."

But sometimes they couldn't explain. There were loose ends. There were issues that might have been resolved but hadn't been yet. There were contradictions, errors, and instances of sloppiness. Haddock seemed to be catching every one.

"What about this?" he'd ask calmly. "I find it hard to understand why you haven't . . ."

"Oh, yes. Well, Henry, we're getting right on that, let me assure you. . . ." And John (or Bob or Phil or Powell) would make a note and flash Haddock a wary look. What was going on? Where was the Haddock they'd always known, that amiable fellow who had such a knack of putting people at their ease? His manner was the same. His smiles were, too. But those disquieting questions . . . that was another matter entirely. He was behaving as though he were actually intent on running the company!

The problems Haddock was examining were more or less the same ones he had tried to deal with for many weeks and that had left him bewildered or bored. Now he was finding them interesting—fascinating, even. For the first time he was beginning to understand how the company actually worked. He had understood before, in a dim and methodical way, and, given enough time, he had been able to comprehend the key points in a complicated issue—but now he seemed to sense them instinctively. He was pulling free of what had constrained him for so long a time. He was moving toward what he'd longed for—the perception of the company in operation as an organic entity, as a series of movements no longer perplexing in their mass of detail but as necessarily interwoven as muscle and nerve. And he saw himself as a part of it, an important part—a vital part, in fact—for what he did as president could move and shake that strange, ungainly creature, the company.

His awareness of Mr. Nicholas had changed, too. It had diminished, or at least it didn't weigh on him now. It no longer made him unwilling to enter his office. On the contrary, he strode in eagerly, ready for fresh proofs of his newfound capacity to handle his job, and once he was plunged into the working day, he forgot about Mr. Nicholas entirely. Even at the apartment he was untroubled by what had so perturbed him before. It was as if his thoughts were so fully occupied by the company that there simply wasn't room for Mr. Nicholas anymore. He felt a sense of liberation—and not from Mr. Nicholas, but from his own limitations, his own timidity and fears.

But he didn't waste time exulting. He had so much work to do, and so many wasted weeks to make up for, that he was annoyed by the slightest interruption in his schedule and impatient if there were the least delay.

One afternoon his office door swung open unexpectedly.

Miss Bottweiler, the chief administrative officer, strode in. "Oh, Mr. Haddock, I hope I'm not intruding," she said, "but there's something I'd like to get taken care of." She approached the desk busily, carrying a sheaf of papers.

Haddock was about to respond to Miss Bottweiler's entrance with some conventional remark of salutation, and in fact an automatic smile of welcome had already formed on his lips, but he said nothing. Instead, he thought: Would Miss Bottweiler have marched so breezily into the president's office if Charles Mersey had been sitting behind the desk? Or Carl Brandt?

She was saying something about insurance. He wasn't listening.

"This is the president's office, Miss Bottweiler," he broke in.

She hesitated.

"You didn't knock," he said.

"Oh, I'm sorry, but I—"

"This isn't a public lounge, Miss Bottweiler."

"Well, I beg your pardon, but Miss Prince was away from her desk, so I thought—"

"You thought you'd just barge on in, is that it?"

"Well—"

"Do you realize how discourteous it is, Miss Bottweiler, to plunge into someone's office without knocking?"

She stood open-mouthed with surprise. Haddock never spoke to anyone like that. She was confused by the fact that his voice was mild and level and that his expression was pleasant, almost friendly.

"Miss Bottweiler, you've just violated a very fundamental rule of respect for the rights of others. Quite frankly I'm astonished and disturbed. If this is the way you behave toward a superior, I certainly wouldn't want to be one of your subordinates."

"I-I'm sorry, Mr. Haddock." She was not a woman who was easily cowed, but she was reddening and bewildered. She stared at Haddock as though she weren't quite sure who he was. "It won't happen again." She glanced down at the papers she held. "I just needed your signature—"

"One moment, Miss Bottweiler," said Haddock coolly. He,

too, was surprised by what he was doing. Ordinarily it wouldn't have occurred to him to make even a joking reference to such a minor transgression. Even when some serious shortcoming on the part of a staff member forced him to utter a reproof, he did so in an apologetic way, prefacing it by lavish praise of the offender's past achievements.

"I think this situation calls for something more than words," he went on, leaning back in his chair and gazing at her quietly without the slightest show of irritation—and he wasn't irritated. He was Haddock in the chair, and it was his mouth that opened and his words that issued forth, and yet he felt a curious detachment, as though he really had very little to do with what was taking place. He was interested in it, true, but this interest was remote. It was a spectator's interest. He was curious to find out how this episode was going to come out.

"There are two ways of doing something," he continued. His voice remained steady, his manner polite. "There's the right way, and there's the wrong way."

Miss Bottweiler continued to gape at him. Her ringed fingers were beginning to crumple the papers she carried.

"You've done it the wrong way, Miss Bottweiler. Now I want you to do it the right way."

She opened her mouth. "I'm not sure I—" She was flushing crimson.

"Do I need to be more explicit?" he remarked. He raised his eyebrows in inquiry. "I want you to go back outside and try it again, Miss Bottweiler. The right way this time."

Miss Bottweiler actually swayed. She had been with the company for twenty-two years. She was honest, efficient, and resourceful. Four previous presidents had valued her ser-

139

vices and had shown it by treating her with due respect. "I can't quite bring myself to believe—" she began, stammering. She was furious.

"Come, come," said Haddock, tapping a pencil on the desk. "We've wasted enough time on this already, haven't we?"

If he had displayed any emotion other than quiet confidence, she might have flung her papers on the desk and stalked out. As it was, she seemed incapable of doing anything.

Haddock raised his hand. He snapped his fingers.

Miss Bottweiler jerked her head back as though he'd slapped her. Then she turned and walked out of the office, closing the door behind her.

She knocked.

"Yes?" he called out amiably.

She opened the door. Her cheeks were patchy; her mouth was set crookedly. "I have the papers on the insurance reorganization, Mr. Haddock," she said hoarsely, approaching with heavy, wading steps. She'd neglected to close the door. Behind her, in the corridor beyond the anteroom, two secretaries passed by, then reappeared, as though drawn by the scent of trouble.

"Yes?" asked Haddock.

"I need . . . your signature."

"Well, I think we'd better wait a day or two on that, Miss Bottweiler," Haddock said blandly.

She remained staring at him, her bosom laboring.

"I want to go over that material first," he went on, "but I don't have time for it right now."

She tried to speak. She couldn't.

"Was there anything else, Miss Bottweiler?" He gazed up

140

at her with mild curiosity. There was an odd, flat look about her. She seemed to lack dimension. It was peculiar—she was standing there shaking with rage and humiliation, but although he could recognize these emotions, the force of them didn't reach him.

"Nothing else?" he remarked as she remained silent. He regarded her dispassionately. There was a wen on her cheek. He hadn't really noticed it before. It wasn't disfiguring, but it seemed to call attention to the fact that Miss Bottweiler was a woman without charm. He'd always thought of her as a sort of head nurse, a bustling, maternal figure. Now he saw her as an ugly, aging, bossy woman. She wasn't particularly likable.

"You seem a little upset, Miss Bottweiler," he added. "Don't you think you'd better try to get a grip on yourself?"

With a little moan she turned and left, walking so unsteadily that she lurched in the doorway and bumped against Miss Prince's desk on the way out. The two secretaries had vanished.

Haddock remained quietly at his desk, reading a memorandum he'd picked up earlier. Several ideas occurred to him. He made some notes in the margin. When he had finished, he set the memorandum aside and picked up another one.

It wasn't until he was seated in the limousine that evening after work that he found time to consider his treatment of Miss Bottweiler. Had he been too severe with her? Well, maybe he had. If so, he ought to apologize. But there was another way of looking at it, wasn't there? That is, he had dealt with her on an official basis. There hadn't been anything personal about it.

141

Right, he thought. In an official sense it hadn't been Miss Bottweiler who had come in without knocking; it had been the chief administrative officer. Likewise, it hadn't been Haddock who had delivered the rebuke. It had been the president. As individuals, he and Miss Bottweiler hadn't been involved at all. They'd been merely bystanders. So there was nothing to apologize for—and no one to apologize to. He felt relieved.

"I've got a pair of opera glasses now, Mr. Haddock," said Mackensen from the front.

"What?"

"Opera glasses." Mackensen looked up cheerfully into the rearview mirror. "I'm increasing my range, sir."

Haddock glanced at him. He had to look into the rearview mirror to see his face, and it occurred to him that this was the way he and Mackensen saw each other for the most part; indirectly, as reflections in a little rectangle of glass. This seemed appropriate, though. It was the limousine, after all, that brought them together, and so it was fitting that their relationship should be visually defined through the medium of the limousine. It was a useful reminder.

He realized that he hadn't paid attention to what his driver had said. "Sorry, Mackensen. What were you telling me?"

"I was talking about my new opera glasses, Mr. Haddock. When I get the hang of them, I bet I'll be reading lips up to fifty yards away."

"Not on company time you won't."

"Sir?"

"Mackensen, the company pays you to drive this car, not to go cruising around the city reading lips."

"Mr. Haddock, I—"

"What you do after work is your business, Mackensen, but

as long as you're wearing that uniform, the company has the right to demand that you concentrate on your job, and if you need something to do between trips, you might give some attention to the condition of the car. It's dusty. This side window—it's streaky. I can hardly see out of it. I might as well be riding in a hearse."

"Honestly, Mr. Haddock—"

"For my own account it wouldn't matter, but from the point of view of the company it's really shameful for the man who holds the office of president to be carted through the streets like a sack of garbage. I'm speaking officially, Mackensen. I hope you understand that. Personally I wouldn't care if you kept pigs in the car and practiced your violin at stoplights, but as president I've got to insist on standards."

"I—"

"It's the position that counts, not the man. Men change, Mackensen, but the position stays the same. Who knows, maybe next year there'll be someone else sitting back here in my place—and maybe there'll be someone else behind the wheel—but they'll still be president and driver, so I think it's time that we get straight about the reason we happen to be here in this car at this particular time . . . not because we're two men named Haddock and Mackensen but because we occupy temporarily certain positions that require us to be here. Do you understand what I mean?"

Mackensen maintained a sullen silence.

"Well, maybe you don't understand, Mackensen, so let me put it another way. Society isn't just a haphazard collection of human beings; it's an organization of functions, and it's an organization that moves at top speed, too, so this means that every individual function has to be clearly delineated and instantly recognizable, or otherwise there'll be inefficiency

143

and breakdown and all the rest. I've got a responsibility to behave like a president, and you've got to behave like a driver—and reading lips, it just doesn't fit in. It confuses things. Anybody watching us wouldn't know what to think, frankly. Lipreading is extraneous to your functional existence, you understand. After hours, fine. But it's got no business in here with us now; that's my whole point."

"Well, nobody's watching anyhow," Mackensen muttered.

"That's where you're wrong, Mackensen. That's where you're dead wrong. I'm not saying that any specific individual person is watching us—but society is watching us . . . that is, there's a general awareness of us that amounts to the same thing. We're riding along a street where there are hundreds upon hundreds of people, and each one of them is aware of our presence, Mackensen, if only for a split second, and all these tiny little awarenesses add up to one big one, in my judgment, so that you might say that society is reading our lips—and doing a pretty damned good job of it, too."

Mackensen mumbled something but in a voice so low that Haddock couldn't hear him.

"But there's another kind of awareness, Mackensen. It comes from within. It comes from our own consciousness of our functions. In fact, I'd be willing to say that this internal consciousness—this awareness—is the very spirit of our functions. In specific terms, there's a sort of president inside of me, Mackensen, and this president is watching me very closely, and when I don't behave in appropriate ways . . . well, this presidential spirit is offended and angry, and it has the right—it has the duty—to call me on the carpet to correct me. And there's a driver within you, Mackensen. Or a chauffeur, if you prefer. And this chauffeur isn't just any chauffeur. It's the essence of the perfect chauffeur. It's a sort of

144

absolute ideal of chauffeurism, Mackensen. It's what you could be if you realized your potential fully. But you won't achieve that ideal unless you're true to it. You've got to pay attention to it, you've got to study it, you've got to give it your honest and undivided attention—no distractions! no lipreading!—you've got to let yourself be possessed by it! And don't kid yourself, Mackensen. It's there, that chauffeur. It's keeping an eye on you. Every minute of the day. You can't escape. And you shouldn't want to escape, either, because . . . because it's trying to help you, Mackensen. It's trying to encourage you. It's trying to show you the way. And when you've done something right at last—and it may be only a little thing, Mackensen, but it's the spirit that counts—well, then, you feel better, and no wonder. You've made some sort of connection with the ideal. You're on the track!"

Haddock knew that his energetic direction of company affairs would bring him into conflict with the executive vice president sooner or later. That didn't worry him. He not only welcomed the prospect, he deliberately precipitated it, by ordering a contract cancellation without informing Imry in advance.

That brought Imry hurrying in, hardly bothering to conceal his annoyance.

"Henry," he said brusquely, "Phil tells me you're concerned about the Denver operation, so I thought I'd better try to put that in the full context for you. . . ." His heavy features were flushed; his balding dome gleamed damply. ". . . too bad you didn't see fit to call me in on that, Henry, because I could have helped make it clear to you that . . ."

Haddock watched him calmly and said nothing.

"... Phil was under the impression that you wanted him to cancel out the contract, Henry, and I can't imagine that you would actually have told him that."

"Why not, George?"

"Well, Henry—" Imry hesitated. Angrily he wiped the palms of his hands along his trouser legs.

"It's the logical step, isn't it?"

"Under the circumstances it's certainly a strong possibility, but there are questions of timing and procedure involved." Imry spoke in a grumbling, exasperated voice, all the while examining Haddock suspiciously, his thick jaw thrust forward, his hairy nostrils quivering. "If I'd known you wanted to review that subject, Henry, I could have laid this all out." He was furious. Haddock had no right even to consider a step of major importance without consulting him. But he was puzzled. Haddock ought to be starting to apologize and explain, he ought to be cringing back a bit now, but he wasn't. He was sitting with a quiet smile, gazing pleasantly across the desk—and finally it was Imry who glanced uncomfortably away.

"I've taken all those factors into account, George," Haddock said. "I've been watching that situation for some time now, and I—" He broke off. He had just made a remarkable discovery. A revelation, really. *He didn't like George Imry.* Was it possible? Yes—it was! For the first time in his life he found himself not liking someone! He leaned forward in his surprise and began examining with keen attention the face of this man he didn't like, as though it was the map of some new and interesting country he'd never been able to visit.

"I fully intended calling you in on this later today, George," he resumed. Oddly enough, he felt a surge of gratitude; Imry had liberated him from an obligation that he now felt had been irksome. "I certainly wouldn't have gone ahead without letting you know about it." He studied Imry's meaty features almost tenderly. It was like first love, in a way.

"So now you do know about it," he went on, "and I suggest you get together with Phil right away and work out the details for me to approve later on in the day."

"Wait a minute." Imry was speaking through his teeth. He was actually grinding them. "This may be premature, don't you think? There are certain considerations against cancellation which . . ." And in a voice hoarsened by rage he began to list these reasons, but with decreasing conviction, for he sensed that Haddock was right, which angered him all the more. In another few days he himself would have come to the same conclusion. He trailed off lamely and sat scowling at the floor.

"Let's don't waste any more time on this, George," Haddock remarked pleasantly. "Let's just get it done."

Imry cleared his throat. "All right," he muttered. "It's your decision, Henry."

"Do you disagree, George?"

"Well, not exactly, no."

"We'll both sign the termination notification, then. Unless you'd rather go on record in a memo to the files as being opposed."

"I'm not opposed," Imry said angrily. Haddock had him boxed in. If he couldn't say "no," he'd have to say "yes." "All right, Henry. I'll get hold of Phil, and we'll get to work on it."

He started to rise.

"Just a second, George," said Haddock. He had nothing particular in mind, but he didn't want Imry to leave; not yet. He wanted something else. Not revenge for the little humiliations Imry had caused him in the past months. It wasn't that. He just felt that more was needed. He swung about in his chair, smiling thoughtfully at the walls.

"Well, Henry?"

Haddock nodded. Oh, yes. He had it now.

"George, that conference next week at the Waldorf. The round-table thing."

"Well, I'm all set on that," Imry said. There was a note of concern in his voice. "I'm all lined up for it, speech and everything."

"Good," said Haddock. "Good." He hesitated deliberately, frowning down at his desk. He had agreed weeks ago that Imry could represent the company at the conference. It would mean public recognition for the first time in Imry's career. He would be known in person as he was coming to be known by reputation as the real driving force behind the company.

"Actually, George," Haddock said, "I've been thinking about that."

"Yes?"

"I've come to the conclusion that I'd better be the one to go."

Imry squinted uncertainly across the desk. He'd bought a new suit. His son was coming down from college to be present.

"Sorry, George, but—" Haddock fabricated a rueful smile and spread his hands apart in a gesture of apology. "It's too high-level for me not to go. It might not look right."

"But—the speech—"

"I'm sorry not to have told you earlier, George, but just send your speech to me this afternoon, and I'll see if I can't modify it for my own use."

148

Imry was perspiring. He had envisioned himself rising at the table, a strong and commanding figure toward whom heads would expectantly turn. His son would see this. But now, suddenly . . . it wouldn't happen. Just like that.

"Henry, I thought we'd agreed—"

"I'll have Miss Prince notify the conference secretary of the switch. I'll get that done today."

"Look here, Henry." Imry had gotten over the first shock. He was starting to react angrily. He wasn't going to surrender without a fight. "I happen to have put a lot of time in on the speech, and as you know perfectly well, quite a few companies will be represented by the number two man. They always are. Quite frankly I don't see that as sufficient reason for you to—"

Haddock was ready for him. "It isn't only that, George," he said quietly.

Imry flashed him a sharp glance. "What do you mean?" He glared at Haddock resentfully. "What do you mean, 'It isn't only that'?"

"Nothing, George." Haddock feigned embarrassment. "I simply meant—"

"What?"

"George, there's no point in going into this thing any further—"

"Tell me what you've got on your mind. I think I've got the right to know, whatever it is."

"It's such a superficial thing, George. It's purely a question of—" Haddock hesitated, as though reluctant to continue. He had a pained look on his face.

"Go on, Henry."

"Well, it's a question of appearance, that's all." Haddock paused to let that sink in. "You know how stupid these things

149

are, George, but they're part of the reality we've got to deal with, and as a business organization, we've got to try to create the right effect."

"Oh," said Imry. He was stunned. Haddock had correctly divined his vulnerability. Imry had been a homely boy; heavyset, squinting, and pimply. As a man, he'd known in a vague way that he was unprepossessing, but never before in his adult life had anyone openly reminded him that his personal appearance was unpleasant. All the torment of his unhappy youth surged up in him. He saw Haddock as one of those handsome, poised, self-assured boys who had always won honors, girls, everything.

"I'm sorry, George." Haddock was watching him with a sympathetic expression.

"This isn't a beauty contest, Henry," Imry said, trying to recover. But he seemed bewildered. He removed his glasses and thrust them into his pocket.

"Of course not. But . . . well, that element isn't completely lacking. For example, we both know why the board picked me to be president instead of you." Haddock was being friendly and sincere now. He wore his confidential smile. "They wanted someone out front as a handshaker who had the particular style they felt would set the company off to best advantage, someone who went to the right tailor and the right barber, someone who—well, someone who had that superficial little knack, George."

Imry looked down blankly at the knees of his trousers.

"You know, some men can pay five hundred dollars for a suit of clothes, George, and it still doesn't seem to fit them. It's a question of body type or something. You're either born with it or you're not."

Imry remained seated with his head slightly bowed.

150

"Well, George," Haddock said. He wondered whether he should go further. No, perhaps not. Not today. "Just have your speech brought in, right?"

He rapped a pencil on the desk. Imry's head raised. He gazed at Haddock with wondering, uncertain eyes. "All right, Henry," he mumbled, and then heavily he got to his feet and walked out.

Haddock watched him go. Then he swung his chair around to the window and gazed thoughtfully out at the city. Had he been too severe with Imry? Had he acted out of rancor or ill feeling? He thought not. No, he was convinced that he had done the proper, necessary thing. Imry had to be reminded that Haddock was the president. True, he had discovered that he didn't like Imry, but it was also true that he didn't *dis*like the man, either. In fact, right now he felt a little sorry for him. But a company couldn't be run on the basis of personal emotions, could it?

"Well, Miss Prince," he said, "things seem to have gone more smoothly for me these past few weeks."

"Oh, I'm glad they have, Mr. Haddock."

He saw that she was really glad, and he was touched by this further evidence of her unselfish loyalty. They were together as much as they'd been before, but there was no longer time for those moments of intimate silence. The work he had shunned before was surging to his office now in response to his growing authority. Miss Prince hastened in and out all day. A lingering cold had made her nose red. When his door was open, he could hear her sniffing as she sat hurriedly typing, trying to keep from falling behind.

But his door wasn't open very often. He had become less

151

accessible to the staff. He no longer encouraged the others to stroll in whenever they felt like discussing something with him. He called them in when he needed them. He didn't particularly care for this new system, but he was obliged to adopt it for the sake of efficiency. He knew what he was doing now, and so his time was more valuable. Partly for that reason he went out less frequently with the others for lunch. But he also had the feeling that he should restrict his familiarity with the men who served under him. A president, he thought, ought to be a little reserved. He shouldn't be seen too much.

As always, he was polite and good-natured. He never raised his voice. He displayed his customary smile and made an occasional joke to put the others at their ease. But his main purpose no longer was to put them at their ease; it was to pull information out of them in order to shape decisions and issue instructions. The other men sensed this, but they didn't seem troubled by it. On the contrary, they appeared to welcome Haddock's new decisiveness. It was a relief, after months of uncertainty, to have the president start behaving with the authority proper to his office.

He arrived early and often didn't leave until eight or nine o'clock in the evening. He stuffed his attaché case with papers to go through after he had eaten his solitary supper. On weekends he remained in the apartment, working. He left only for social engagements of a business nature. During the week he refused all but the most pressing obligations that took him away from the office.

Under this regime he became thinner. He lost that disarming boyishness that had marked him before. Tired as he often was, he stood straighter and walked more purposefully. He wore a slight, preoccupied frown, as though he

152

wasn't ever completely pleased with the way things were going. He wasn't, either. There was always too much to do, and his staff couldn't move quickly enough to meet his expectations.

His knowledge of company operations was extensive now. Even where his information was imperfect, he managed, by adroit questioning, to make it appear that he knew as much about a particular department as the man who actually headed it. At meetings he might sit back and say little, letting others do the talking, but in silence he was more impressive still, and his associates would defer to him, breaking off in the middle of arguments to ask: "How does that strike you, Henry?" Frequently he'd merely shrug and tell them to go ahead, reserving his own opinion, so that they'd have to proceed on their own but more than ever aware of the watchful presence of the president of the company.

He had moments of intense happiness and of pride. He was making progress. He could feel it. Every day his confidence increased. He was careful to maintain his outward composure, but inwardly he was exultant. What Mr. Nammers had predicted would happen was in fact starting to happen. He was hurrying toward the conquest of presidential power. At the same time, his old fears and fancies were dwindling. Wasn't that a final proof that his original hunch had been correct—that what he had referred to as Mr. Nicholas was really his own anxiety about his work?

He still had that particular sensation, but it was fainter, much fainter. He didn't mind being alone in his office. He even went into the conference room alone sometimes, with hardly a qualm. At the apartment he was only vaguely conscious of what had once weighed on him so heavily; moreover, he was sleeping tranquilly every night. Yes, he

153

thought, he was talking over the presidency—and he was consequently liberating himself from "Mr. Nicholas."

One day late in May he received a call from Mr. Nammers, inviting him to lunch at the chairman's club. This was an unusual mark of favor, a tacit recognition of Haddock's new and forceful handling of the presidency. More than that, from certain allusions made by Mr. Nammers during the meal Haddock understood that his name might one day be proposed for membership. This was no small honor, for although the club somewhat resembled a mausoleum, being huge and dim and gloomy, with antiquated old gentlemen doddering about like windup toys with their pacemakers ticking away, it had considerable prestige in the city.

Mr. Nammers listened attentively as Haddock reported the latest information on the company's proposed establishment of a plant in Argentina, a project that had been advanced in recent weeks toward the point of final decision.

"Good, Henry, good," the chairman commented, pushing his dessert dish aside. "When you've got all the figures together, we'll give them a careful review, you and I. This will be a landmark for the company," he observed. "Our first move into direct production overseas! But not our last, Henry. By no means. First, South America . . . then Africa, and Asia—the whole world!"

"That's a very compelling vision, Mr. Nammers," Haddock responded with an appreciative smile. He felt a little tired, though. The lunch had been a long one, and he had work waiting for him back at the office.

"I can remember the early years of commercial radio, Henry," Mr. Nammers continued expansively, his bulbous eyes gleaming in the subdued light of the dining hall. "And the first overseas telephone service—I remember that, too. It seems a million years ago. And we thought *that* was something. Well, it was child's play compared to what's happening now. Why, with government and science and industry working together to spread communications far and wide, we're helping knit a fabric that will grow progressively tighter, denser, more intricately linked, more powerful . . . systems capable of penetrating the most intimate secrets of the sky, the earth, the sea—and of man himself!"

"You paint a really inspiring picture, Mr. Nammers," Haddock said, but he was troubled by a slight feeling of discomfort. His food lay heavily on his stomach. He hoped that Mr. Nammers would soon bring their luncheon to a close.

"But enough of my ramblings, Henry," Mr. Nammers said, shifting his bulk in his chair. "One step at a time, eh? That Argentina project will keep us busy for a while, I should think. Which reminds me of what I wanted to broach to you." He gave Haddock a confidential glance. "What would you say, Henry, to our naming that new plant after Edgar Nicholas?"

Haddock hesitated, caught offguard. It was the first time in weeks that he had heard the founder's name mentioned. It had given him an odd flash of alarm.

"Oh, that sounds like a very fine idea," he said hastily.

"I thought it would be appropriate," the chairman remarked. He leaned forward, turning the full force of his huge eyes on Haddock. "You see, this plant will be important not only in itself but as a symbol of our reaching out on an international scale. Edgar foresaw that, Henry. A worldwide system was always his dream."

"Yes, I see," said Haddock, shifting his gaze away from Mr. Nammers' basilisk stare. There was a faint pulsing at his temples, perhaps the beginning of a headache.

"In his quiet way Edgar was something of a philosopher," Mr. Nammers went on. "I remember the things he used to talk to us about back in the old days. He had a deep and abiding faith in man's ability to dominate his environment, not just through inventive genius but also through the persistent and unflagging exercise of willpower."

Haddock nodded but kept his eyes on his plate, his glass, his coffee cup, to avoid the chairman's penetrating gaze.

"And what Edgar believed, he practiced. Once he got an idea in his head, Henry, there was no shaking him off. Not only that, but he prosecuted these ideas to the very limits of their potential to assure himself that he'd left no possibility unexplored."

Haddock stole a glance at his watch. It wasn't as late as he'd thought, but he wanted to leave. He was ready to get up that moment. He had no interest in hearing any more about Mr. Nicholas.

". . . I remember one of his favorite phrases," Mr. Nammers was saying. "He used it time and again. 'Observation is power'—that's what he used to tell us. By that he meant that what man can observe, he can study. And from that study comes knowledge—the capacity to use and control the social and natural forces that surround us. That was Edgar's message to us, Henry. And of course he was right. The whole thrust of human history over the ages is toward that knowledge, toward that control—and when every square inch of space under the sun is subject to our observation, then we'll have achieved the ultimate in the control of our destinies!"

Haddock managed to produce a smile of enthusiasm, but

156

he was bothered by that pulsing in his head. He wished that he could simply push back his chair, rise, and walk out of the room.

"So that's why I think we ought to name our first overseas venture in Edgar's honor," Mr. Nammers said. "I don't know whether he'll agree to it, but I'll sound out his nephew on the subject. It's certainly time we did something like that. And it would give me great personal satisfaction. Edgar is a very old and valued friend."

Haddock glanced unwillingly at his host. "Do you . . . see him often?"

"No, no. Edgar lives in pretty strict retirement. But I manage to keep in touch." Mr. Nammers signaled the waiter to bring the bill for him to sign. "I won't see you down to the door, Henry," he said as they left the dining hall. "I have to save my steps, you know." He chuckled as he shook Haddock's hand. "The communications business is the old man's friend, Henry. It lets us keep up with things by remote control. Not that there's much for us to do with fellows like you in charge!"

Outside the club Haddock declined the doorman's offer to call a cab. He decided that a brisk walk in the bright air might clear away his oppression, which had been caused, no doubt, by something he'd eaten, perhaps the pie. And if that little headache didn't clear up, he'd stop at a drugstore and take something for it. In any event, he was relieved that the lunch had ended. What a waste of time it had been, he thought in irritation. When he became chairman one day, he certainly wouldn't subject the president of the company to such a windy ordeal.

He strode along frowning, with his fists clenched. "Philosophy," he muttered contemptuously. Those old men had nothing better to do evidently than sit around mouthing pompous phrases—while he was the one who had the burden of responsibility, he was the one who had to do the actual work. Yes, he was far too busy to trouble himself with such high-flown notions. He resolved to dismiss them from his mind. He would refuse to think about them at all—and that was a sign of how secure and confident he was now, wasn't it? Why, just a few weeks ago he would have pondered and agonized over every scrap of information about Mr. Nicholas. Yes, the old Haddock, nervous and tormented, would have seized on each ambiguous remark and tortured out insidious implications!

But those days were over. He was finished with all that suspicion and trembling. Now he could meet the challenge of the presidency with his concentration keen and his energies undistracted.

As he walked along, he found that the afternoon was not quite so fine as it had first seemed. The sun was hazed by smog, and the air had a bitter scent. There was a cool breeze, too. He wished he had worn his topcoat. He could feel the current against his back; it made a cold spot there. And he still had that pulsing in his head; not a headache, really, but more the intimation of a headache. Still, it bothered him.

He paused at a crossing, waiting for the light. The traffic, he saw, was moderate, and the sidewalks were not crowded. It was a typical midafternoon scene. Most people were already back at work. It was the best time of day to take a stroll, and he was annoyed that his slight physical unease prevented him from enjoying it fully. Had it been the pie that had produced that whisper of a throb in his head? The extra glass of wine? More likely it was the pollution in the air. Even on clear days it was there. You couldn't help breathing it in, and

158

some of the worst elements were odorless, weren't they? You might saunter along congratulating yourself on how fresh the air was, but all the time, without knowing it, you'd be inhaling those poisons, and finally they'd build up to the point where you'd have to acknowledge that something was definitely wrong.

As he reached the next crossing, he realized that the breeze had died down and vanished. But he still had that cold spot between his shoulders. The current had left its imprint there. But it was faint. He hardly felt it. It wasn't so much a cold spot as the suggestion of a cold spot, as though something had touched him there and gone away. It was barely noticeable, like the pulsing in his head.

Well, he knew he was unusually tired. He'd been working hard. He wasn't afraid any longer, true; on the contrary, he worked zestfully, in a state of exhilaration almost, but that carried with it a special tension that was bound to have an effect. He was more irritable now, although he took pains to maintain a calm manner with his staff. It was partly impatience. He saw quickly the answers to problems the company confronted, but the others lacked this swiftness of comprehension, and it irked him to wait for them to catch up. Sometimes he found it difficult to keep from expressing his impatience intemperately. So his irritability was a presidential irritability—another indication of his increasing mastery of the job—and if from time to time he might be vexed by a little headache, that was a small price to pay. Not that he actually had a headache. It was more a tingling sensation, almost as though—

He stopped and turned around. No, there was nothing out of the ordinary back there. Just the customary afternoon crowds walking along. No one had the slightest interest in him. He started off again at a quicker pace. In the middle of the next block he hesitated and then turned around once more, for a few moments examining the traffic, the pedestrians, even the buildings.

Then he decided that he'd done enough walking and hailed a taxi.

Back at the office he felt better. There was work to do, and as long as he was busy, he wasn't troubled by those nagging little sensations of discomfort.

But when he left his desk at the end of the day, he became aware of them again. That dim tingling in his head, that light chill between his shoulders—he felt them in the corridor, in the elevator, and in the lobby, too, and even in the limousine as he was being driven back to the apartment.

They remained with him the following day and the day after that. He seemed unable to shake them off. Later in the week he made an overnight business trip to Washington; they went with him. On his return, he took an evening off, going to the theater; he was bothered by them there, too. He took headache pills and digestives; he began eating blander foods and cut out alcohol altogether. Nothing seemed to help. He thought of going to the doctor, but decided not to. He would have to describe these symptoms to the doctor, and he didn't want to do that. He didn't want to speak of them at all. If he refused to define them—even to himself—then they might fade away, and so he fought against what rose insistently in his thoughts, mocking him, challenging him to recognize it.

His resolution failed finally. He couldn't hold out. He had to admit to himself that the sensations that now worried at him were the same as those he had lived with for so many weeks. He had the feeling that he was being watched. Except

160

that now it wasn't just in the conference room, in his office, and at the apartment.

He was being watched everywhere and all the time.

His original obsession with Mr. Nicholas had been founded on a possibility of truth. The old man *might* have gone on monitoring the conference room. It was conceivable, too, that he watched the office as well. That he monitored the apartment was highly improbable; nevertheless, it was not beyond the reach of the company's technology.

But for this new phenomenon there was no conceivable basis. Was he supposed to persuade himself that in a burst of extravagance Mr. Nicholas had hired a fleet of mobile units to track him through the streets? It was fantastic. It was maddening. If reality had been stretched to the breaking point before, it had snapped now. He was confronted by a monstrous dilemma: he felt that he was being watched . . . and he knew he couldn't be.

If this had happened a few weeks earlier, he might have concluded that his failure in the presidency was driving him insane. But he wasn't failing any longer. He was succeeding. There still were pressures but of a radically different kind. *He* created them. *He* was in command. He had never felt more sure of himself. His tenseness and irritability were on the surface. Within, he was moving toward a state of quiet certainty. There was not the slightest question about his sanity.

Think it through, Haddock, he told himself. *Reason it out.* If anything, his new predicament offered a final proof (if such proof were needed) that Mr. Nicholas didn't exist. The sensation of being watched had spread—but the possibility that

161

Mr. Nicholas caused it hadn't. Mr. Nicholas couldn't watch *everywhere*. Therefore he didn't watch *any*where. He didn't watch at all. Nobody watched.

What remained, then, was the initial premise: that the sensation was the invention of his own neurotic suggestibility. On the day of his election some psychic spring within him had been touched by Mr. Elphinstone's little anecdote, and he'd created the original version of Mr. Nicholas. And then Mr. Nammers' remarks at their recent lunch had been enough to produce the new, omnipresent one. That unexpected reference to the founder in connection with the expansion of the company had been distorted into the expansion of the synthetic Mr. Nicholas himself.

Very well, he thought. The problem was irrational, but irrationality had its own logic, and he'd arrived at a satisfactory explanation. Why, then, did the sensation persist? Why couldn't he explain it away?

He was angry and disheartened. More than that, he felt unjustly treated—and this emotion he found disturbing in itself. He was reacting as though he were facing a real situation in which he was literally being watched by someone . . . by Mr. Nicholas. He caught himself thinking resentfully that the old man ought to be making things easier for him, as a reward for his successful management of the company. Instead, there was this malignant and incredible increase in monitoring activity. It was grossly unfair!

And yet, of course, no one was watching. He knew that. No one *could* be watching. Not everywhere!

As the days went by, he remained in his office more and more. It was there, ironically, that he felt most comfortable. He was accustomed to it there. He avoided going out for lunch; he had his meals sent up. Finally he realized that this was cowardly. He'd surrendered to Mr. Nicholas when he'd been weak, but now he was strong and had no excuse. One day when Miss Prince asked him if he wanted her to order something for him—he realized from her question what a habit this had become—he told her no, he wouldn't eat at his desk that day, and then he pushed aside what he was doing, took his hat, and left.

He entered the first restaurant he came to. While he waited for a table, he stood at the bar, looking at the people who were already dining. They began to irritate him. Whatever troubles they might have, they didn't have *his*. That fat fellow sitting alone in the corner, reading his newspaper while he ate—he wasn't worried about anybody reading over his shoulder, was he? He wasn't glancing around nervously from time to time. If anybody suggested to him that for all he knew he might be under constant observation . . . well, that fat fellow would laugh, wouldn't he? Of course. It **was** ridiculous.

He examined the others, each in turn, and with a mounting sense of outrage. Why did *he* have to be the one to feel that incessant watching . . . ? Let *them* be watched for a while, he thought, fuming. Then they'd begin to understand—

"Your table's ready, sir."

"Oh. Thank you."

He studied the menu restlessly. When his food was brought, he ate little. His appetite was gone. He'd come out to prove a point of courage, but what use was it when he was challenging what didn't exist? And yet . . . he was compelled to look around. Nothing there, of course. Well, oddly enough, there was something. Up in one corner of the ceiling a convex mirror had been installed, presumably so that someone back in the office could check the house. Or keep an eye on the waiters. Well, he thought wryly, here was a good sales opportunity. He could go back and explain how, at a reasonable cost, a monitor system could be set up that would make that little mirror look sick! Why, the proprietor would be able to zoom in with the magnifier lens and count the peas on a customer's plate if he wanted to.

Still, he didn't care to sit there with the mirror peering down at him. Not that it bothered him. It didn't. But it reminded him of . . . of what he was thinking about anyway.

It was no use. He couldn't finish his meal. He summoned the waiter, paid his bill, and hurried out, humiliated and angry. Couldn't he even enjoy a quiet meal in an ordinary restaurant without being covertly watched? Couldn't he walk through the streets without feeling that mindless, anonymous, insatiable gaze? "It's got to stop," he muttered.

Back in his office he sat tensely behind his desk, glancing resentfully about the room. "It's got to stop," he said again. He went into the bathroom, doused his face with cold water, and toweled himself vigorously. That usually helped restore him. It didn't now, though. He was as tense as ever. When Miss Prince called him on the intercom, he was startled and hurried back in annoyance to his desk.

"What is it, Miss Prince?"

"Mr. Imry and the other men are waiting for you in the conference room, Mr. Haddock."

He was momentarily puzzled. Oh, yes. He'd forgotten. It was the final staff conference on the Argentina project. "All right, Miss Prince. I'll go right in."

He closed his eyes for a few moments, trying to compose himself. Then he crossed to the side door to the conference room, entered, and took his place at the oval table. "Good

164

afternoon, gentlemen," he said, nodding to the other executives. He opened the portfolio of project papers that lay before him. "Evething's here, I suppose."

"We're all ready, Henry," Imry said.

But it turned out, after some discussion, that certain important cost elements had not been precisely worked out. Mr. Probstein, the elderly comptroller, who was in charge of the estimates, explained that he had been forced to put in some contingent figures because he had been unable to obtain all the data he needed from the firm of consulting engineers that had been hired for preliminary surveys.

"You had three weeks to pull this information out of them," Haddock said.

"I realize that, Henry," said Mr. Probstein apologetically. "I've been on the phone night and day, and right up to the last minute I expected them to come through with it."

"If I'd known about this," said Haddock, "I'd have postponed this meeting. I frankly don't see how we can go ahead without solid estimates."

"Oh, they're solid enough, Henry," said Mr. Probstein. "I made the contingencies high enough to cover any differences that may crop up when the actual figures are available."

Haddock made no comment. He sat frowning down at the papers.

"I certainly wouldn't have brought in any estimates I felt were faulty," Mr. Probstein added. He waited for Haddock to make some remark, but Haddock remained silent. "I stand behind these estimates," Mr. Probstein said. He glanced around the table at the other executives, who also were expecting Haddock to say something further. "Of course," Mr. Probstein ventured with a propitiatory smile, "if you'd prefer to wait a couple of days..." But Haddock wasn't looking at him. Mr. Probstein's smile faded.

George Imry intervened. "Actually," he said, "this represents a very small part of the total, doesn't it? I'd say less than two percent, if I had to guess."

"That's just it," said Haddock. "You'd have to guess. I'd rather not guess."

"But if Joe has got that element blocked in on the high side—"

"George, you know very well how many hundreds of unknowns there'll be, operating in a country like that. I don't see any reason why we need to add our own."

"My figures are adequate ones, Henry," Mr. Probstein said worriedly. "I'm honestly convinced of that."

Haddock pushed the papers away. "Well, frankly," he said, "this is a disappointing and disturbing situation. I told Mr. Nammers we'd be ready, but obviously we aren't ready." He rose to his feet. "Do you expect me to go in to him pretending that we've got everything properly lined up?" He looked with irritation at the faces around the table. "Mr. Nicholas has a very keen eye, I can assure you." He caught himself, annoyed at his error. "I mean Mr. Nammers... and if there are any weak spots in a program, he'll find them. Particularly those involving costs."

"Well, Henry," said Imry, "I'm sure that Mr. Nammers will understand the situation and be prepared to make a proper allowance—"

"How do you know what Mr. Nammers will choose to understand? *I* certainly don't know. What I do know is that this project is extremely important for the future development and expansion of the company and that it has a very

166

considerable symbolic importance as well, and for me to be forced to make an inadequate initial presentation to the chairman of the board on such a vital matter—well, it puts me in a potentially humiliating position."

"Henry, I can't believe that this is such a serious thing," Imry said placatingly. "I think we've got a pretty sound basis here for judging the project. Granted, it would be better if Joe had been able to get those figures, but it's hardly his fault if the engineers—"

"The fault will be mine," Haddock said sharply. "I'm the one who is ultimately responsible. And Mr. Nammers, as chairman, has the duty to hold me accountable."

"No one is denying that, Henry, but this present problem hardly seems to justify—"

"What you don't seem to grasp is that there are certain expectations that as president I'm obliged to satisfy! There are certain understandings I'm a party to, and I intend to honor those understandings! But I can't do it on the basis of supposition and guesswork!" Haddock's face was flushed, and his breath was quick. "I've got to have real figures! Otherwise I've got nothing solid to move ahead on! One way or the other, I've got to know the truth!" The other men shrank back in their chairs; they had never seen Haddock lose his temper before. He glared angrily around—not at them but at the portraits on the walls. The painted faces seemed to mock him. He felt their sneers, their scorn. "All right, gentlemen," he said, his voice shaking. He was still looking at the portraits. "Let's get one thing clear, anyway. As of this moment, I refuse to accept these ambiguous and uncertain situations! I'm finished with that! I've had enough of them!"

Mr. Probstein was shuffling his papers in consternation.

167

"Henry," he exclaimed in a frightened voice. "Henry, I—"

But Haddock had turned away. He went over to the inter-communications box by the side window and pressed a key. "Miss Prince," he said, "would you get Mr. Haeggler to come to the conference room right away, please?"

He returned to his place at the table, his features sternly set. The other executives looked down at their portfolios. Haeggler was Mr. Probstein's assistant. Why was Haddock summoning him to the meeting?

Mr. Probstein was agitated and confused. "Henry, I doubt that Bob Haeggler would have any additional information to offer us. . . ." His voice trailed off. Haddock wasn't looking at him. "But of course," Mr. Probstein resumed uncertainly, "if you want to ask his opinion on any of these—of these—"

Again he hesitated. Haddock didn't seem to have heard what he'd said. Mr. Probstein cleared his throat nervously and began fingering the edges of his papers. He stole glances at the other men, but they avoided his gaze. No one cared to break in on Haddock's silence.

The door opened, and Haeggler entered. He was a tall, bony man with anxious eyes magnified by thick-lensed glasses. Haddock spoke to him at once.

"Bob, you're familiar with the Argentina estimates?"

"Well, yes. I've worked on them with Mr. Prob—"

"Good. Then you're aware of the fact that they've been presented to us in incomplete form. What I want to know is when they'll be finished. Can you tell me that?"

Haeggler peered doubtfully at Mr. Probstein, who sat stiffly in his chair, his hands gripping the edge of the table. "Well, maybe later today. Or tomorrow. Day after would be safer."

168

"Day after tomorrow," Haddock repeated. "You can give us a guarantee on that?"

"Well, if Mr. Probstein would agree—"

"I'll tell you what," said Haddock crisply. "I want you, Bob, to take charge of these estimates, and I want you personally to get on top of them and see them through, all right?"

Haeggler started to mumble some demurrer, stealing a sidelong glance at his superior, Mr. Probstein, who was too shocked and affronted to speak.

"I'm counting on you to pull us out of this little mess, Bob," Haddock went on authoritatively, "and I'll tell you what I want you to do."

"Henry," Mr. Probstein interposed in a shaking voice.

Haddock ignored him. "Bob, I want you to report to me personally tomorrow afternoon on how the situation stands at that time, and in the meanwhile—"

"Henry," said Mr. Probstein again.

"—in the meanwhile, gentlemen," Haddock continued, addressing the others, "we'll provisionally set the time of our meeting for day after tomorrow at ten o'clock, right here."

"Henry."

"Any questions?" Haddock inquired blandly, looking around quickly from one face to another. "None? . . . Very well." He slapped his palm down lightly on the top of the table. "Meeting adjourned."

He got to his feet. No one else moved. The other executives sat numbly staring at him. Haeggler stood awkwardly where he was, blinking and fidgeting. Mr. Probstein had paled. His lips were twitching.

"Day after tomorrow, gentlemen," Haddock repeated, closing his portfolio. He prepared to leave.

"Henry," said Mr. Probstein once more.

The other men began to arrange their papers, push back their chairs, and get up. Haddock went briskly to the door.

"Henry!" cried out Mr. Probstein, his voice cracking. He rocked forward in his chair, his fingers clawing at the table as he attempted in vain to rise.

Haddock paused in the doorway and turned inquiringly.

"Henry, I don't understand—" Mr. Probstein was laboring for breath. "—I don't understand why you've chosen to bypass me in this way—"

The others were crowding toward the door in haste to leave.

Haddock was looking not at Mr. Probstein but at the portraits on the wall beyond. He was frowning at them in a thoughtful, abstracted way.

Mr. Probstein coughed rackingly, a cough that made him shudder. "I've served five presidents, Henry, and never before—" He had to twist sideways in his chair to see Haddock. The veins on his neck were swollen. "Never before have I—" He pushed almost petulantly at the table, as though it were preventing him from gaining his feet. "I've received honest criticism when I deserved it, Henry, but never before—" His mouth worked soundlessly. A trickle of saliva appeared at one corner. "Never," said Mr. Probstein, panting heavily.

Haddock didn't seem to be listening. His full attention was directed at the portraits.

Mr. Probstein's forehead was beading with sweat. "To be held up to—" He coughed again, and his head swung weakly forward, so that he could no longer see Haddock. "A department head has certain rights, Henry," he said unevenly, staring at the portrait of Mr. Cagle. "Certain rights—"

170

Haddock remained poised at the door, still with that musing frown on his face.

"I—" But Mr. Probstein said nothing further. He was leaning against the table, breathing stertorously.

Haddock gave an almost imperceptible shrug, glanced at his watch, nodded to those who still remained in the conference room, turned, and departed.

A few days later he visited Dr. Despard again.

He sat down across from the internist and glanced about the consulting room. It seemed even more elegant than he had remembered it, and he asked Dr. Despard if it had been redecorated.

"Oh, I had it touched up a month or so ago," Dr. Despard replied. "It needed painting, and the rug was worn, and then I wanted a little structural change made, so I went ahead and got it all done at once."

"Very impressive," Haddock commented, and they sat smiling amiably at each other for a time while the doctor waited for Haddock to describe his symptoms. As Haddock hesitated, however, Dr. Despard decided to prompt him. "Well, Mr. Haddock, have you been sleeping well lately?"

"Oh, yes. I don't have any trouble sleeping. I drop right off."

"Your appetite. How's that?"

"Pretty good, Doctor. I have a good appetite."

"And your digestion?"

"That's fine, too," said Haddock, and he gave similarly positive replies to other questions, which didn't daunt Dr. Despard, for he was experienced in treating important executives, and he knew that they frequently sought him out for counsel on the psychological problems produced by their demanding careers. He was confident that sooner or later, Haddock would indicate what was troubling him.

"And your work," Dr. Despard remarked. "Is that going along well, Mr. Haddock?"

"Very well, yes."

"You're working hard, I suppose?"

"I work like a dog, Doctor."

"But you feel that it's worthwhile?"

"Oh, absolutely."

"I see," said Dr. Despard. He leaned back in his chair, and gave Haddock an amused look. "Well, Mr. Haddock, if you have no medical problems, and in fact no problems of any kind, then I take it that you came here today to pay a social call."

"No, no," said Haddock quickly. He smiled, chagrined. "There is a reason, Doctor. I just don't know quite how to put it. Something happened," he said, clearing his throat. He glanced down at his crossed knees. "Earlier this week," he added.

"Yes?"

"Well, at a meeting of my staff, I found it necessary to discipline one of my subordinate officers for a certain shortcoming that inconvenienced me. I may have been harsh with him—well, I *was* harsh. I was worried about something else, and I've got to admit that I took it out on him. He's near retirement age, and he hadn't been in good health. Anyway, he became upset, and later I was informed that after the meeting . . . he suffered a stroke."

"I see."

"He's in the hospital now. I don't suppose he'll be able to work again. Provided he survives, I mean."

172

"Ah."

"That's about it."

"Well, this must be very distressing for you."

"Yes, it would have been."

"*Would* have been, Mr. Haddock?"

"Let me try to explain that, Doctor. You see, I've got to acknowledge the fact that I was responsible for that stroke. It would have happened sometime, I suppose, but I certainly brought it on right then. I precipitated it. Now, before I became president, I would have been crushed by such a thing," Haddock said, regarding Dr. Despard earnestly. "Actually, I never would have put myself in a position where anything of the sort could have happened, because then, you understand, I would have considered that this man's personal feelings were of paramount importance. But the presidency is a special sort of job, and the standards of judgment and behavior are special, too. Oh, it's taken me a long time to get used to it, and there are still a lot of things that puzzle me. Let me give you an example. Just yesterday I asked my secretary to ring our corporation counsel for me. He's a man I've known for years. I have lunch with him a lot—or I used to, anyway. Normally I'd have said to my secretary: 'Would you get Mr. Hall for me, please?' That's his name—Hall, Ted Hall. But I didn't say that. I said: 'Would you get the corporation counsel for me?' And then I sat there at my desk for a bit, Doctor, and I was baffled—not because I'd used his title instead of his name, but because I couldn't think of his name at all. It was a couple of minutes before I remembered what it was."

"I see," said Dr. Despard with some interest. "Well, that's not uncommon, Mr. Haddock."

"No?"

"Not at all. You've been concentrating on the functional operation of the company, and so you've become very much aware of the functional roles played by your staff members —but less aware of their personal characteristics and individuality."

"Oh," said Haddock. "I guess that's it. And this . . . this is normal?"

"For a man in your position it certainly isn't unusual, Mr. Haddock. Among men who exercise command—and I have quite a few of them as my patients—it's actually fairly common. But getting back to the man you criticized at that meeting—"

"I didn't criticize him, Doctor. I ignored him. I didn't do it deliberately, or at least it wasn't completely deliberate. But what you just said about my being aware of people's functions, that really helps me to understand. You see, this fellow had come to the meeting to exercise his particular function, and since he failed to exercise that function, that meant he wasn't properly at the meeting at all. He didn't exist in a functional sense, that is. And so I didn't ignore him. There wasn't anything to ignore."

"Yes, I see." Dr. Despard opened a pad on his desk and took some notes. "That's very interesting, Mr. Haddock. I've never heard it put quite that way before, but tell me, do you regret what happened? The stroke?"

"No," said Haddock.

"No?"

"I realize that sounds cold-blooded, Doctor, but I'm speaking to you as a company president in private conference with his internist, so I know you'll understand. The man who suffered that stroke was becoming something of a weak link, and he should have retired earlier. Now I'll be able to put a

174

younger and more energetic man in the job, so we'll be better off."

Dr. Despard continued to take notes. "What you're telling me is that this episode has been a beneficial one for you and the company, is that right?"

"Generally speaking, yes, that's my view."

"But still . . . you did come to see me, Mr. Haddock."

Haddock's expression became shadowed by uncertainty. "Well, yes, Doctor. That's true."

"And that means you must be troubled by this in some way."

"I am troubled, Doctor. I admit that. You see, I have the feeling sometimes that I'm . . . that I'm not a free agent. It seems to me that I'm imposing on others the same sort of thing that's being imposed on me." Haddock leaned forward and lowered his voice. "It's as though there's something behind me that's driving me on. Something that's taken possession of me." He cleared his throat self-consciously. "I don't want to sound melodramatic, Doctor, but this goes back to what I told you on my earlier visit, about being under observation. At that time this feeling was restricted to my place of work and where I live, but lately I've begun to feel it just about everywhere and all the time, too. Why, to be honest with you, Doctor, I feel it right this minute, and it makes me want to turn around and take a look to see what's behind me."

He did turn around to take a precautionary look about the consulting room. What he saw directly behind his chair made him pause. He hadn't noticed it before.

A window had been fixed in the interior wall, providing a view of the reception room.

"What's that?" he asked.

175

"That? Oh, that's just a little window, Mr. Haddock. Now, as you were saying—?"

"I don't remember it being there, Doctor."

"Well, I had it installed last month."

"No, I mean I didn't notice it when I was in the reception room waiting to come in."

"Actually, Mr. Haddock, on the reception room side it doesn't show."

Haddock craned around to look at the window again. In the room beyond, the receptionist sat at her desk, examining a file folder. No one else was there. "You mean to say that you can see into that room but no one there can see you?" he asked.

"That's the way it works, Mr. Haddock," Dr. Despard replied. "Lots of physicians have them now. But you were about to tell me—"

"You can watch the receptionist, then."

"It has nothing to do with the receptionist," Dr. Despard said. "It's a protection against drug addicts chiefly. There've been quite a few cases lately. They sneak into doctors' offices looking for prescription pads, drugs, anything—and this gives me the opportunity to see who's come into my office, that's all."

"You could phone the police."

"In extreme cases, yes. I haven't had anything like that to deal with yet, and I hope I won't, but getting back to your own situation, Mr. Haddock—"

"Do your patients know about this window?"

"Oh, I imagine most of them have noticed it, Mr. Haddock."

"Does it have an effect on them, then? I mean, do they like the idea?"

"I don't suppose they think much about it one way or the other, really."

"And do *you* like it?"

"What?"

"Do you like sitting here and watching them?"

"I'm not sure I understand you."

"I mean, I've never had the opportunity to talk to anyone in your position, and what I'd be curious to know is what goes through your mind when you're watching."

"I don't watch. It's not a question of watching. I occasionally glance up—"

"Look, Doctor. Someone's coming in. He's wearing dark glasses. Now he's talking to the girl at the desk. Too bad we can't hear what he's saying. Don't you have it wired for sound?"

"Mr. Haddock, I wish you'd turn around so we could continue your own examination."

"Those dark glasses are suspicious, Doctor. Better keep an eye on that fellow. He's sitting down now with that magazine, but he probably knows about the window, so he's being very careful to behave normally."

"That's my next patient."

"And now he's looking straight at us! Isn't that something? All *he* sees is wall—but we can see *him* plain as day! We can watch his every move, Doctor! See—? Now he's sneaking a look at his watch!"

"He isn't sneaking anything. He's presumably verifying the fact that he's on time for his appointment, and he's a very busy man, I can assure you."

"Just one more question, Doctor," Haddock said. He was still gazing toward the window. "This little arrangement of yours . . . doesn't it have an effect on your receptionist? Look

177

at it this way. She knows that you can see her but that she can't see you, right? But more important, she can't tell when you're watching and when you're not."

"Really, Mr. Haddock. I don't sit here all day spying on that girl."

"I realize that. You had it put in because of the drug addicts. But the things we choose to live with, Doctor, they have their own purposes. We use them, but they use us, too. That window doesn't just show you the addicts. It shows you everybody—addicts, yes, but also patients and delivery boys and the receptionist . . . see what I mean? It's for *watching*. That's what it's there for. And so you watch, Doctor. Oh, you say you're watching for the addicts, and I don't doubt you for a minute, but you watch more than that. You can't help watching that girl, too!"

Dr. Despard put his pad away. "Mr. Haddock, I'm afraid I fail to see the relevance of—"

"Believe me, Doctor. It's relevant. Highly relevant." Haddock turned to smile ingratiatingly at Dr. Despard but then turned back again. "Don't misunderstand me. I'm not saying that watching is wrong. I honestly haven't come to a final conclusion on that subject, but now that I'm here with you on the other end of it—the watching end, Doctor—it occurs to me that my experience has been a little limited, and there may be more to it than I thought! I mean, as far as that girl in there is concerned, it could be a very beneficial thing."

"Mr. Haddock—"

"No, please let me make this last point, Doctor," Haddock went on eagerly. "It's important to me, I honestly feel that. This is a sort of revelation. Well, what I'm saying is that this little window is bound to make your receptionist more conscious of her job. For example, suppose she wants to do her

178

nails instead of typing a certain letter? Well, the knowledge that at any given moment you may be watching—and this is the crucial part of it—this will tend to inhibit her from doing her nails. She'll be psychologically inclined to type that letter instead. And not because you would object to her doing her nails. No, I don't mean that. It's just that the existence of this window acts as a subtle reminder of what she's supposed to be doing rather than what she may want to do. In other words, she'll become more aware of herself as a receptionist, do you see what I mean?"

Dr. Despard checked his watch. Then he pushed back his chair, preparing to rise.

"But beyond that, Doctor, I'm willing to bet that within a few months, she'll be so accustomed to the job-consciousness that this window produces—she'll be under its spell, you might say!—that even when she knows you're away from the office, she'll still have the sensation of being watched, and she'll act accordingly without fully realizing it. So you see that this window of yours is helping make her a better receptionist."

"This is frankly a bit ridiculous, Mr. Haddock."

"Oh, I wouldn't be too sure of that. My experience has taught me that you can't be sure at all in this field. For instance, that wall behind *you*. The one that seems to be a wall. How can you tell? Suppose that's a one-way window, too? Did you ever take that into consideration?"

Dr. Despard involuntarily cast a glance at the wall behind him.

"Anyway, I understand now that I really can't be opposed to this sort of thing," Haddock continued. "Why, it's my business, in a way, and a man can't be opposed to his own business! I don't mean windows. Windows are pretty primitive devices, frankly, even though they illustrate the principle involved."

"Mr. Haddock, unfortunately we've run out of time. I've got that other patient waiting, and then after him there are others—"

"But tell me, Doctor. Doesn't this watching have an effect on you, too? That's what I'd like to know."

"We'd really better make another appointment for you, Mr. Haddock."

"I've never watched, so I don't know. I've *been* watched. I know that part of it, all right."

"I'm afraid we'll have to continue this some other time. I'll have my girl work you into my schedule, and then she'll call your secretary."

"Do you think it helps you do *your* job better, too? Maybe it makes you more aware of yourself as a doctor. Except that when you're watching, you're not actually being a doctor. You're something else then. And so the question is—what *are* you when you watch?"

Dr. Despard got up. "I'm sorry, but—"

"That's what I don't know," Haddock said, also rising. "I mean, what actually happens to you when you watch? When Alice went through the Looking Glass, Doctor, she found everything distorted on the other side—but maybe everything had been distorted before, so the other side was the right side—wasn't that the point of the story?"

"Good-bye, Mr. Haddock."

"Oh. Well, good-bye, Doctor. And thank you. Thank you very much. This little visit has certainly helped me to crystallize my thinking on the subject. It's put the whole thing into a new light."

180

In the reception room, before he reached the outside door, Haddock turned toward the wall and cheerfully waved farewell.

Instead of returning to the office, he went to a movie. He was too tired to pay attention to it. Almost as soon as he took his seat, he closed his eyes and fell asleep.

It was past eight o'clock when he awoke. Late though it was, he decided to go back to the office. He'd left his brief-case there, and it contained some documents that he wanted to glance over before morning, so he took a taxi back to the company building and had the night watchman let him in.

He paused in the anteroom. Miss Prince, as usual, had left her desk in tidy fashion. There was nothing on it but the desk calendar and an array of pencils. Those pencils looked odd, though. They were scored and indented. Why was that? He picked one up. Oh, those were toothmarks. Miss Prince chewed her pencils, then. But she must do it on the sly. He'd never seen her do it, not once in all the years she'd been his secretary. Why, she must have gone through whole boxes of them. He'd caught her at it now, though. "Sorry, Miss Prince," he whispered. "Didn't mean to pry. Go ahead, though, if it makes you feel better."

He stepped into the corridor. It was dim there. Only one light was left on at night, and it was all the way down at the turning for the elevators. The offices were dark. The whole floor was deserted. The typewriters were hooded. If a telephone rang, no one would answer. The memos would lie on the desks all night unread, while the flowers wilted in their vases unseen.

181

There was a stale, secretarial odor of perfume and carbon paper in the corridor. But that was the way the company smelled after a busy day. He didn't really mind it. It was even pleasant, in a way.

He stopped at Miss Bottweiler's office and snapped on the lights. He'd never seen it without Miss Bottweiler in it. She wasn't there now. The room was empty. Even so, it seemed still to be occupied by Miss Bottweiler. She'd dwelt in it for so many years that it was part of her, like a shell. Her real life was lived in that room, and that life didn't cease when she left. It was almost as though Miss Bottweiler wasn't actually the middle-aged woman with a wen on her cheek who picked up her hat and purse each day at 5:15 P.M. and walked out, but was instead that thick-legged desk, that flat-chested file cabinet, that graceless chair. "Good evening, Miss Bottweiler," he said, addressing the furnishings with mock cordiality. "I see you're working late again. That's a sign of real job satisfaction, isn't it, Miss Bottweiler!" But he knew that Miss Bottweiler was not at all satisfied. She had a distraught air about her these days. When she passed him in the corridors, she flushed and averted her eyes. She had been particularly fond of Mr. Probstein.

He smiled amiably down at Miss Bottweiler's desk. "What's that, Miss B.? Don't tell me you're thinking of looking for another job!" She undoubtedly was doing just that. The desk would contain the evidence—some notes, phone numbers, perhaps even a few letters. "Mind if I take a look, Miss B.? Let's see what you've been able to come up with, shall we?" But the desk was locked. The drawers rattled but wouldn't budge. The file cabinet was locked, too. This was annoying. It was all very well for the staff to keep the offices tidy—and locking up was officially recommended—but he was president. He had the right to see whatever he wanted to see. "This isn't your private property, Miss Bottweiler! This belongs to the company!"

The next office belonged to the comptroller. It was empty by day and night as well. Mr. Probstein was still lingering at the hospital. Well, the company's insurance was taking care of the costs, and, then, Mr. Probstein was a widower, so no wife would be left grieving. It could be worse.

He looked in at the adjoining office, Haeggler's. Haeggler was acting comptroller now. His desk wasn't very neat. It had a stack of papers on it and a scattering of pencils and paper clips. And what was that beside the phone? A page of doodles. He picked it up. Haeggler's doodles weren't the usual aimless designs. They were sketches, sketches of cats, carefully drawn and neatly shaded. Not bad. But what was the acting comptroller doing drawing all those cats? Didn't he have enough work to keep him busy? If he had a spare minute or two, why didn't he check over his figures or something?

He crumpled the sheet into a ball. He was about to toss it into the wastebasket. Then he decided not to. He left it, crumpled, in the center of the desk. That would give Haeggler something to think about tomorrow morning. He'd come in and see it there. He'd know he hadn't done it himself, and he'd know that the cleaning women probably wouldn't have done it. So he'd be left wondering: who had come in and crumpled his doodles?

He came to George Imry's office. It had been weeks since he'd been in it. He remembered meeting there with Imry in the old days, before he was president. Imry had impressed him from the first as a bluff, tough fellow; decent enough, really, and honest. He'd liked Imry then. Hadn't he? Or had he never really liked him? Perhaps he'd just been afraid of him. Well . . . Imry was the one who was afraid now.

The air was sour in there. When he switched on the overhead fluorescent light, it stuttered, shedding a fitful glare. The yellowish walls seemed to blink resentfully as he approached, and the desk shrank sullenly back. It wasn't so much an office as a lair. Imry had dragged his wounded pride into it. How many times he must have sat right there behind that desk, seized by silent rage—if only the board had chosen *him* as president!

"Sorry, George," said Haddock genially. "Breaks of the game!" He leaned against a corner of the desk, smiling at the empty chair. He tried to envision Imry there when he was working away all by himself. Was Imry the same then—or different? Did his expression lose that tough guardedness? Did he sometimes smile . . . or frown? Did he pace or put his feet on the desk or pick his teeth? What *did* a man do when he was alone in his office?

What had *he* done? He couldn't remember. The sense of being alone in his office was too remote.

He switched off the light and left, sauntering on along the row of offices. He had a pleasant sensation of lightness. He seemed almost to float along the corridor, so softly did he move. Why hadn't he roamed the floor at night before? Now he could enter these offices as he pleased, without having subordinates rise up out of their chairs at the sight of him. He could do whatever he wanted, and no one was the wiser. The offices were empty, true, and yet he could easily imagine that their daytime occupants had left the essence of their working selves behind, as had Miss Bottweiler—that they were really there, perusing reports, fussing over correspondence, tapping their pencils, and lighting their cigarettes . . . yes, and that he, therefore, had managed to achieve some exalted condition of authority that enabled him to drift in and out, unseen and unsensed—an invisible president, a severe and watchful presence. Like Mr. Nicholas. Yes, like Mr. Nicholas. "Mr. Nicholas," he said aloud, and his words, caught up by the walls, caught up in the emptiness and darkness, seemed to come echoing back. . . . *Mr. Nicholas.*

"Henry, I'm sure you realize that what you're proposing is out of the question. It—it simply can't be done."

"Of course it can be done."

"Technically, yes, but as a matter of policy—"

"You'd better leave policy questions to me," Haddock said. It was the following morning. He had made another visit to New Jersey and was sitting in the office of his research director, Andrew Cooley.

"But, Henry, what you're suggesting—"

"I'm not suggesting anything. I'm telling you what I want done."

"Henry, a thing like this—I don't see how I could possibly authorize it without at the very least a directive from the board itself."

"That's unnecessary," Haddock said. "The only authorization needed for this I'm providing right now. Do you think I have to go running to the board every time I want to get something done?"

Cooley picked up a paper clip and started working it in his fingers. A summery breeze came in from an open window, bringing with it the whine of distant traffic, the mindless thumping of a nearby factory, the groan of jets descending. "Well," he said, "this puts me in a very awkward spot. What you're asking—"

"You still don't seem to understand the situation, Andy," Haddock said, smiling agreeably. "I'm not asking. I want this done this weekend."

Cooley snapped the paper clip. He picked up another one. "I'm sorry, Henry. I couldn't possibly consider a thing of this kind unless I had a signed order from Mr. Nammers."

Haddock's smile became less agreeable. "Well, Andy, I hoped you'd accept my instructions without raising any objections—although I can well understand your position—because I wanted to keep the background out of this particular picture." He paused, as though reluctant to go further. "But I guess I've got no choice. You mentioned Mr. Nammers, Andy. Well, Mr. Nammers knows all about this. It has his full approval."

"It does?"

"Do you think I'd say that if it weren't true?"

"No, no. I didn't mean that. I just . . . well, I didn't realize he knew." Cooley gave Haddock a doubtful glance.

"It's an experiment, Andy," Haddock went on. "Mr. Nammers himself had the original idea, you see, and if it works out, it could be a very important contribution, Andy."

"I don't quite grasp that, Henry, but listen, I'd like at least to talk to Mr. Nammers about this. I mean, I've never had to deal with anything like this before, and it would give me some reassurance if—"

"Sorry, Andy. I'm afraid not," Haddock said smoothly. He'd foreseen this possibility. "As you can imagine, there could be some rather unpleasant consequences arising out of this—I mean, the whole purpose of the test would be ruined

186

if the subject found out about it, you see—and, anyway, since I'm the one who'll actually be doing the . . . conducting it, well, we thought it best if Mr. Nammers' name were kept out of it entirely. That is, as a matter of policy, Mr. Nammers and I have concluded that he doesn't know a thing about it. Officially, that is."

Cooley nodded, but he kept his eyes lowered. "I see," he said glumly.

"This will be absolutely and completely my responsibility and mine alone, but rest assured, Andy, that if anything does go wrong—and it won't, provided we maintain a proper security—well, you won't be called to account for any of it. Mr. Nammers wanted me in particular to make that clear to you."

"So I can't phone him."

"That's the way he and I decided to play it, Andy. And he would react very unfavorably if you decided on your own initiative to take action contrary to the program he has approved and that I've just lined out here, understand?"

"Well, I understand what you're proposing, Henry, but I still wonder—"

"We've got this set up on a tight schedule, Andy. If you use three or four men, you can get the work done over the weekend, and that's precisely when it's got to be done, or else the whole thing will be out of gear. I've got to report to Mr. Nammers at the end of the week on the results of the first stage, you see, so any deviation from the program would be unacceptable. Now I'll need your acknowledgment of this, Andy."

"Well, I guess we . . ." Cooley hesitated, frowning down at his desk. "All right, Henry," he said. "If that's what you and Mr. Nammers have decided."

"Fine. I don't have to tell you that your cooperation will be appreciated," Haddock said, getting to his feet. "This company is moving ahead fast and in a big way, and the opportunities for executive advancement are multiplying fast, too. I don't want to make any promises, Andy, but Mr. Nammers is very much aware of your capabilities, and the successful execution of this little research job will really nail down that picture in his mind. And in mine, Andy." He picked up his hat.

Cooley got up slowly. "Henry, I still can't help being concerned about the implications involved here."

Haddock grabbed his hand and shook it. "Don't you worry about that. That's my department." He grinned and stepped back, turned, and went to the door. "You just do your job, Andy, and I'll do mine. But if you're afraid that this will somehow be contrary to the spirit and best interests of the company, let me assure you that you don't need to have a single doubt on that score!"

On Monday morning he arrived a little early at the office. The key was in his pocket. He kept fingering it, just to be sure it was there.

"Good morning, Miss Prince."

"Good morning, Mr. Haddock. If you want to get that dictation finished—"

"No, no. Not now. Later, Miss Prince. There's something I want to get out of the way first, so kindly hold all incoming calls until I buzz you, right?"

"Yes, Mr. Haddock."

He entered his office, closed the door, and leaned against

188

it. The hand he kept in his pocket was doubled into a fist, gripping the key.

He had to force himself to follow his usual routine of going over to the closet to dispose of his hat.

Only then did he approach his desk—his new desk. It was exactly like the old one, except that it had a drawer underneath on the right side, a drawer large enough to contain a standard typewriter.

He sat down. He took the key out of his pocket, keeping it concealed in his hand. He looked slowly all around the room, smiling. Then he opened his fist and sat contemplating the key. He was breathing rapidly, and he had to keep swallowing.

He unlocked the drawer.

There it was inside, smaller than he'd expected it to be, but neat, he had to admit that. It slid easily out on metal runners and was tilted back so that its smooth glass face was raised toward him.

He turned it on and waited.

The image swam up dark and fuzzy. He had to experiment with the controls until he'd managed to achieve a picture that was bright and sharply defined. Now he had it.

What he saw was a head-on view of a desk with a chair behind it and a blank space of wall beyond. The installation had been made right above the door, according to his instructions, so that he was seeing more or less what he would have seen had he entered the room himself.

But no one was there. The office was empty. He glanced at his watch. It was 9:15 now. Surely by this time . . . He frowned, annoyed and suspicious. Had they gotten the wrong room? It looked like any office. There were no identifying objects in sight—the desk could be anybody's desk. Suppose the damned fools had put it in Probstein's office by mistake?

No—there he came.

It was George Imry, all right. Bald spot, dandruff, heavy shoulders in a suit already wrinkling from the strain of containing that awkward bulk, shirt collar stained with perspiration . . . and now he had reached the desk, now he was pulling back the chair, now he was sitting down.

Haddock watched, fascinated. That little monitor was a marvel, all right. A twist of the knob, and it zoomed in, magnifying the image. He could virtually count the hairs in that patch of stubble on Imry's right cheek that the razor had missed! He could study close-up that heart-shaped mole on Imry's chin! And look at Imry's eye—the left one. A bit of a swelling on the lower lid. If the picture were in color, that swelling would show up pink. Imry was getting a sty in that eye—and he, Haddock, probably knew about it before Imry did himself!

Imry began picking his nose. That was disgusting. Didn't the man have the decency to use his handkerchief? Of course, he supposed he was alone there.

Imry leaned forward, reaching out for his intercom box. His mouth was opening and closing. He was saying . . . what was he saying?

Oh, the sound. He'd forgotten about the sound.

". . . that stuff I didn't have time for Friday . . ."

Imry's voice came booming so loudly out of the monitor's speaker that Haddock, alarmed, turned the set off and pushed it back in its drawer. Well, he'd turned it up too high. It had startled him, though. He'd have to be more careful.

190

He pulled the monitor forward again and snapped it on, cautiously lowering the volume this time. He turned it down to a whisper, in fact. He didn't care about the sound. Watching was the main thing.

Imry was saying something off to one side. Was somebody in there with him now? Zoom back. Ah . . . the secretary had come in and was taking dictation. There she was in profile —legs crossed, pencil flying on the pad, jaws working fast, too, on gum. A vulgar girl, really. Miss Kohl, that was her name. Miss Prince would never dare chew gum in the presence of the president, and she wouldn't wear a skirt like that, either. See how it rode up that girl's thighs? And her blouse was one of those flimsy summer things, and so low-cut she was practically hanging out.

Zoom in again on Imry. He was keeping an eye on Miss Kohl, too. A lustful eye, it was . . . the lid half closed, the pupil cloudy. Even that incipient sty was throbbing. And those wet dictating lips, smacking hungrily! Well, what was Miss Kohl doing to protect her modesty from Imry's bestial leers? Nothing. Less than nothing. She was crossing her legs the other way, giving her bottom a little wriggle as she did so, and—zoom—Imry was ogling her like a satyr. His nostrils were steaming. See? A tiny drop of moisture was clinging to that tuft of nasal hair! Even more revolting, he was laughing—look at those crooked teeth, that ghastly tongue awash in bubbly spittle! With the volume so low, Haddock hadn't caught what he'd said. Something funny evidently. Probably vulgar. Miss Kohl was laughing, too, and not just to be polite. She had tipped her head back, eyes closed, mouth agape, gum and all, and was bouncing in her chair, her bosom virtually exploding out of that peekaboo blouse. Why, Miss Kohl was hardly more than a slut.

On impulse, he reached over to his intercom box and punched Imry's key.

"Good morning, George," he said.

Imry wasn't answering. The monitor showed him still guffawing with Miss Kohl.

"George . . . are you there, George?"

Now Miss Kohl was eyeing the intercom box on Imry's desk. Imry turned toward it, too, with a look of disgust, leaned forward, and punched Haddock's key.

"Good morning, Henry."

"George, I was wondering about that negotiation with the electrical workers."

"Yes, Henry?"

On the screen Haddock saw Imry make an obscene gesture at the box—and worse, he and Miss Kohl were snickering together. Laughing at him!

"George," he said into his box, struggling to control his anger. They were making fun of him! Well—he'd have the last laugh! "George—I'd like to discuss that situation with you—provided you're not too busy with your dictation."

A faintly puzzled look passed across Imry's face. "Be right down, Henry," he said.

Haddock flipped off the monitor, pushed it back in the drawer, closed the drawer, locked it, and pocketed the key. He sat back in his chair, frowning. He hadn't intended to say that about the dictation. Well, it wasn't much of a slip. It was customary procedure to get the dictation out of the way first thing in the morning.

Still, he knew he'd have to be careful. He didn't want Imry to suspect anything. At least, he didn't want his suspicions aroused in that particular way. Imry would sense something soon enough. A man couldn't be watched the way Imry was going to be watched without shadows edging into his mind. Yes, Imry would start to feel those vague, unsettling doubts. He'd find himself troubled without apparent cause. He'd start wondering. He'd start worrying . . . about what? Ah, he wouldn't know! But he wouldn't be quite so relaxed and comfortable there in his office. And then he might think twice about making disrespectful gestures. He might think twice about fooling around with that tramp of a secretary on company time!

He watched Imry all Monday afternoon and most of Tuesday, too, begrudging every minute that took him away from the monitor. His appointments he cut short, canceled, or postponed. He raced through his dictation. As his work began piling up, he passed batches of it on to Imry with hastily scrawled notes: "George, would you mind handling this?" A few minutes later he would see Miss Kohl appear on the screen to lay the latest presidential packet before Imry, and he would note the look of dismay with which it was greeted and hear a grumbled complaint: "Can't that bastard do his own work?"

He watched quietly and attentively. Every so often he would lean forward to make some subtle adjustment of the controls, but otherwise he remained immobile, alertly studying the monitor. Each fleeting expression that passed across Imry's meaty features was of profound interest to him. Even when Imry sat stolidly minute after minute, his face as blank as a plate, Haddock wasn't bored, and in fact it was at those times that he became particularly vigilant, waiting with mounting tension for his subject's inaction to end in a smile, a frown, a yawn. Watching, he lost track of time. He was fully absorbed. He didn't regard himself as a passive observer; he felt, instead, that he was actively participating in something that required his full attention and something, moreover, that he really had to do. It wasn't a question of choice. He felt compelled to do it. And it didn't strike him as being a strange sort of occupation for a man in his position. It seemed quite natural. Necessary, in fact. He was already accustomed to it, as if he'd been preparing himself for a long time in order to function efficiently as a watcher.

It wasn't easy. He couldn't relax, not even when his eyes began to smart and his head to throb. Nothing he had ever done was as demanding as this. And if watching Imry was hard, *not* watching Imry was worse. Every time Imry left his office, Haddock became ridden by anxiety. *Where was he going? What was he doing? Why didn't he come back?* And he'd stare at the image of the empty desk and the blank wall as though by the force of his will he could draw Imry back again.

On Wednesday morning he had a conference in his office with Imry and several others on the Argentina project, which was still hanging fire. He couldn't make his mind up on that proposal. He didn't really care about it now. It seemed of minor importance, and he took little part in the discussion. He was impatient to get the meeting over. He found Imry in person to be far less interesting than the Imry on the monitor. There seemed to be no connection between them, as though they were literally two different persons. He gave the flesh-and-blood Imry hardly more than a glance. "Let's get on with it, gentlemen," he kept saying, looking at his watch. He wanted to get Imry back in his office as soon as possible.

Later, to make up for the lost time, he ordered his lunch sent up to the office. The waiter who brought it headed for the conference room. "No, no," Haddock told him. "I'll eat it here, thanks. Just put it on the desk." It was only after the waiter had departed that he realized that Imry would be going out to eat, as usual. He switched on the monitor anyway. Watching Imry's empty office would be better than nothing, he thought. Then he saw that Imry wasn't going out, after all. He was right there at his desk. He'd had a sandwich and a cup of coffee sent up. And why was that? Ah, yes. He had to stay in to get through all that work Haddock had passed on to him.

So he watched Imry munching the sandwich and gulping the coffee and moodily scratching notes in the margins of the papers he'd been sent. Haddock barely nibbled at his own food. He was hungry, but he didn't want to be distracted for an instant. His hunger to watch was greater.

Imry's head lifted. He smiled sourly right into the monitor, but of course that meant that someone had entered. It was Haeggler. He'd dropped by for a little lunch-hour visit evidently. Haddock was irked. He preferred to have Imry alone. Visitors were distracting elements. Now Imry was responding to Haeggler's presence. He was listening to him or talking to him, nodding or shaking his head, and in short, the purity of the watching relationship had been muddied by the intrusion.

In annoyance, Haddock pushed the monitor back in the drawer, and as he waited for Haeggler to leave, he signed some correspondence and disposed of a few other items of business. Meanwhile he kept the volume on, turned low, so that he could tell when the visit had ended.

Ah . . . now Haeggler had gone. Haddock pulled the

monitor out again and settled himself into his customary viewing position.

He knew that it wasn't really Imry he was watching. Imry as the object of his concentration had become depersonalized. He wasn't Imry any longer—that is, he was more than just Imry. He was a living abstraction, the expression of a highly satisfying ideal state that existed only when Haddock watched, and therefore, in a sense, he was created by Haddock and was dependent on Haddock's will. And if that were true, then he was a part of Haddock, actually. Haddock was really watching himself.

But he didn't trouble himself much with such reflections. The watching absorbed all his energies. He was concentrating intently, determined to drive his way into Imry's consciousness. His success as a watcher evidently depended on Imry's success as a subject, and so he found himself silently urging Imry on. *Don't you feel it yet, George? No? Well, you will. You will.*

And look ... wasn't Imry sensing something already? Once in a while he glanced about in a puzzled way, as if a remote corner of his mind had been fleetingly brushed and some animal instinct had bristled. A message was whispering through his veins. No doubt of it now. Imry was restive. He'd lift that jowly, scowling head of his and look around. Sometimes he'd give himself a shake, as though to throw off that sensation. But he couldn't throw off Haddock's gaze!

Haddock knew it wouldn't be easy for Imry. It would hurt. It might hurt a lot. He almost wanted to flip on the intercom and say: "Listen, George. I know what's starting to bother you. You've got the sensation that you're not alone in your office, right? And yet you know for a fact that you *are* alone.

196

Nothing's there. Exactly. Nothing . . . it's there. And it'll get worse. It may become agonizing. But after a while—maybe after a long time—you'll begin to see that there's something about it that's . . . well, fine and good. Something that lifts you up. Something that helps you re-create yourself as a better, stronger man!"

But he couldn't do that. Imry would have to suffer as he had suffered. He *wanted* Imry to suffer, but not out of meanness. Suffering was part of it. Sometimes, indeed, as he recognized in Imry the early symptoms of his own ordeal, he felt a surge of sympathy and commiseration.

Mr. Nammers telephoned him that afternoon while he was watching.

"Henry, I wanted to check on the status of the Argentina project. What about that market research report?"

"We're analyzing that, Mr. Nammers. George is reading the last part of it right this minute, and—well, what I mean to say is that I sent it to him this morning for his views, and so I assume he's checking it over." He switched off the monitor and pushed it back in its drawer. "Obviously I don't know for a fact whether he's reading the last part or not, but I would guess—"

"Well, Henry," Mr. Nammers interrupted testily, "it seems to me that this whole thing is lagging, and I think you'd better give it a shove, all right? And then give me a progress report soon."

"Sure will, Mr. Nammers."

He was annoyed with himself. He'd made a slip there. Not a bad one, luckily. But it had better serve as a warning.

He kept the monitor locked up for an hour and got some of his own work done. It was half past four when he permitted himself to resume watching. Imry wasn't there, though. He'd gone to some meeting. That was a disappointment. But he'd probably come back after it was over.

Haddock inspected the empty office. Imry's briefcase wasn't there. Well, he might have needed to take it with him. But his hat was missing, too. That was a bad sign. It indicated that he intended to go straight home after the meeting. Maybe not, though. Besides, he might have forgotten something and have to come back for it. So Haddock kept watching. At five o'clock Miss Kohl appeared. She put some papers in the in-box, yawned, scratched herself under one arm, turned, and left. After that . . . nothing. Haddock remained where he was. He watched the empty office after everyone else had left the building. He watched until the summer sun had finally set and the light had faded and failed, and only then did he turn off the monitor and close the drawer and sink back in his chair, exhausted.

He spent his days before the monitor. It was only after Imry had left at the end of the afternoon that he had time to attend to company business, and even then, working late into the evenings at his desk, he kept the monitor on, for companion-ship, although it merely registered a dark and empty room. Imry sometimes worked late, too. He had to, in order to handle the extra work Haddock sent his way during the day. But the longer Imry worked, the less time Haddock had available to clear his own desk—and the more he was forced to send along to his executive vice president.

Earlier Imry would have complained about the additional burden. But now he plowed through it doggedly, almost as if he realized that Haddock had to be free to carry out the most important duty of all, that of watching. Imry was tired, though. His features were drawn, and he'd lost weight. There was an apprehensive look in his eye. Sometimes he'd stiffen in his chair, his eyes narrowed and alert, shifting here and there about the room . . . or he might glance surreptitiously at his wristwatch, as though aware of Haddock's searching gaze, and then, with a sigh, he'd bend over his work again. Occasionally he'd glance up wonderingly, his expression strangely altered. It became softer, almost timid, even beseeching in a way, as though he were on the verge of smiling—yes, on the verge of smiling at the walls!

At such moments Haddock was suffused with pride. If only he could give Imry a friendly pat on the back or whisper an encouraging word in his ear! *You're doing fine, George! Keep it up!* When he happened to encounter Imry in the corridor or sat next to him in meetings, however, he had no difficulty in mastering these impulses, for the Imry he watched vanished when the watching was interrupted. For his part Imry betrayed not the slightest sign of suspicion that Haddock had any connection with the peculiar sensations he was experiencing while sitting at his desk. It sometimes seemed to Haddock that the watching existed independently of either man. More than that, he wondered if he stopped watching Imry, would he still have the sensation of watching him . . . and would Imry, in his office, feel watched all the same?

That didn't seem likely. In any event, his compulsion to watch persisted. He hadn't finished yet! He kept making progress. Miss Kohl was a confirmation of that. Imry hardly gave her a glance now when she entered. He seemed anxious to get his dictation over with in a hurry, so she would leave. Miss Kohl seemed puzzled. What was wrong? She ran a few tests of her own. But all her wriggles were in vain. Imry

199

might sneak a look or two, but that was all. When she brought in fresh memos for his in-box, she'd bend over the desk so that her plentiful bosom was practically thrust in Imry's face. Imry seemed embarrassed. He drew back from her—and no wonder, for Haddock was putting on the pressure. He'd hover above the door like a gnat and then zoom in until his gaze sat on one of Imry's bushy eyebrows, or he'd sweep back and forth across Imry's forehead and dart into the pupil of Imry's left eye. No, it wasn't Miss Kohl that Imry was aware of!

But it was tiring, that incessant watching. Haddock's neck ached, his eyes burned, his whole body seemed numbed by the strain. Even when he was away from the office, he had the sensation that he still was watching, as though a monitor were fixed in his inner eye and the world he saw was no more than a miniature reflection of some remote reality.

He was beginning to feel confused. He was being watched everywhere and all the time, and he himself was watching now, too, and these two sensations—watching, and being watched—were merging, so that what he saw and what he felt were identical. His own identity seemed to have flattened and become distant, as though he were literally being re-duced to a grayed image on a glass screen. He was his own reflection . . . but where was the reality, where was his literal, corporeal self?

This sense of having lost himself, of being a man displaced, increasingly alarmed him.

"Listen, Mackensen," he said one day in the car, "I want to ask you something about your lipreading. I realize I told you not to do it on company time, but it's an interesting subject, and I have a question to ask."

200

"Sure, Mr. Haddock," said Mackensen, who wasn't a man to hold a grudge.

"Well, with all the lipreading you've done, have you ever had a problem controlling it?"

"Controlling it?"

"For example, have you ever found yourself reading lips when you didn't intend to?"

"Not to my knowledge, Mr. Haddock, but what did happen once is I got to mumbling without knowing it until my wife got after me and made me stop."

"Mumbling to yourself?"

"No, not to myself. Mumbling to other people when I was talking to them. It was the lipreading, see. I was so used to listening to people speak without hearing them that the sound of words didn't mean much to me, and I guess I got into the habit of speaking without sound myself."

"That's interesting, Mackensen. You were concentrating so hard on your lipreading that you got to the point where you lost your power of speech."

"Oh, well, it wasn't that bad. I could control it, like you said."

But Haddock couldn't seem to control his watching. By day he sat staring at the monitor as in a trance. By night he seemed to be monitoring still, in his dreams. He had poured all his energy into watching and hadn't enough left over to stop. Sometimes he felt that the monitor had taken possession of him, sucking out his vital juices as a spider empties a fly, leaving only the dry husk hanging in the web. Even his little triumphs with Imry didn't seem to be his now. They belonged to the monitor. And worst of all, he felt obscurely betrayed. In his compulsive watching he was neglecting his job. The presidency was slipping from his grasp—just when he had finally seized it!

Miss Prince was afraid that something was wrong. Haddock was spending long hours in his office with the door closed. He would see no visitors then, nor would he accept any calls. When he emerged, he was drawn and spent, his face tight with fatigue, his eyes sunken. She could only suppose that he was engaged in some vast company project that required absolute secrecy, but at the same time she was worried. He was doing little of his customary work. What he didn't pass on to Imry he sent to other executives or neglected outright. Unanswered letters evoked other letters, which went unanswered, too. There were phone calls as well, but Haddock wouldn't take them. He couldn't be disturbed. She protected him as well as she could, inventing excuses for him to mollify offended callers. She began handling certain minor matters herself, which she would never have thought of doing before. She had time for that, at least, since Haddock gave her virtually nothing to do. And so, while he remained mesmerized before the tiny screen in his office, she sat anxiously at her desk in the anteroom waiting for the next outside call, to which she would have to respond: "I'm terribly sorry, but Mr. Haddock is tied up at the moment. May I take a message?"

On the infrequent occasions when he summoned her she lingered in his office as long as she dared, hoping in a vague way that she might cheer him, for she sensed he needed that. She didn't have the heart to press him too hard to attend to the work that had piled up.

"I brought some fresh flowers, Mr. Haddock. Some roses. I saw them on my lunch hour, and I thought—"

"Fine, Miss Prince. They're lovely. Thank you very much."

He was impatient for her to leave, and yet he longed for her to stay. It was soothing to look at her, and he thought how restful it would be if she would lightly pass her fingers across his forehead. But then he would feel the surge of his guilty, helpless, fateful fascination—the monitor was blazing in its hiding place. Time was ticking away. He wasn't watching! He felt choked, as if all those unseen images were clustering in his chest, suffocating him.

"Just put them anywhere, Miss Prince, anywhere. And I'll buzz you when I need you."

He needed her then. He needed her always. He yearned for her voice, her presence, her touch. If only he could tell her, if only he could share it with her! But that was impossible. She couldn't stay. She had to leave. He was trapped in his obsession, alone.

One June morning Haddock's intercom box buzzed busily, startling him.

"Miss Prince, I thought I said I wouldn't take any calls until eleven today."

"I'm sorry, Mr. Haddock, but Mr. Nammers is calling from his club."

"Oh. In that case, put him on, Miss Prince. Put him on right away."

He kept watching the monitor as he lifted the telephone receiver. "Yes, Mr. Nammers?"

"I want to see you, Henry. I'm coming into the office this afternoon at four thirty."

"Yes, Mr. Nammers. I'll be here."

"It's about the monitor."

Haddock was momentarily confused. "Which monitor, Mr. Nammers?"

"*Your* monitor, Henry."

"Oh," said Haddock. "That one." With his free hand he snapped off the monitor and shoved it back inside its drawer. "I see," he said, closing the drawer. "My monitor." He turned the key in the lock. "For a moment there I thought you might have meant some other monitor, Mr. Nammers." He pulled the key out but dropped it on the floor. He put one shoe on it, covering it. "I suppose Cooley told you about it, sir."

"Cooley? No, it wasn't Cooley." Mr. Nammers sounded cold, but then he frequently sounded cold.

"Well, might I ask who it was, then?"

"It was an old friend, Henry," said Mr. Nammers shortly. "Remember—four thirty. I'll see you then."

He hung up.

Haddock sat unmoving, frowning down at the desk. An old friend? *What* old friend?

Then he stood, the perspiration breaking out on his face, and stared around at the walls, ceiling, corners, door tops.

"So . . ." His voice broke. He swallowed and moistened his lips with his tongue. "So . . . you're there," he whispered. "You're . . . really there. You've been there all the time." He was trembling, and his breath came quick. "I see," he muttered, his gaze shifting around the room again. "I understand now. It was you. You told him. But . . . why? Why did you tell him?" He still had the telephone receiver in his hand. He'd been gripping it ever since Mr. Nammers' call. He managed to replace it without dropping it, although his hand was shaking. He stooped and picked up the key and put it in his pocket. Then he wiped his face on his handkerchief and took a deep breath.

"I'm . . . better now," he said in a low voice. He achieved the semblance of a composed and dignified smile, but his eyes still swung about the room, searching. "It was . . . a surprise, that's all. I didn't really expect it. But now . . . I'd like to know why you did it. Why you told Mr. Nammers."

He stood at the desk, his head tilted inquiringly to one side, waiting. "Well . . . ?" Then he frowned and went to the door to the conference room. "Are you in there, then?" He opened the door. The room was dim. "I'd appreciate some response," he said louder. The blinds were drawn. The portraits were dark rectangles on the walls. "I've been shaping up as president, haven't I? I know I have. I've been doing a good job. Until lately maybe. Until I began watching. But I was drawn into that. It wasn't my idea. It was . . . suggested to me. It was . . . forced on me." His voice sounded muffled, for there was no resonance in the empty room. The air was dry and dead.

He closed the door and turned back in his office. "You didn't want anybody else to do any watching, was that it?" He cocked his head to listen. "Yes, that must be the answer. But now, you see, my position—it's impossible. If Mr. Nammers insists on my resignation, what can I do?" He was still perspiring and leaned back against his desk for support. "I couldn't conceivably take this before the board, could I? That would be out of the question. And he knows it. You know it, too. You both know. So . . . did the two of you plan it that way?"

He swung around and fumbled at his intercom box. "Miss Prince? Would you mind stepping in, please?"

When she entered and saw his face, she paused, wide-eyed and apprehensive.

"No, wait," Haddock said quickly, heading toward her. "Not in here." He hurried her out again, through the anteroom and into the corridor, where he hesitated, and then led her down to the only vacant office, Mr. Probstein's. He guided her inside and shut the door behind them. "Sorry," he muttered. "I don't mean to alarm you, but I wanted a word with you in private."

"Mr. Haddock, what's wrong?"

"Nothing," he said. "Nothing." He began pacing the office, running his hand through his hair. "I just wanted to . . ." He turned, facing her. "I needed to see someone," he said. She was watching him anxiously. He noticed that from habit she had brought her dictation pad and a pencil—one of her chewed ones. He could see the marks. "A certain problem has arisen," he said, resuming his pacing. "A certain . . . difficulty. Which will undoubtedly result . . . in some changes. That's what I wanted to say, Miss Prince. There'll be some changes here. Very soon. I think I can definitely say that." He saw how bewildered she was and hesitated, wondering what to say. "I'm sorry I can't be specific," he said finally, trying to master his agitation, "but . . . there's something about this place that inhibits—well, I find it impossible to speak frankly here." He glanced at her apologetically. Then he turned away. "But at least this isn't the only place in the world."

He was facing the window. Beyond were the smoky Manhattan peaks, the dusty air, the blotched and swollen summer sun. "No," he said. "There are other places." And if he were forced out of the company, wouldn't he be free to go to those other places? Wouldn't he be liberated from the watching then? "Other places," he repeated in wonder, as though the thought of leaving had never seriously occurred to him before. Why, yes, he thought, there would be no watching in those places. And there were hundreds of them. Thousands. He would find them in the little towns and villages. In the cities, too. Out in the countryside, in the fields and forests, and down along the shores of lakes and beside the sea.

He drew a deep breath and turned, his face alight. "It's all a question of having a choice to make, Miss Prince—and making it. And I do have a choice. That's the most important thing. I'd almost forgotten." He moved toward her. "But you helped remind me, Miss Prince. Oh, I know you don't know exactly what I mean, and I'm sorry I can't explain it, but anyway your being here, it's been very . . . very . . . "

Someone passed by in the corridor outside. The clicking steps alerted him. He turned aside, frowning. His anger leaped up again. "There's something I've got to do first, though," he muttered.

He went to the door and put his hand on the knob. "One last thing, Miss Prince, if you wouldn't mind. Please call the garage and ask them to send Mackensen around with the car as soon as possible."

He opened the door and ushered her out. "Oh, my hat," he mumbled and hurried past her, through the anteroom and into his office, where he got his hat from the closet.

Before he left, he paused and looked around the room. "I want to tell you that you can't treat a man the way I've been treated," he said in a low and even voice. "You can't raise him up and drive him through what I've gone through and then . . . betray him." His jaw was set; his fists clenched. "Do you hear that, Mr. Nicholas?" He turned around in the center of the room, staring at the ceiling, staring at the walls. Then he shouted:*"Do you hear that, Mr. Nicholas?"*

* * *

It was a windy day. Clouds raced low, making the wooded Pennsylvania countryside flicker between brightness and shadow. A sunny stand of trees would suddenly dim into dark forest; then the cloud would pass and the bright grove would leap up again, only to vanish as another cloud swept above it. Those flashing woods seemed to mock him. He'd have a surge of hope, dashed by doubt; his thoughts of freedom would flare and quickly die. Bright, dark; bright, dark. *Which?* Finally he closed his eyes, to shut it all out.

"I guess this must be it, Mr. Haddock." Mackensen had slowed the car and was pulling over to the side.

A neatly trimmed hedge ran along the edge of the property. Beside the driveway entrance stood a mailbox with the name *Nicholas* lettered on it.

"You want me to go on in, Mr. Haddock?"

"All right."

The driveway was lined with flower beds and fruit trees. On one side an ancient stone boundary wall lay crumbling in luxuriant vines. The air, delicately beaten by butterflies, had a drowsy, summer sweetness. The wind had died. The clouds had gone.

"This sure is a nice place, Mr. Haddock."

"Mmmm."

The house, set back some fifty yards, was built of whitewashed brick. It was a modest old place, comfortably settled into green lawn. It looked scrubbed in the sunshine and cheerful with climbing roses.

The car pulled up to the front and stopped. Haddock got out. "I won't be long," he said, but he didn't know. He had no clear idea of what he would do. He wasn't even sure now what impulse had brought him there. All he felt was what he

208

always felt—the watching, that clinging suffocating watching, fitted to him like his skin, imprisoning him.

He shook himself, as though to cast it off. Then he set his face into an expression of dignified resolve. *Hello, Mr. Nicholas,* he thought.

He rang the bell.

In a few moments the door was opened by a plump little middle-aged woman wearing an apron.

"I'd like to see Mr. Nicholas, please."

"Well, he's got a cold," the woman replied. She took a long look at the limousine and the uniformed chauffeur and self-consciously smoothed her apron.

"I'm sure he'll see me," said Haddock, extracting a card from his wallet, "if you'd be kind enough to give him this."

"Who's that, Mrs. Blake?" inquired a sluggish voice from the upper floor.

"It's a man," she answered, taking the card and peering nearsightedly at it. "You want to step in, sir?" she said to Haddock. She turned and went up the stairs.

Haddock entered. He looked carefully around. There was nothing much to be seen. The stairs rose sharply ahead of him. To the right was a closed door. He opened it. That was the dining room, smelling of furniture polish; beyond it presumably was the kitchen. On the left side of the hall was the living room, long and low-ceilinged, with a raised hearth, bookcases, cabinets. The hall itself angled around the stairs and ran straight on to the back door, which stood open, framing a patch of sunlit green.

He heard shuffling steps overhead. A floorboard creaked. The banister shivered. Someone was descending the stairs.

"Mr. Haddock?"

A pair of slippered feet came into view.

"Good afternoon, Mr. Nicholas," said Haddock.

The slippers were followed by a bathrobe, then a hand that held Haddock's card; a puffy and unshaven face, rimless glasses askew beneath sparse, graying hair. "I seem to remember the name, Mr. Haddock. I believe you telephoned once. I didn't realize that you were the president—"

"Yes, yes," said Haddock pleasantly. It was the nephew, of course. He'd expected the nephew.

"—but if it concerns my uncle, I can only refer you to his attorney in Philadelphia, as I did before."

"The attorney won't do for this, I'm afraid."

"Unfortunately he'll have to do," John Nicholas replied, straining to be polite. He had a summer cold, and he'd had to get out of bed to deal with an unnecessary visitor. "My uncle doesn't receive visitors."

"I see," said Haddock. The two men stood regarding each other with blank expressions of courteous reserve as Mrs. Blake descended the stairs, edged past them, and went off along the hall to the rear of the house.

Haddock cleared his throat. He felt choked; his heart was hurrying, with stumbling strokes. "Well, maybe you'd be willing to satisfy my curiosity on a particular point," he said, and he marveled at the evenness of his voice.

"Yes?"

"Some years ago your uncle had a television monitor installed in the conference room of the company headquarters in New York."

"Yes, that's right. I recall that."

"The purpose of that monitor was to enable him to keep in direct touch with the board of directors during the monthly meetings at a time when he couldn't make the trip himself."

210

"Yes."

"That monitor was never removed."

John Nicholas adjusted his glasses. "It wasn't removed? Well, I wouldn't know about that."

"And apparently it remained in good working order."

"No, you're misinformed there, Mr. Haddock."

"I'm sorry, I don't understand."

"I don't know about the New York end of it, but here we had it taken out."

Haddock squinted at him. "Taken out?"

"Dismantled. You know . . . removed."

"I-I don't quite . . . When was this supposed to have been done, may I ask?"

"Oh, seven or eight years ago. Seven, anyway."

"That's . . . that's not possible."

"I can assure you it was done. I was here at the time."

"You must be wrong. There's a mistake somewhere—"

"I have no idea what you mean by that, but I can tell you—what's the matter, Mr. Haddock?"

"Nothing . . . nothing." Haddock edged back against the wall. The hallway was uneven, with its worn old boards; he'd felt it tilt beneath his feet. He gazed all around in bewilderment. Perspiration was flooding down his forehead.

"Mr. Haddock, are you sure—?"

"No, no. It's all right. Just a touch of sun. Or something." Haddock pulled out his handkerchief and wiped his brow. His hands were moist, too. "Well, the fact is," he said, "that I had the impression . . . the impression that your uncle might still be using that monitor. I had that distinct impression. That he might use it. Once in a while."

"Well, he doesn't. And I can tell you—excuse me, Mr. Haddock, but if you'd like to sit down a minute—"

"I'm fine, really. Fine. It's the heat. But about your uncle, you say you're certain that—"

"He couldn't use it anyway."

"Beg your pardon?"

"Even if the monitor hadn't been removed, it would be useless to him now."

"Useless? I don't—"

"My uncle is blind, Mr. Haddock."

"Blind."

"He's been blind for five years."

"Oh, God. No. You can't mean that."

"Unfortunately it's true."

"Blind?" Haddock whispered. He stared around at the walls, the stairs, the narrow hall that led to the back. "No. He can't be blind. Not really blind."

"I assure you that my uncle is blind, Mr. Haddock."

"But not completely. Or . . . or you're joking."

John Nicholas eyed him severely. "I would hardly have the bad taste to joke on a subject of that kind."

"I'm sorry, I didn't mean that exactly. I don't know what I meant."

"Mr. Haddock, this question seems to have some special meaning for you."

"It does, it does. I can't explain it to you—that is, I couldn't expect you to understand it completely, but if I could be sure one way or the other—"

"You won't take my word for it?"

"Oh, it isn't that. It's just that if I could see for myself, with my own eyes, then my doubts would be . . . well, they'd be laid to rest."

"But there's nothing to see, Mr. Haddock. The company

212

sent some technicians to remove it, you understand. If it were still here, I'd be glad to show it to you."

"That wouldn't prove anything anyway."

"What do you mean?"

"Well, he might have another one somewhere. One you don't know about."

"Mr. Haddock, this is becoming outrageous. My uncle is blind."

"Right. You told me. I don't doubt your word, not a bit. But . . . just to nail it down, suppose I took a look at him. At Mr. Nicholas."

John Nicholas stepped back a pace and blew his nose. "My uncle is an old man," he said, his voice thick with cold. He regarded Haddock disapprovingly. "I don't want him disturbed in any way."

"Oh, I wouldn't disturb him."

"Strange voices bother him."

"I can understand that. But I wouldn't need to say anything. I wouldn't speak at all. I'd just . . . look at him for a few seconds. You see . . . your uncle—well, as the founder of my company, he's come to represent something to me. As a kind of symbol. And if I could just take one look at him. Well . . . it would mean a lot to me."

John Nicholas turned aside and sneezed twice into his handkerchief. "Damn this cold," he muttered. He glanced at Haddock in irritation. Then he sneezed again.

"Please," said Haddock.

John Nicholas removed his glasses and dabbed at his watering eyes. He put the glasses back on again fretfully. "All right," he said shortly. "But remember, Mr. Haddock. You're not to say a word, is that understood?"

213

"Absolutely."

"And walk quietly." He turned toward the rear of the house. "My uncle's sitting out in back."

They went along the hall and out through the doorway to a flagstoned terrace, shaded here and there by pear trees. An old dog lay sleeping beneath a wooden bench. Someone had dropped a green garden glove nearby. Bees flashed through the patches of sunlight; a dragonfly whirred clumsily above a watering can. At the far end of the terrace someone was reclining in a lawn chair that faced the house. It was an old man, Haddock saw. A bald old man, sunning himself in a bathing suit. He had a protruding old man's belly; his arms and legs were thin and hairless, with creased and sagging skin. His head was tilted back to receive the sun.

Some ten paces away John Nicholas stopped, putting a restraining hand on Haddock's arm.

Mr. Nicholas straightened his head. He was gazing directly at them. He resembled his photographs in the company files, except that he was brown from the sun and his face was blotchy with age spots. Feathery tufts of white hair flared above his ears. His eyes were pale blue.

"Is that you, Mrs. Blake?" he asked in a cracked and whistling voice.

John Nicholas glanced meaningfully at Haddock, but Haddock was staring at Mr. Nicholas.

"Mrs. Blake?" Mr. Nicholas said again.

"No, it's me, Uncle," John Nicholas replied.

Mr. Nicholas nodded, relieved, and settled back in his chair. Then a puzzled expression crossed his face. "Is someone with you, John?"

"No, Uncle."

"Funny, I thought—"

"No, there's no one."

"All right, John."

"I'll be back later, Uncle."

"Good," said Mr. Nicholas. "Good."

John Nicholas turned. Haddock was no longer staring at the old man in the lawn chair. He was looking anxiously about at the grass, the stones, the sky, the garden, and the grove of trees beyond it, as though he expected the real Mr. Nicholas to rise from the earth like a wizard or drift grinning out of the woods.

John Nicholas touched Haddock's elbow.

Haddock swung around and headed back to the house. He stubbed his toe on the doorstep, winced, and limped along the hall.

John Nicholas followed him. "I don't want to be impolite," he said, opening the front door, "but I've got to get back in bed."

"Yes, of course," Haddock mumbled, nodding. "I'll be on my way, then. Sorry for the trouble I've put you to."

"No trouble, really."

Haddock stepped outside. He turned. "It's a strange thing, though." He hesitated, glancing all around, as though bewildered. "I've had a sort of . . . a sort of sensation, a peculiar sort of sensation that I somehow attributed—well, it's a long story, and I won't go into it, but anyway this sensation was based, you might say, on a supposition which . . ." He stood smiling uncertainly.

"Yes?"

"Well, this supposition—I mean, you've shown me that this supposition is . . . that it's groundless."

"Well—?"

"So the sensation I referred to . . ." Haddock took a slow

215

breath and gazed around once more. He seemed to be listening for something.

John Nicholas twisted the doorknob impatiently, making the catch snap.

"Well," Haddock said, so softly that the other man couldn't hear him clearly, "the sensation is a real one, you see. I still have it. More than ever, actually. So . . . what's the reason for it? What's the explanation, then?"

He turned and walked, still limping, to the car, where Mackensen was holding the door open for him.

The limousine trundled down the graveled drive, turned onto the paved road, and headed back toward New York.

Haddock slumped in the back, fingering his hat, his gaze darting from one side window to the other. He kept thinking: *He didn't watch. But somebody did. Somebody's been watching all the time.* He swung around to look out the back. The curving country road was empty. No one was following. The sky was blank. Not even a bird was up there. But the watching was stronger than ever. It flowed all around him. He sucked it in with every breath.

"Oh, God," he muttered. He shrank against the seat, trying to make himself small. There was no refuge from it, no relief. He tried to veil his imagination with thoughts of Miss Prince, but all that came to him was her name, which he turned over and over in his mind like a charm. He closed his eyes, the better to concentrate. *Miss Prince,* he thought in desperation. *Miss Prince, Miss Prince.* If he could get back to her, then it might stop.

"Can't you go any faster, Mackensen?"

"Well, I'm at the limit already, Mr. Haddock, and they've

probably got radar on this road. It's not posted for radar, but sometimes they don't post it just to fool you, so you don't know if they're clocking you or not."

Haddock opened his eyes. "What are you talking about, Mackensen?"

"About the radar. You know, the radar they got for speed limits. You never can tell, Mr. Haddock, but I've got a sixth sense about radar, and I've got the feeling they may be clocking us right now."

Haddock leaned forward, frowning. "Wait a minute, Mackensen. Are you telling me you've got the feeling of being watched, is that what you're saying?"

"That's right, Mr. Haddock."

"Watched by something you can't see, is that it?"

"Well, the radar, it's there, but you can't see it, and that's the whole point, Mr. Haddock."

Haddock expelled his breath slowly. "Listen, Mackensen. This sensation of being watched. You actually feel it? You really have that sensation?"

"Sure. When I'm driving, it's always in the back of my mind. I mean, they don't clock everybody all the time because that's impossible, so they set it up so you won't know when it's you, see?"

"Yes, I see," said Haddock. "I do see. I understand that." He gazed out at the undulating fields and woods, a look of surprise on his face. "I just never imagined . . . well, I never thought anybody else had that sensation. It simply never occurred to me." He ran his fingers over the fabric of the seat, staring in mute conjecture at the familiar objects inside the limousine—the ashtrays, the armrests, the back of Mackensen's cap—as if he were noticing them for the first time. "Why, you've been driving me every day for months,

217

and I never for a moment had any idea that . . . that you sometimes . . ." He cleared his throat. "But it isn't just you, Mackensen. No, it can't be just you. Other drivers . . . they must feel it, too, don't they?"

"Guess so, Mr. Haddock. If you don't want a ticket, you've got to think about it when you're on the highway."

"On the highway, right," said Haddock. "That's where you feel it. You—and the others, the other drivers." He swallowed, amazed. "My God, there must be thousands who feel it. Millions." He sank back, his eyes fixed on the back of Mackensen's hairy neck, as though that were the critical center of a possibility whose implications spun through his mind, dizzying him. "That's extraordinary," he muttered. "Really extraordinary. I mean, it's normal. It's a very normal reaction. That's what I mean. I just hadn't—" His pulse had quickened; he could feel it pounding. "It happens when you're driving, Mackensen. That's when you feel it. But why do you feel it then? I mean, why not other times, too?"

"Well, I don't know, Mr. Haddock, but when I'm driving, I'm working, and I've got to be on my toes for stuff like that. You know, for other cars and cops and signs and radar, whatever they throw at me, see?"

"God, yes. I see that. Right. You feel it when you drive because your job forces you to be aware of it. You're functionally involved with it then. That's how it works! But when you're not involved that way, then you wouldn't feel it. You probably wouldn't be aware of it." Haddock was perspiring now, although the air-conditioned car was cool. He impatiently wiped his brow and leaned forward again. "Tell me, when you go into your bank to cash a check, you don't feel that same sensation, do you?"

"I don't get you, Mr. Haddock. The banks, they don't have radar."

"No, they don't have radar, but they have hidden cameras that snap your picture when you step up to the window, in case it's a holdup, and then they may have television monitors trained on strategic locations—watching the vaults and the tellers' cages. As an ordinary customer, you probably wouldn't feel it—even though it's there, all right—but the tellers would feel it. Why, they'd feel it all day! Like you feel the radar on the highway! It's part of your job—and it's part of their job! And with me . . ."

"How's that, Mr. Haddock?"

But Haddock didn't answer. Yes, he thought, with him it wasn't only part of his job, it *was* his job. His job . . . his life. He lived with it all the time—and so he felt it all the time. It was more intense for him, but others felt it, too. Others felt it.

He glanced wonderingly through the window. They were cruising through a dim business district in the northern reaches of Trenton. Down at the end of the block was a bank . . . a bank! Monitors in there for sure. And beyond that was a high school. The company had sold systems to hundreds of schools, and that very well might be one of them. Why, there were probably monitors posted in the halls, so that if a student sneaked out of class for a smoke, the principal would know who it was. In some schools they had them right in the classrooms, so if the teacher's back were turned . . . well, the teacher's back was *never* turned. Those kids were watched every second.

Schools, yes, and banks—and hospitals, factories, hotels, supermarkets . . . the list was almost endless. "Good God," he muttered under his breath. There were monitors in subways, in public toilets, bus depots, on ships and airplanes . . . in every direction his mind turned he saw those silent sentinels, saw them by the thousand. He blinked and shook his head. It was incredible. He'd sold those systems for years—for years!—but he hadn't really understood what he'd been doing. No, he hadn't had the slightest suspicion of what it all amounted to. He'd thought he was alone, despite the obvious and overwhelming evidence that there were millions of people, literally millions, who were bound to be aware that during at least some portion of their daily lives they were subject to observation, whatever they might be doing and wherever they might be.

Wherever they might be . . . which meant anywhere and everywhere, almost literally everywhere. Not only in ordinary places, either, for there were systems installed in remote locations, watching what men could not watch and doing what men could not do . . . systems within the earth, in the mines, and down in the sea, too, for marine research, and there were military sensing devices that could scan a jungle and determine what was a man and what wasn't, and there were the special aerial cameras that created archaeological maps . . . they could see right back through time!

And then there were the greatest of all watchers, spinning and clicking through the sky.

"Listen, Mackensen. You know about the radar, but do you know about the satellites?"

"The satellites, Mr. Haddock?"

"You know, the satellites we've been firing up into orbit around the world."

"Oh, sure. They use them for TV news and for the Olympic Games."

"Yes, but I mean the other ones. The spy satellites."

"Oh, those. Well, they put them up there to watch the Russians, as I understand it."

"But they pass over our heads, too, Mackensen. They're looking down on us. Or they might be looking down on us. That's the point. We don't know for sure if they are or not. Maybe they aren't all the time, but they are some of the time, and . . . it's not just me they're watching, and it's not just you. It's everybody. Everybody everywhere."

It was late in the afternoon when they reached the city. The streets were clogged with rush-hour traffic. The buildings flooded out office workers. Police were trying to keep the cars moving, but there had been an accident somewhere up ahead, and everything came to a halt.

"I might as well walk from here," Haddock said. "It isn't far."

"Sorry about this, Mr. Haddock."

"That's all right. It doesn't matter."

Haddock got out with some difficulty, for pedestrians were crowding along the sides of the stalled vehicles. He pushed his way through to the sidewalk and started off in the direction of the office.

The air was foul with exhaust, and the pavement was filthy. People hurried along, sweating in the heat, their faces angry, their eyes suspicious. Grit and dust were everywhere, and the sour smell of too many bodies too close together. It had been months since he'd found himself in a rush hour like this. He'd avoided it with his executive schedule and his limousine. But he didn't mind it. He was buoyed up by a sense of kinship with the people who went elbowing past him. *They feel it, too,* he kept thinking.

221

He stopped to watch them more closely, but they were rushing by so quickly that he couldn't focus on an individual face, and he could do no more than marvel at their sullen discipline. Look at those buses, loaded to the bursting point, and down below, in the subways, what suffocating masses of people would be crushed inside those grimy steel boxes! And when they got home, most of them wouldn't be much better off, cramped in tiny flats, with paper-thin walls, so if their neighbors sneezed, they'd hear it. Even on their vacations, they'd have to wait in line for a yard of sand at some packed public beach. At no moment in their lives were they out of range of someone else's awareness. Someone was always listening, always watching. And if they did find themselves alone, perhaps just for a few minutes, wouldn't they still have that same sensation?

So what difference did monitors make to them? They were watched anyway. They watched each other. They couldn't help it. The monitors couldn't take away their privacy. They'd lost that already.

The crowds surged around him, shoving along the street. He was moved by pity, but then he thought: Why pity? These people had faced up to what was inevitable. Their world was too crowded for privacy. They'd learned to get along without it. They held fast to their only obligation—survival. Yes, they couldn't have privacy, so they'd forgotten about it. They didn't even think about it anymore. Survival was the main thing for them, and if monitors helped them to survive, then they wanted monitors. They wanted . . . Mr. Nicholas.

He stood there, a solitary figure in the wash of the crowds. How could he have failed to understand that? They knew about Mr. Nicholas. They accepted Mr. Nicholas. They *wanted* Mr. Nicholas. If they hadn't, if they had insisted on trying to save what few shreds of privacy remained, then there would have been rioting in the streets when the first satellites went up, and there'd be mobs right now running around ripping out the monitors. But there hadn't been any rioting, and there weren't any mobs. Why, the company couldn't produce enough to meet the demand.

Yes, they'd chosen Mr. Nicholas—the real Mr. Nicholas, the true Mr. Nicholas, a selfless, tireless presence, secretive and quick, always alert, missing nothing. Oh, he might not be lodged in the office walls or crouched in the ceilings back at the apartment, but he was in countless other places. Why, Mr. Nicholas was the faithful companion of old Mrs. Haddock down in Florida, wasn't he? And he'd been the one to send the nurse running in when Mrs. Stern fell out of bed. It was Mr. Nicholas who counseled Mackensen against speeding and who reminded Dr. Despard's receptionist of her duties. And how many others did that busy old fellow watch and protect and guide? Thousands. Hundreds of thousands. Millions. Mr. Nicholas ranged far and wide, in an amazing variety of forms. He might be a billion-dollar electronic ganglia, at whose command a thousand rockets would spring into the sky . . . or he might be a pane of glass. He knew no bounds, no limits. He watched the streets, jails, banks, schools, hotels, hospitals, factories, planets, ships . . . why, there was hardly anything he *didn't* watch. He told the archaeologist where to dig and the pilot where to bomb. He reported the birth of stars and the death of cells. He might not be everywhere yet, but where he wasn't, he would be soon. No job was too big for him to undertake; none was beneath his notice. Mr. Nicholas watched the fish in the sea.

223

He squatted in the belly of the earth. He flashed like a comet in the heavens. He even had time to keep an eye on the men's room.

And this phenomenal Mr. Nicholas was there along that street somewhere—perhaps down at the corner, counting cars, or scattered here and there in some of the buildings, or winking down from the sky. He was in a dozen places at once, right then and there—watching.

Through the din of the street there sounded the half-hour stroke of a clock. He glanced at his watch. It was five thirty —and wasn't he supposed to have met Mr. Nammers back at the office at half-past four?

He called Miss Prince from a public telephone booth and was told that after waiting until five o'clock, Mr. Nammers had returned to his club.

"Was he annoyed, Miss Prince?"

"Y-yes, Mr. Haddock. He did seem rather annoyed."

"I see. Well, his club isn't far from where I am now. I suppose I'd better go directly there and see him. And you might as well go home, Miss Prince. It's late as it is."

He hurried along the street, somewhat surprised to find his steps so light and quick, for he knew he ought to be sagging with fatigue, he'd had such a wild, unnerving day —and with the worst to come, surely, for he realized how untenable his position was. It didn't matter now who had told Mr. Nammers about the monitor. The fact was that the chairman knew about it . . . and he would undoubtedly insist on Haddock's immediate resignation.

And yet, strangely enough, Haddock wasn't apprehensive at the prospect of facing an enraged Mr. Nammers, nor was he particularly disturbed by the likelihood that his career was ruined. He was too full of the moment to worry about the future. The walls of his isolation had crumbled; the truth had come flooding in. He was no longer alone. *Everybody feels it,* he kept thinking as he strode along, glancing about with alert curiosity. *Everybody.* The only difference was that he felt it more, he knew it more intimately, it was a part of him, it had been burned into his bones and tissues. He alone had the full awareness of it, he alone could visualize completely that hidden world, those million fragments of sense and sight fixed in a million different places, like a secret galaxy of stars, shining with invisible light.

His buoyant sensation of discovery diminished only slightly when he reached Mr. Nammers' club. He went briskly up the stairs and into the cavernous lobby, where he gave a message to the steward on duty at the desk. As he waited, he paced back and forth, idly jingling the coins in his pocket. His fingers closed on the key. He smiled wryly. Had he imagined that he could copy Mr. Nicholas by watching one little monitor? He might as well have sneezed in imitation of a hurricane.

Mr. Nammers stumped into the lobby and beckoned Haddock into a small, dimly lighted sitting room off to one side. "We can talk in here," he said curtly. The room was empty; its musty air smelled of yesterday's cigars. Heavy draperies deadened the noise from the street.

Mr. Nammers eased himself into an armchair and waved away a waiter who had come up to see if they wanted drinks. "All right," he said in his deep, hoarse voice. "Let's get on with it, Henry." His face was impassive, his gaze somber and intent. "You undoubtedly know, Henry, that I have always had great hopes for you as president. I've always felt that you would grow in the job, gaining in experience and insight, learning new lessons each step of the way."

"Yes, Mr. Nammers. You've been very encouraging."

"What I'm concerned with right now is whether my judgment about you was correct or not," the chairman went on gravely. "In the past few weeks I've realized that the company has suffered from a lack of direction and authority, and of course I could only assume that you were neglecting your job. But I was puzzled. I couldn't understand why—or at any rate, I didn't understand until this morning, when I received a call from—" He paused for a moment. "Well, I won't be violating a confidence if I confirm the obvious. My informant was one of the technicians who installed it."

"You said it was an old friend."

"I've known the man for years," Mr. Nammers said shortly, "but all this is beside the point." He turned his luminous eyes squarely on Haddock. "What I want to know right here and now, Henry, is how you can justify what you did."

Haddock sat silently, examining his clasped hands. "Well, I'll be honest with you, Mr. Nammers," he said finally. "I can't justify it. I suppose I made a mistake. Yes, I realize that now. It was a waste of my time. I neglected my job, as you put it."

Mr. Nammers regarded him quizzically. "Is that all you've got to say—that you wasted your time?"

"Essentially that's what it amounted to."

"But didn't it occur to you that there might be an ethical issue involved?"

"An ethical issue? No, that didn't occur to me."

"That didn't occur to you, did it?" But Mr. Nammers seemed neither displeased nor surprised. His features remained immobile, although his eyes glinted for an instant, as though he had been in some way diverted. "Surely you realize that you were violating another man's privacy?"

"Oh, yes. I did realize that."

"And?"

"Well, it didn't seem important."

"I see. It didn't seem important. You spied on a fellow officer of the company. You kept him under surveillance for weeks, but the question of his right to privacy meant nothing to you." Mr. Nammers' remarks were hostile and sarcastic in form, but his voice remained neutral, his face without expression. "Well, would you mind telling me, Henry, how you arrived at such an interesting conclusion?" he asked, and again his eyes gleamed, hinting at some hidden amusement.

Haddock gave him a curious glance. He found the old man's manner puzzling . . . where was the righteous rage he had expected? When would the storm of denunciations begin? "I don't know if I can explain it," he said. "I felt very strongly at the time that it was something I had to do, and the means to do it were available within the company itself, and so—"

"Wait a minute, Henry. You can't blame the company. Our systems are intended for public purposes, not private spying."

"The question isn't that simple," Haddock said hesitantly, trying to order his thoughts. It was so quiet in the little room that he could hear Mr. Nammers' wheezy breathing, and so dim that the old man appeared to have merged with the squat and heavy chair he sat in. Only his eyes seemed vigilant and alive.

"What are you trying to say, Henry?"

"Well, when you've got some systems operating privately

227

in public places, like banks, and other systems operating publicly in private places, like apartment buildings . . . then the distinction between public and private becomes blurred, doesn't it?" He looked questioningly at Mr. Nammers—and once more seemed to catch in his eyes that subtle, perplexing trace of irony.

"Are you talking about our work in the public sector, Henry? Our defense work?"

"Well, no. That distinction is totally absent there."

"Really? Why?"

Haddock was puzzled. He had the odd sensation that the old man was prompting him, but he couldn't understand why. "Well," he said slowly, "the chief focus of defense communications is, as you know, the satellite program—and that's changed everything. I mean, with the satellites, we've got a surveillance system on such a vast scale that the question of privacy is simply obliterated. It's technically impossible to recognize the claims of privacy in that program. The satellites see everything."

"And so?"

"Well, that means it's a program of surveillance that has no ethical limitations. The only limitations are engineering ones."

"But it's justified for reasons of national security."

"Oh, I'm not saying it isn't justified. It is. But more than any other single thing, it's gotten people to see surveillance as a security measure, and there are many different kinds of security, Mr. Nammers. You've got to have security in the streets and in the factories and in the schools . . . you've got to have it everywhere, and if you think about it enough, then you realize that it's the only thing that really counts. I mean, if you don't have security, you don't have anything, so the more security, the better—and therefore, the more surveillance, the better. That means that the only standard of judgment about surveillance is a practical one—whether in a given instance it's an efficient use of time and equipment. Well, what I did in George's case can't be justified on that ground. It was wrong because it was impractical."

"But not morally wrong?"

"Well, no. If what I did was wrong, then the company is wrong. The whole country is wrong."

"And you don't think it's wrong?"

"I don't know whether it's wrong or not, I honestly don't, but it's what everybody's involved in, so it's probably right."

"But is it necessary?"

"Necessary? Well, I . . ." Again Haddock had the impression that the old man, giving him cues, was leading him through some peculiar catechism, deriving occasional private amusement at Haddock's fumbling efforts to arrive at answers that in themselves were no surprise to him. "Yes, I think it's necessary," Haddock said, and then in sudden earnestness he went on: "Listen, Mr. Nammers. I was in the rush hour this afternoon, and it was terrible. I'd forgotten what it was like. All those people in the streets, they could very easily have turned into a mob. But they didn't. They moved along under their own self-discipline, knowing that if they didn't voluntarily control their behavior, then society would have to move in and force them to do it, and that would mean a police state, wouldn't it? So a democracy has to be based on self-discipline. And how do you get people to discipline themselves? You encourage them to do it by giving them little reminders. A policeman is an external reminder

. . . but the most effective reminder is the one you plant right in a fellow's thoughts. So maybe that's our job, Mr. Nammers. We let people know they're being watched, watched in a friendly and constructive way, let's say, but being watched anyway . . . and this reminder reinforces their latent inclination to behave responsibly. And people want that, Mr. Nammers. They want those little reminders. Watching, that's nothing new for them. They weren't brought up on television for nothing. They're *used* to that screen. They're used to watching what can't see them . . . and now the only difference is that they're getting used to *being* watched by what they can't see."

"That's an interesting thought, Henry," said Mr. Nammers quietly, "but it sounds a bit tenuous. After all, how can people be influenced by something beyond their senses? They can't hear it, they can't see it—"

"That's exactly it, Mr. Nammers. You've put your finger on it. What we're selling isn't only a material thing, it's an idea. It's the concept of monitors that's crucial. I hadn't really grasped that before. Yes, it's the idea that's important. And . . . why, we're helping create a new consciousness, a new awareness—a whole new dimension to modern life. People are gradually beginning to realize that wherever they go and whatever they do, no matter how private the circumstances may seem to be—who can tell? They may be under observation. So what does this mean? Well, it means that the more a man suspects that he may be held accountable for his actions, the more hesitant he will be to act in ways that may be contrary to what's expected of him. This is happening right now, Mr. Nammers. It's happening in thousands and thousands of individual cases. And probably at some time in the future we'll reach the point where each man will be . . .

well, monitoring himself, consciously or not. He will condition himself to behave as if his private actions were under public inspection—as some of them certainly will be. And so he ought to become a better citizen. And if that's true, then we ought to have a better society, with all men acting the way they ought to act."

Mr. Nammers nodded solemnly, although his reserved manner remained intact. "That sounds like a reasonable projection, Henry," he remarked in his dry way, "but I still can't help wondering about the ethical element." He permitted himself a small, sardonic smile. "It may be an old-fashioned attitude, but privacy still means something to a lot of people."

Haddock caught up his last phrase. "Well, maybe privacy is old-fashioned now, Mr. Nammers. You're right. Maybe it just won't work anymore as an ideal. It's a sort of luxury item now, and in times of trouble you can't afford luxuries. Luxuries become . . . selfish. That's right, Mr. Nammers. It's selfishness. Think of it this way. When there's a famine, the man who hoards food is a sort of public enemy, isn't he? Well, there's a famine coming in the world for living space and breathing space—privacy—and so the man who hoards privacy, he'll be a public enemy, too. He's got to share. Everybody's got to share. What we're moving toward is the opposite of selfishness. We're developing a society based on sharing, based on self-restraint. On a democratic self-restraint. People will freely restrain themselves, you see, in the interest of the common good. They'll *have* to. So you understand what we're doing, Mr. Nammers—we're helping create a new kind of social being, a person who is no longer a private individual but a *public* individual. One who accepts the full weight of his social responsibility and who is re-

231

minded of that obligation every minute of his waking life."

Mr. Nammers gazed at him searchingly for some time. "Tell me, Henry," he said quietly. "Do you honestly believe that?"

Haddock hesitated. "Well, yes," he said. "That's the way things seem to be shaping up, and I—"

"All right, Henry," Mr. Nammers said with sudden decisiveness. His manner became more expansive, his voice boomed louder; he even seemed, authoritatively, to swell physically. "I've always felt you had it in you to give our company forceful and dedicated leadership," he declared, "and I find no reason to believe that my judgment was in error. What we need in the presidency, Henry, is a dynamic vision of the future, and you've certainly got that, even though I can't say that I would agree with you in each and every particular." He withdrew his cigar case, opened it, peered at its contents, and then regretfully snapped it shut again. "My doctor keeps me on short rations," he grumbled. "I used to smoke a fistful of these things each day." Defiantly he reopened the case, selected a cigar, thrust it into his mouth, and lighted it. "I'll tell you frankly, Henry," he said, squinting through the smoke, "that some members of the board might not be willing to overlook your little mistake in judgment, and for that reason I have no intention of raising the question—provided you have that monitor removed."

"Oh, definitely, Mr. Nammers. I—"

"Have Cooley take it out over the weekend, though. I'd just as soon we kept this strictly between ourselves."

"Yes, I'll certainly—"

"And then back to work. Right, Henry?"

"Right, Mr. Nammers."

"Fine," said Mr. Nammers. He rose to his feet. "That's the

232

spirit, Henry." He led the way out into the lobby again, where he shook Haddock's hand. "And I want that Argentina project wrapped up in a hurry. Is that possible, Henry?"

"Um, can do, Mr. Nammers."

As he descended the stairs to the street, Haddock was overtaken by such a rush of accumulated fatigue that his shoulders sagged and his legs began trembling. He had to ask the doorman to summon a taxi.

By the time he returned to the company headquarters the floor was deserted, the offices empty. Even George Imry had left.

Miss Prince was still there, though. She got up as he entered the anteroom.

He looked at her, surprised. "Oh, I supposed you'd have gone by now, Miss Prince."

"I thought you might . . . might need me," she said timidly. He trudged into his office, dully wondering: Did he? Did he need her? She followed him. "I hope everything was all right, Mr. Haddock."

"Oh, yes. Everything's fine." He eased himself into his chair. "There was a little misunderstanding, that's all." She was tired, too, he saw. Her eyes were darkly circled and her cheeks drawn. He realized how worried she must have been during these last few weeks, how she must have been tormented by her confused awareness that he was faltering, sinking, failing. "Poor Miss Prince," he murmured—but he hadn't intended to say it out loud. She caught her breath in a half sob. "Sorry," he said. She was sniffing rapidly, as if on the verge of tears.

"It's going to be all right, Miss Prince," he said sympathetically. The thought occurred to him that he might go to her and comfort her, but he was too exhausted to move. "There, there," he said soothingly. He wanted to say more to her. She was really his only friend, the only one who cared for him, the only one who thought of him not as president but as himself—yes, the only one who loved him, loved him generously, hopelessly, with no thought of being loved in return or even of being recognized.

He leaned forward in his chair, smiling at her—and then his eye was caught by the windows of the building across the street, glinting with the reflection of the setting sun. In the heat that rose from below, the windows seemed to quiver, as though their glassy surfaces were shifting this way and that, searching and tracking.

He watched, bemused. That strange and glittering light confused him in his weariness, stirring his fears and doubts. When he spoke, he spoke not of her but of himself. "You know, Miss Prince," he said in a low voice, "I was ready to quit this job. I was ready to resign." She sank into the chair across from him, studying him uneasily. "I'd thought about it a lot," he said muzzily, still gazing at the shimmering windows. "I thought if I went somewhere else, it would be better. I thought I had that choice." He raised his hands to his face and began rubbing his forehead and temples. "But now I see that it would be more or less the same anywhere. There isn't any choice, really." He drew his fingers down his cheeks until they joined, prayerfully, beneath his chin. "There used to be a choice, though. Even just a few years ago, you could find . . . find a place where you knew you were by yourself. Where you knew that for certain." He sighed and sat straighter in his chair. "But now . . . there's a difference. Maybe a small difference, but a difference all the same. You can't be sure anymore. You can't be absolutely sure." He smiled faintly at her. "Oh, I suppose that in a practical, everyday sense you can be reasonably sure, and most people don't worry about it—it doesn't even enter their minds—but . . . even if they don't realize it, they may sometimes sense that something's changed, that things aren't quite the same any longer, that there's a tiny doubt which didn't exist before . . . but it's there now and growing. Growing. You can't be alone anymore. I mean, you can't be sure. That certainty—it's gone. And isn't that an extraordinary thing? That every human soul on this planet has lost that assurance . . . of being alone? Of being unobserved?"

He gave her a questioning look. She was watching him in anguished perplexity, one hand raised to her mouth. "But, then," he said, "being alone—that can mean loneliness, too, can't it? And loneliness can be a terrible thing, Miss Prince. So if in perhaps a limited but very definite sense loneliness has been abolished forever from the face of the earth . . . well, that's not such a bad thing. Not if you try to look at it in . . . in a positive sense. Anyway, we've got to accept it. It's here. It's a fact. There isn't any choice. Life is supposed to be a series of choices, but if the choices have already been made, then it's simply a question of recognizing them and accepting them. Yes," he said thoughtfully, "we've got to accept, don't we?"

"I-I don't know," she whispered, although he hadn't really asked her the question. He smiled at her ruefully. No, she wouldn't know. She couldn't understand him. But even if he tried to make it all clear to her, she wouldn't understand. How could she? He'd seen the invisible. He could see it still. But she . . . she saw only what met her eyes. Him she would see as the same man she'd begun working for years ago—his

235

hair a little grayer, his face thinner, his manner more intense and subdued. Why, she was closer to him now than any other person in his life, and yet she had no idea of the visions that swarmed before his inward gaze. She still regarded him with that same shy tenderness, as though nothing had changed.

On impulse, he went to the door to the conference room and opened it. "You know, Miss Prince," he remarked, "I used to be afraid of this room. Can you imagine that? Actually afraid of it? Afraid to go in?" He grinned back at her. "I'm not now, though." He stepped inside. "It's only a room like any other room." He wandered about, touching the chairs, trailing his fingers along the surface of the oval table, smiling at the portraits on the walls. "No, Miss Prince," he said, "there's nothing to be afraid of here. It's just so much plaster and wood and leather. . . ." The blinds were partly closed. The dying sunlight slanted through them, striping the rug. She had followed him and was standing just inside the doorway. "All inert matter, Miss Prince. No spirits. No ghosts!" He chuckled and perched himself on the end of the table, swinging one leg. "I used to have all sorts of fantastic notions about this room, Miss Prince. You couldn't begin to imagine the kinds of things that passed through my mind." He cast an amused glance at the portraits. "Well, that's over now—and high time, too. Fear makes a man humble, Miss Prince, and while a touch of humility may be good for the soul, you certainly can't run a business enterprise on it!"

He eased himself off the table and adjusted the set of his suit jacket. "Anyway, I've finally reached the point where I can stand in this room and look these old fellows straight in the eye. But it hasn't been easy. No, not by a long shot. A job like the presidency, you don't just walk in and take it over. You have to conquer it." He squinted around at the portraits

236

again with an ironical, challenging expression. "Well," he added, smiling, "I can't go on congratulating myself all night, Miss Prince. I've kept you too late as it is, but if you wouldn't mind taking a few notes for tomorrow's calendar—"

"Of course, Mr. Haddock." She sat in the nearest chair, her pad and pencil ready.

"Well, first thing, I've got to telephone the research director, and then I want to see Mr. Imry and Mr. Haeggler together, and then . . ." His weariness persisted, but it seemed to lift him now. He had a light, exultant feeling, and he saw everything touched with a special radiance—the oval table glowed, and the portraits seemed to have a three-dimensional depth, as though the painted men had come to life for some supernatural board meeting.

". . . as for the correspondence, pick out the half-dozen or so most important items for me to do in the afternoon. The rest I'll take back to the apartment tomorrow evening and dictate on tape."

"I'll have it all ready for you, Mr. Haddock," she said, her pencil moving over the pad.

He was gratified by the sense of clarity and quickness he had in organizing his work. He'd be able to take care of that backlog with Miss Prince's help. He guessed that she had kept matters from falling into complete confusion in these past few weeks. She was really quite a good secretary, he reflected. Alert and intelligent (within limits, of course) and hard-working. She could be a little tougher, though. Less sensitive. That habit she had of gazing at him adoringly—it was flattering to his ego, but only up to a certain point.

He began pacing about the room, snapping his fingers as he spoke. There was too much work to make up quickly. He couldn't jam it all into one or two days. Miss Prince could take

237

care of some of it, though, with no more than a word or two of guidance from him. She had all the details at her fingertips. ". . . better get me that market research report on Argentina, Miss Prince. I haven't really read it yet, and we're going to be pushing on that project now."

"I'll be sure it's on your desk in the morning, Mr. Haddock."

"Good," he said. "Good." He paused, trying to recall what else he would need to review. He glanced at her. She was giving him her customary reverent attention, and right now that was a little distracting, when he wanted to concentrate on his schedule.

"Wait a minute," he said, frowning. "Don't I have a speech to give at the end of the week, to the manufacturers?"

"You had me cancel that, Mr. Haddock."

"Oh, yes. I forgot. Well, maybe I'd better put in a brief appearance there anyway. Maybe they could work me in on a panel discussion. Get hold of their secretary, and see if there isn't a round-table group on Friday, say. . . ."

As he spoke, he paced away from her. Why did she have to gaze at him in that fond way she had? Just when he was trying to think about his work, she was thinking about him—he could tell, it was so obvious—and the two things simply didn't mix.

But he immediately reproved himself. He shouldn't be critical of that girl. She was loyal, after all. Intensely loyal. Why, she would practically die for him, and you didn't find that kind of attachment everywhere. But that was a problem in itself, wasn't it? It was an excess of devotion. A really first-rate secretary would know where to draw the line. That woman who was Ted Hall's secretary—what was her name? Luft. Mrs. Luft. Mrs. Luft was a quiet, dry, matter-of-fact woman who got her work done with no nonsense. She wasn't making eyes at Hall all the time. Well, she was married. That might make a difference.

The room was heating up. The air-conditioning system was shut off after regular hours. He was beginning to perspire. He removed his suit jacket and hung it over the back of a chair. That was better. He circled the oval table, restlessly eyeing the portraits. He cleared his throat. It felt tight. And he'd forgotten what it was he'd been trying to deal with.

"What were those last items I was talking about, Miss Prince?"

Her soft voice, reading from her notes, didn't soothe him. He was more discomposed than before. "Yes, yes," he grumbled as she finished. "I've got it now." But he couldn't seem to find the words for what he wanted to add next. That galled him. The clarity he'd felt before had vanished. He was fumbling now.

"Would you like to finish it in the morning, Mr. Haddock?"

"No," he snapped. He caught himself. "Sorry," he mumbled. "I'm just—" He broke off in vexation. He had been about to explain that he was tired, but he didn't owe her any explanations. If Mrs. Luft were sitting there in her place, he'd have gotten his thoughts out clearly and in good order.

"Did you say Mr. Peterson wanted to see me?" he said fretfully.

"Yes, Mr. Haddock. He's asked for an appointment several times, but I—"

"Well, put him down for tomorrow, then, but near the end of the day. I don't want to get stuck with him too long."

He paced moodily about. He really ought to hire an executive assistant, some energetic young fellow who could deal with routine things, leaving him free for broader questions. He'd considered that possibility before. At one time he'd thought Miss Prince might fill such a job. But she didn't have the background for it or the temperament. She was too pliant and submissive. She'd served him well enough when he'd been sales director, but anybody working out of the president's office had to be tough and hard and on occasion even ruthless. Look at the portraits . . . those old boys didn't get where they were by coaxing and wheedling and being nice—no, they used whips when they had to. Cut a few throats, too, in their time.

"Listen, Miss Prince," he said suddenly. "I want to see Mr. Harris tomorrow." Harris was the personnel director. "Work him in wherever you can—but I definitely want to see him." He resolved to broach the executive-assistant question with Harris, as part of a proposed reorganization of his office, which would expand anyway, with the overseas operations not far in the future. A reorganization was long overdue, frankly. In a company of that size it just didn't make sense for the president's office to be served by one little secretary. With an executive assistant—maybe two of them ultimately—his contact with Miss Prince would be considerably lessened, which would be a shame in a way, for he certainly owed her a debt of gratitude, and he would never think of her without sincere appreciation.

He stole a glance at her. Yes, she was watching him. She was always watching him, always, with those soft, those tender, those adoring eyes.

He passed his hand across his forehead. It was damp. Why did he keep thinking of her? He had to stop. He turned to face Mr. Elphinstone's portrait. The artist had cleverly caught Mr. Elphinstone's expression of barely controlled

240

annoyance. Mr. Elphinstone wouldn't stand for any sentimental nonsense, not with those savage little eyes. Mr. Elphinstone was watching him. So were Mr. Carpenter and Mr. Brandt and the rest . . . all glaring at him, bristling with admonitions. Mr. Nicholas was, too. Yes, Mr. Nicholas was watching. He ran his fingers through his hair, trying to recall the exact phrasing of something he'd said to Mr. Nammers. "Privacy is selfishness," he muttered, and Miss Prince had to strain to catch his words. "That's right . . . selfishness. But when everything is out in the open, then there'll be no more hypocrisy, no more lies, no more pretense." His heart was pounding. He kept working his fingers and frowning around the room. "There won't be any choice, because . . . because concealment will be impossible. Yes, that's the way it'll be. There'll be no place to hide from the awareness of social responsibility, no place to hide from . . . from the monitor."

He paused, breathing hard, and looked at her. The last light of day struck in through the blinds behind her. Her hair was kindled with it. He stared at her. He couldn't seem to tear his eyes away.

She glanced up from the dictation pad and saw him looking displeased. His face was pallid. She could hear his breathing. Was something wrong? Her pencil slipped from her fingers.

"Mr. Haddock, is there anything—?"

"What?" His voice cracked. It startled him.

"Nothing, but you seem—"

"I'm quite all right," he said irritably.

She bent to retrieve the pencil and sat up again, her cheeks flushed. A curl of hair strayed over her forehead, making her look younger and more vulnerable.

241

"I've got a little headache," he muttered. He felt exhausted and dizzy. He thought he'd better sit down. He came up to the table unwillingly, pulled out a chair across from her, and eased himself into it.

"Don't worry, Mr. Haddock," she said falteringly. "Everything will be all right." Her hand moved toward him in an unconscious gesture of sympathy. It lay before him on the table: slender fingers, bitten nails. He stared down at it wonderingly. He had an impulse to reach out and seize it . . . and then what? Press it to his cheek? Wrench it off? He clasped his own hands together so tightly that his fingers ached.

"I know what you've gone through, Mr. Haddock," she said, flustered by her daring, "and if it's any help to you—"

He drew back stiffly.

That dismayed her. "I mean, all the problems you have to—to—" she stammered, blushing.

"All right, all right," he muttered, keeping his head lowered.

"—and all the pressure . . ."

"Never mind," he said harshly. "I think I've proven that I'm equal to the pressure, Miss Prince."

"Oh, I'm sorry. I didn't intend . . ."

Her voice wavered. She fell silent.

He glanced up at her and then quickly away again. She reminded him of his past weaknesses and failures. He'd hidden for a while in her sentimental adoration. Didn't she realize that was over? Didn't she know that hiding was impossible now? It seemed incredible that this girl should trouble him so. Hadn't he withstood a force far greater than hers? But of course that had been without shape or substance, whereas she was living, she was real, she was there before him, gazing at him in that timid, tender way . . . and it would go on, too. Day after day he would be subjected to the constant irritation of a sentimentality that was grossly inappropriate for a man in his position. There was something maddening about it.

He glanced sharply around at the portraits, as though he had sensed them grumbling behind him, and felt the weight of their disapproving stares. But that was nonsense now. He had liberated himself from that. If anyone was watching, he was the one. Hadn't he just perceived that? *He* was the watcher now. He was monitoring himself! *I'm free at last,* he thought. *I'm free to act according to my conscience and my sense of duty.*

He took a breath. He pulled his hands apart and rested them on the edge of the table. *Free,* he told himself again. Ah . . . he felt better now. His hands were perfectly steady and his breathing untroubled. He glanced over at her and found that he could gaze at her steadily without flinching.

"Miss Prince," he said gently, "I've been meaning to speak to you about something for some time. I've put off doing it because it's not easy to find the right words, but . . ."

She watched him, confused. His voice was so mild, his expression so sympathetic and earnest, that his words meant little to her at first. For a moment she was even gripped by a wild hope—could it be that he was at last about to confess to her that he, too, felt—?

And then she realized that he was discharging her.

". . . I can't tell you how much I regret taking this step," he was saying, "but frankly, for your good as well as for the good of the company . . ."

She sank back, paling. Her hand crept away from him. No, he wasn't really firing her. He needed an older, more experienced secretary, that's what he was talking about. She would be transferred somewhere within the company. Or if she decided to seek a job elsewhere, he would give her a first-class recommendation. It would all work out splendidly. He spoke with increasing ease, his voice kindly and considerate. His smile became paternally benign.

She slumped in her chair, both hands pressed to her mouth. She was beginning to shake with sobs. Tears ran down her cheeks.

"Control yourself," he said. Her weeping disturbed him. "Don't be foolish, Miss Prince." His face flushed unpleasantly.

She couldn't stop weeping.

"Get hold of yourself." He was perspiring. "This is ridiculous, Miss Prince. All I'm talking about is a transfer. It happens all the time. I can even speak to Miss Bottweiler about your moving into some administrative work if you want. You could use a change of scene, frankly." He was furious. He never would have expected her to behave so badly. It was shocking. He glared at her. "In a new department you might find—" he paused to wipe his brow "—you might find some new interests. How old are you, Miss Prince? Twenty-six? Twenty-seven?"

She looked at him, terrified, as though she knew what he was about to do.

"You might find a marriageable man there, Miss Prince," he said, leaning forward. "It wouldn't be such a bad idea, would it? At your age?"

She whispered something he couldn't hear. Her hands were shaking, her lips trembling; her eyes implored him to stop.

He dug his fingers into the arms of his chair. "You might

244

find a husband, Miss Prince. Some young man all your own—"

"Oh, please, Mr. Haddock—"

"—and then you wouldn't go mooning around the executive floor like a schoolgirl."

"Oh, please, please—"

"These little secretarial infatuations are amusing for a while, but then they become a little boring, a little ridiculous—"

"Oh, please." She covered her face with her hands.

"—and pathetic, really. I'm a patient man, Miss Prince, but I've put up with it for years—"

She closed the dictation pad, her hands shaking.

"—and now it's become an annoying impediment to my work. There's no room in the company for—" he hesitated "—no room for that sort of thing!"

She rose hastily, clasping the pad in her arms.

"It's . . . disgusting!"

She gave him one last horrified glance and then hurried out.

"Disgusting," he repeated softly to himself. "Disgusting." She'd swung the door shut. He sat rigidly at the oval table, waiting for his anger to subside, counting silently to ten, to fifty, to one hundred. By now she would be out of the building, he thought. It would be unlikely that she would ever return. Well, he would speak to Miss Bottweiler in the morning and have her take care of the necessary details. He'd be better off now. He didn't need Miss Prince.

He stood, took his jacket off the chair, and put it on. There was something in the pocket. It was his tape recorder. He took it out. It had a welcome feel in his hand, and he studied it thoughtfully. What was it he'd been saying before? "Self-ishness," he mumbled, trying to remember. "No more self-ishness. No more . . . self." He glanced around the room. "A new kind of society. Watched, watched all the time. Watched—and watching . . . like God. Yes, like God."

He nodded. That was it. "In the old days," he said into the tape recorder, "people used to feel the presence of God in their lives. They believed that God was watching their every move. That belief gave them a sense of importance and worth, and it kept them from . . . from violating the commandments." He felt better now—calmer and self-possessed once more. "Those old beliefs have long since worn away," he said, his voice stronger. "They've gone. But nothing has been put in their place—and the world has become more chaotic and more dangerous. But now . . . now maybe something else is . . . is happening. It might not be too much to say . . . that a new belief is arising. A new . . . state of consciousness. Perhaps that's it. A new . . . awareness. Founded not on the faith that God is watching but on the fact that man is watching. Man, not God—"

He broke off then. Something had caught his eye. It distracted him. It was lying on the rug . . . a yellow pencil. She'd dropped her pencil. In annoyance, he went over to it and picked it up. It was one of those she'd nibbled. He stared at it for a few moments. Then he broke it in two pieces and hurled them away.

He slipped the tape recorder into his pocket. He went to the door and paused there, wondering. Hadn't he forgotten something? Had he left something behind? He looked all around, puzzled. No, the room was as it had always been, orderly and solid, its neatness marred only by the broken halves of the pencil lying in a corner.

He'd left nothing. Nothing was there. Nothing . . . everywhere. Nothing inside, nothing outside. For a moment he was tempted to explore that other nothing. He might go over and open the window and step out into it. Then he stiffened, holding tight to the knob of the door, and forced his eyes away from the broken pencil, away from the window. He looked instead at the portraits. Yes, that was better. He let his gaze move slowly from one to the next, all around the walls. He was among his peers now. His club. He'd arrived at last, and on his own. Well, he thought ironically, almost on his own.

He bowed; he smiled. "Thank you, Mr. Nicholas," he said, and then he left.

247

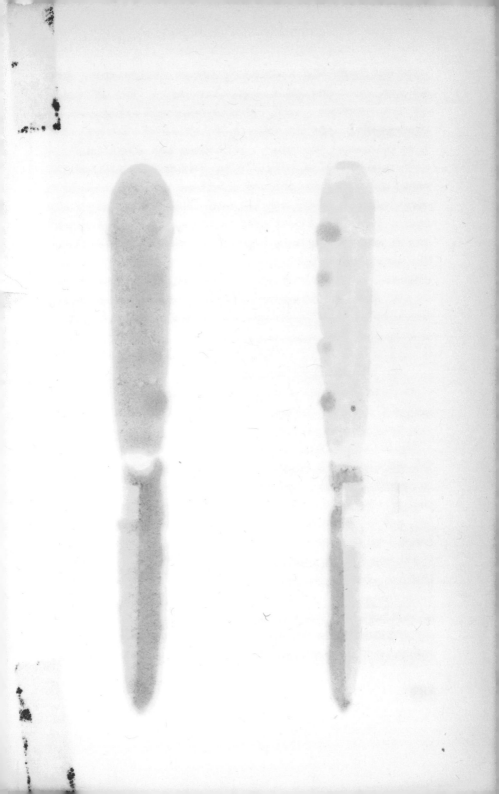